THE
GATHERING

THE
GATHERING

THE GIRL WITH THE 18

A NOVEL BY

MATTHEW HOLMES

I dedicate this book to the ones who believed in me the most.
The A team.

Anastasia Law

The Gathering – (ga-ther-ing) The day they will sentence you to death and your new life awaits.

INTRODUCTION

THE BLUE BAR AT THE bottom of the 60-inch Panasonic slowly filled to a hundred.

"It seems… yes. Yes, we have him now." The news anchor flustered, shifting in her rolling chair and turning to a different camera view, the producer of Channel 6 News sure to be yelling into her right ear.

"Yes, everyone, I'm sorry. Bear with us; it seems we're having a bit of technical difficulties."

"Hello?" a voice called from behind a frozen picture on the TV screen, a man in a white smock and glasses smiling awkwardly.

"Yes, David. Are you there?"

"You're breaking up pretty bad on this end, Cathy."

"David, we can hear you fine. Just go ahead," Cathy said. She was the last of the employed news anchors, and Channel 6 was the final working station, even coining the slogan, *Here with you to the end,* the fatal words scrolling across the bottom of the screen similar to a toll free number. For three long days, the entire country, including Thomas Edwards, had been waiting on pins and needles for NASA to speak after making that emergency announcement. Thomas stood from his khaki-colored couch and tossed the Xfinity remote to a cushioned corner.

"Naomi! You gotta come hear this!" he called, turning to see his spouse, who was staring hopelessly, like a child who had lost her parents, at a picture hanging in the hall.

"One landing in the Pacific, the other off the coast of Africa, the last one landing in the Arctic," David Gillespie said from his half of the now split screen. He was the young-faced poster boy scientist from Harvard University, credited with having spotted the ice rocks plummeting through space.

"A third of the human population will die from the tsunamis caused by the impact alone."

"With it not being expected to hit land, David, should that at least buy us some time?" Cathy said, crossing her legs under a red dress and stroking her chin.

"Time!" David laughed, a fearful laugh. "These rocks of ice are over a mile wide each. We're talking catastrophic destruction. The ice caps in both hemispheres, gone. The earth… will flood, Cathy, then water will cover the planet. Think of it like the era of the dinosaurs—"

"Naomi! Naomi! Come listen," Thomas shouted at his wife, who was still gazing into a gold-framed picture.

"Honey? Don't you hear me calling?" he asked, walking across the vinyl plank floors, scrubbing at his eyes. The hall seemed much longer than usual; with every step his slippers made, Naomi receded furthered away, then multiplied before him like in a house of mirrors.

"Honey," he breathed, touching her shoulder when he arrived on the hundredth step, elated.

"Huh? I'm fine. Sorry, I didn't mean to ignore you, but I was just admiring this picture. How long has it been up here?" she asked, gesturing to the composition nailed to the gray-colored wall. They owned and collected many paintings, but this one? He tilted his head; this one was unfamiliar. It was a wet painting of a peninsula, the kind he used to see the legend Bob Ross himself draw every morning when he was a kid back in the 80s. Bright colors with mountains, sloping hills, and a fog-covered lake were the gist of it.

"I'm not sure when we got this one. Didn't we go here on vacation once, or something like that?" Thomas said, squeezing his wife into a loving hug from behind, brushing up against her hazel hair and kissing her on the neck.

"No," she whispered, "I don't think that's it." Her face scrunched like it did when staring at the sudoku puzzles she enjoyed at the table for breakfast.

"Maybe we got it from your mother on our anniversary," Thomas said.

"My mother! I'm sure my mother wouldn't know the first place to buy such art," Naomi intoned, almost insulted.

"So, what do you think we should do?" he asked.

"It is beautiful, isn't it?" she said.

"It is." Thomas reached out to touch the picture, then pulled away when his hand came back wet and sticky.

"The paint's still wet?" he said, rolling the lush blue and green colors around with his finger and thumb. He sniffed at the dripping hues, then turned to Naomi, whose cheeks had sagged to the floor.

3

The tan of her skin smeared together with the colors of her pink blouse as she collapsed into a giant, flowing puddle.

"We have been told by the authorities that 60 percent of the planet will be underwater by tomorrow. Ships and submarines of all sizes are being prepared." Words trailed away from Cathy the news anchor, who was now a talking skeleton sounding like an old record player as the TV sizzled and popped. Thomas spun to the painting, backing away and stumbling into one of the eight cushioned chairs that lined the dinner table. The plant centerpiece inside a matching gray vase came crashing down over the wood-like floors. *Why can't I recognize that island?* he wondered. Without warning, a brightly burning ball ripped through the sky, setting off a sudden explosion. The impact boomed and shattered the windows as high, roaring waters burst through the walls, dragging Thomas outside to an endless ocean.

CHAPTER ONE

NIGHT SEVEN HUNDRED AND FIFTY fell aboard the massive vessel *Lady Luck*. He had carved the days one by one into the wooden floor in Roman numerals, marking the spot where he slept in a starboard corner of deck three of six. It had been the main lounging spot of the once-luxurious cruise ship, equipped with ziplines, basketball courts, lounge chairs, and more lounge chairs. Now they had turned all space into living quarters for the 6,000 passengers on board, floating alone in a dark, endless ocean.

The air was thinning as the boat rocked and moaned against crashing waves. Thomas Edwards' pale fingers re-gripped Naomi in his arms, as he awoke coughing into the sleeve of his Navy military pullover sweater.

"Naomi...you asleep?" he whispered, then shivered, staring past the metal rails at the black sea, air clouds emerging as he breathed. The ocean and sky smeared together, a murky pink, black-and-blue like they had been badly bruised and beaten. A star that appeared so close he could pluck it from the sky and a full moon being obscured by forming clouds completed the scene. They wouldn't last much longer. Death was finally among them, in this beautiful nightmare of a moment, and to some it was a welcoming idea. Thomas peered over at a cry that suddenly burst from a few feet away. It came from deep inside a woman's belly. The kind he would hear at the church a few blocks from his old home during a funeral. He wasn't much of a religious person, but a few morning jogs left an impression when he heard the cries of someone who had lost their loved one. It was a feeling they all shared now, no matter the age, race, or beliefs.

Mrs. Elanor bawled into her purple bandana, pressing a small boy's head into her breast. Thomas, eavesdropping on the conversation, fumbled a small gold compass from his layered sweatpants and clicked the button that started a ticking red dial to spin around the face. North, south, east, west. The dial spun with no control. Closing it, he focused back on the argument rising between the others.

"Fifteen years!" Bill said.

"Fifteen years, you say," Frank remarked half-heartedly, as he stood at the railing, flicking his once-collectable coins into the black ocean.

"Yeah, a long fifteen years, too. A man learns a lot that long on the job, studying the clouds and the atmosphere. All that jazz. One thing I'm sure of is… those clouds ahead don't look good. I hate to be the one to interrupt the therapy session, but somebody had to say something. Or have you all gone insane?" Bill shouted at the group.

He was once a heavyset man, a storm tracker who had spent half his life staring at the sky. His aggression could make him seem more intolerable than he meant to be, and too often he spoke loud and out of turn, even when his opinions warranted it. Elanor, a sweet old woman from South Africa swaddled in a plaid cotton blanket, silenced her sniffles in the folded bandanna, choosing not to slap him in his face like she was prone to do when he was being rude. Surprised, Thomas turned and looked up at the clouds and bright lightning strikes.

Most were complete strangers to Thomas and his family, meeting them at the docks in Tampa Bay, Florida during the escape. Many more ships had set sail back then, back when the crisis first happened. Six thousand people made it aboard *Lady Luck*, Thomas and his family included. Fifteen ships, most of them military, a few cruise liners, and ten or more submarines had left from the piers of Franklin St. that night, and it had been over two years since they'd seen any of the other vessels. Now, the survivors were down to their last supplies; the ship was barely afloat, and hope was a more fragile dream than reality.

"No, no, he's right." Mrs. Elanor shivered with watery eyes; the others crammed on deck 3 at the testimony chimed for Big Bill to put a cork in his fat mouth.

"His father… my son… my boys… he's all I have left in the world, Bill, that's all I was saying," she said, clutching the boy like a newborn, even though he was all the age of twelve.

"I'm telling you, Frank!" Bill continued, pushing his squared bifocals up the brim of his nose and scratching at his patchy beard. "If we keep heading in this direction, we are going to run smack dab into that brewing storm. My guess is twenty minutes, that's all we got. Ship this size can't turn on a dime. We don't have enough spare boats or enough life jackets. Do you all understand that?" he shouted, his voice shaking out over the silent night. "We need a plan!"

"Is that right?" Frank said with a blank stare, clearly not in the mood for arguing. "Why don't you tell the captain then? He's lying right over there. I'm sure he could use your expertise." Frank threw the fistful of collectable coins into the sea with a back-arching stretch.

Thomas, still catering to his wife who had become ill, hadn't moved from that spot in days, eaten, or bothered to bathe either, glared at Bill, who flicked his sight away and back to the ocean.

"I'd rather not. He seems busy enough with his wife. It's just a thought, is all," Bill said.

"Aw, give it a rest, Bill!" Charlie said, from where he lay on the deck, fingers laced behind his head. He was Thomas's younger brother. "Tommy knows what he's doing. If there was a storm coming, I'm sure he would have already said something."

A wave smacked into the hull, forcing Charlie and others who were lounging on deck 3 to their feet with a unified moan. The stars and moon fully disappeared behind rumbling clouds; in seconds a batch of cold, stinging rain fell from the lightning-filled sky. Bill, not sparing another word, headed inside through a shattered glass door.

Thomas nudged Naomi.

"Try to stand, my love. He's right, you know. Seems like we got us a storm," he whispered. He secured a spot against the rail at the bow, one arm wrapped around the bar, the other around Naomi. The wind strengthened to a deep whistle like a blaring Pan flute, hurricane winds at near-freezing temperatures pushing against his grip. The icy water spewed over the lower decks; the winds rocked the ship without mercy.

"Everyone, brace!" Thomas screamed as the ship rose in the air from a forming wave, crisp winds pushing against his stomach as they plummeted back down with a slap.

Sending an unlucky few tumbling overboard.

The ship continued to rock and moan as Thomas limped Naomi to the life jackets on the wall.

"Captain, what do you think we should do?" a man asked with child in hand, pulling nylon straps that cuffed at the chest. Thomas whispered to Naomi, then spun to the surrounding chaos. "I, I, I don't know… I have no way to steer the ship," he said.

Appearing from the broken glass door of deck 3 was Big Bill.

"We're sinking! It's flooding inside. Release the lifeboats: women and children should be first, Thomas!" Bill shouted over the booming thunder. A flash of lightning with an explosive bang sent everyone's hands to their heads. The zip line, once a party favorite, a suspended cable of stainless steel meant to send smiling passengers from one side of the ship to the other, struck by a blinding blue bolt. It cracked and whipped in the air like a power line in a tornado. It whooshed, ripping from the ship, then wrapping around the legs of Mr. Wallace aka Big Bill amongst others and dragging them into the water with horrified screams.

The remaining passengers scrambled for the 32-person lifeboats that lined the sides of the ship. There were only 10 available, and each of these were collapsing into the choppy waves in a brawl and chaotic fashion. Thomas turned to the shouts from his brother.

"Tommy!" Charlie yelled. "We need to get a lifeboat, here! You and Naomi! Strap on your jacket," he screamed, tugging at Thomas's arm, who was still clinging to Naomi; she could barely stand on her own.

"No! We gotta stay on the ship as long as possible. They're going to drown out there. Let 'em go. I need to find my son! That's what I need to do."

"Jacob's fine! But we got to get a lifeboat ourselves or—"

Charlie's words halted, and a silence descended over the growing chaos. Thomas turned, looking at the ocean and bruised sky; his chin dropped onto his chest at what he was witnessing. Leaping from the water with a terrifying screech was a snakelike monster, casting a shadow twice the size of *Lady Luck*.

"What in the hell is that?" Thomas yelled as it maneuvered in the air, silhouetted by the moon. Charlie tugged from behind as the three of them scrambled across the upper deck. The creature landed, causing a high wave that crashed down on the ship. The waters forced him to lose grip on Naomi and tossed his brother overboard with a last scream.

Thomas slid across the deck, his head banging against a cluster of iron chairs, and then slid into the starboard railing that stabbed at his back. Gripping a bar, he dangled over the cold water as the boat continued to rock, his legs slapping against the ship.

"Naomi! Charlie!" he screamed, a shout swallowed by the drumming of thunder.

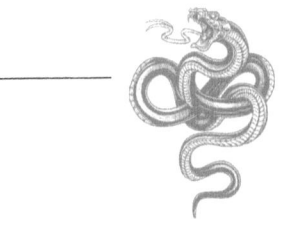

CHAPTER TWO

I TOSSED AND TURNED ON MY wooden cot. The constant tapping on the glass window from a tree branch that thinned at the tip like a finger, begging to get inside, kept me awake.

"I got to get some sleep..." I muttered, curling tighter into the thick cotton comforter. Usually, its fluffy white bundles of wool made me feel like I was sleeping under a cloud, like a member of a flock of sheep. Yet here it was, my third night in a row, without even batting an eye.

Tonight, it was the tree keeping me awake. Last night, the lack of shuteye came courtesy of a riveting nightmare of my Gathering. I've had that same one a few times now. A soldier, weapon drawn, barges into the house, dragging me by my hair as I kick and scream. I awake, panicked, kicking and flailing my arms into my pillow. Other nights were because of my mother in the bedroom next to me. All night long I listened to her grieving, bawling in hysteria, beseeching any god who would listen to stop the approaching Gathering.

All I could do was lie in my bed, staring up at the log ceiling, listening to the cries of my mother as a tragic, heart-wrenching lullaby.

I squirmed a little more in the fit-to-size cot, my eyes focusing back on that stupid tree. Accompanying my list of distractions was an orange glow that landed on the floor of my room, fading out right before being any real help in the dark. It was coming from the lone streetlight that stood tall over the neighborhood a few cabins down. The one and only streetlight in this section of Quadrant Three Sector rd. The rest of the quiet neighborhood was otherwise pitch-black at this hour; directional signs, unreadable, created roads and paths impossible to navigate without excellent knowledge of the terrain. Not to mention beasts of all kinds that lurked in the woods, which made traveling at night not only against the law for most islanders, but dangerous.

Turning away from the window, I stared at the darkened hallway that led to the kitchen. The worst distraction of them all was present. One that I couldn't see or hear but felt. Something's here again, this time hovering in the hall, watching me as I lie in bed.

It's like when someone enters your room and catches you daydreaming. They smile and say, "Sorry, I didn't mean to scare you," and then talk about whatever it is they were sneaking up on you for. But after my long stare, without blinking, there were no smiling faces appearing from the dark. No one there but the presence and its undeniable existence.

Slow drips of rain, sounding like tiny ice drops, tapped on the shingles of our cabin's roof. It was that time of year, cold and rainy. The noise mingled with the tapping branch, shrieks of wind, and other sounds of nature forming a symphony. It was peaceful. My eyelids fluttered in coordination like its conductor, first the winds, then the tiny ice drum section, very nice tapping tree. Before my eyes, slowly...closed...shut.

A blinding, blue flash of lightning acting as a crescendo symbol illuminated the room. Lightning has the tendency of revealing things that hide in the dark, and this flash was no different. As my eyes snapped open from the following boom, the shadowy figure standing at the edge of my bed vanished with the rest of the resounding thunder.

"Who's there?"

I sat up, quieting my breaths, though my heartbeat hammered out of my chest, in sync with the tree's fingertip.

"Okay, never mind, I'm up."

The plush comforter fell to the floor, exposing my socks and matching pajamas set. Bottoms and top, handstitched from a soft fabric mother and I both enjoy. Cotton. With decorative flowers painted on the pants leg, nothing upscale like you would find in Quadrant 4, but it keeps me warm at least. In the room's corner, I arrive at my old wooden desk. Handmade by my father and I on my twelfth birthday. He got the idea as we strolled the local market when we crossed paths with a musician. His name evades me, but he was superb at his craft, he drew a well enough crowd but had only made one coin. Father, being the woodsman he was, tipped him well and had a long discussion on where to purchase such fine wood of all things. "Every real artist needs a workstation," Father whispered to me on our way back home. I flopped down in the seat, reaching toward the lamp, and flipped its switch several times.

Nothing.

"Stupid generator."

I fumbled through the pullout compartment near the desk leg. Inside were stacks of papers from school, a chewed-on pencil, a used candle with dried wax spilling over its side, and an almost empty box of matches.

The rain continued its ice drops as the shadow of the orange flame danced on my wall and hanging portraits. My favorite portrait was the one of my father in a heavy, brown, wool jacket that looked like he was carrying a big, black bear over his shoulders. Staring straight ahead with that piercing glare, hair cut short and clean with thick, bushy eyebrows scowling inward. I painted that one on Mother's birthday a few years back, although Mother didn't enjoy looking at it much nowadays. I can hear her now:

"Rachel, please take that down. For me." With those sad blue eyes that she's now known for. I miss him too. I must glance at it fifty times a night whenever I'm scared. It makes me feel like he's still protecting us.

"Much better," I mutter, waving out the match as a soft vanilla scent permeated the surrounding air. I put the candle next to a black leather journal with my name, Rachel Patterson, stenciled on the cover in gold coloring from crystals. I brushed my fingers across the surface before skimming through the pages, smiling at an entry I once wrote that read, *Learn to drive, get married, become a painter. 1 for 3 is not so bad, I guess.*

Smiling and grabbing the chewed pencil, I find a clean page for a new entry and begin writing.

Three days. That's all I have, then they will sentence me to my Gathering. My new life awaits, as they say. . . I'm in all the papers this week, the most popular girl on the island. "Step right up. Cry for the girl with number 18." The nerve of the reporters printing that. Although a good cry might do me some good, but what do they know? I have seen a few Gatherings before when I was much younger. Some years are worse than others, but nothing can prepare you for the reality itself. The leading up to it turns out to be the hard part, if you ask me.

A wailing alarm blared outside, sounding over the entire neighborhood.

"Last curfew call already?"

I ran to the window, catching sight of the soldier truck, puffing by the lone streetlight and carrying that screaming horn as it traveled until it faded in the dark parts of Sector road.

The feeling returned, a distant presence crawling across the room.

"Who's there?" I said, spinning, not sure if I expected or perhaps even wanted a reply. I gazed out at the darkened hallway, the faint sight of the kitchen's entry only a few steps down the hall.

"Why is it so cold in here?"

A loud BANG! came from the kitchen, timed perfectly with another lightning strike. Briefly illuminating the cabin.

"Mom!" I shouted. *You're being paranoid, Rachel.* I thought, the words repeating in my psyche, not by my doing, but orders of a male islander by the name of Dr. Pooshay: it's pronounced—but spelled with an e so it looks like Poo-se on the name tag. Say that five times fast, some name for a doctor. I couldn't help but smile like an immature schoolgirl when we were first introduced. Dr. Pooshay, and all of his fine wisdom, saw fit to prescribe me some pills—nicknamed kickers by the local school junkies—who offered more than once to buy me out. These little green balls of poison meant to help me sleep.

Death pills, they should call them. With all the jitters and raging paranoia, I stopped taking them after only three days. The few hours of sleep they provided me with was an unhealthy balance.

I picked up the small plate and candle. The mystery of the bang needed solving as much as the generator needed restarting. Glancing at the picture of my father for comfort, terror crawled down my spine. A pair of black and blue marble-colored eyes, reflecting, peered down from where they stalked in the ceiling's corner. They watched through slits of long, black hair that floated as if it was underwater. I spun to where it hovered and lifted the candle, expecting to see something horrifying. The flame's light bounced on the ceilings of space and wooden logs. Nothing was no longer there. The hairs on my arms jumped out of my skin, my heartbeat hammering away.

"Mom!" I hissed, too afraid this time to shout it louder. In the hall, my sole light for comfort was the burning candle. I peered into my mother's room on my left. Her door was open, and mother, wrapped tightly in heavy white blankets she had taken from work years ago. I paused and listened to the snores that started and stopped, then gave a sigh of relief. At least one of us was finally getting some rest. I softly shut her door as more pounding and thuds against the walls came from the kitchen.

"I swear, Ashton, if that's you, I'm going to kill you for scaring the crap out of me." My best attempt at trying to sound brave as the wooden floors creaked beneath me.

I raised the plated candle in the air. Everything seemed normal enough. The kitchen table and its chairs were where they should be; the screen door that led to the back porch was still closed. Mother's rusted hanging pots and pans, however, played tricks on my mind, forming monsters that normalized to regular rusted kitchenware after a blink or two. *I'm definitely paranoid.* I pulled open the screeching back door of the home and headed outside for the generator out back.

It was running on powerful crystals that supplied the energy for the house. They built most homes in the neighborhood to work the same, the entire island when you really thought about it. You could purchase crystals from the local market, but no legal storefront or legit crystal dealer would be open for business after curfew. It was common for them to lose their power from time to time. So, an outage at this hour was not so strange.

The rain continued as I walked through the wet grass, dampening my socks. I arrived at the old generator and squatted on a patch of dirt. It was a block of a machine, red dials and yellow switches and knobs that lined its side. The rain extinguished the candle to a sizzling smoke trail as I spotted that the crystal in its rear part was out of place. An easy fix.

It gave a raspy buzz that sounded as if it was trying to clear its throat before the three crystals in its back shined blue. The lamp inside my room flickered a bright maroon light that shone through the window, reflecting off the scraping tree.

"That wasn't so bad."

As I stood, a beastly growl arose, low and menacing. Appearing in the bushes behind me was a pair of blue shining eyes. Running would only excite the animal snarling behind the bushes. The back door was only a step away; I would have to be quick.

At first budge, it leaped from amongst the hedges and launched itself on top of me as I let out a terrified scream, shielding my face with my arms. Relief washed over me when I felt his slobbery tongue, instead of a mouthful of carnivorous death, licking my face.

"Tojo, I only hoped that was you," I said, patting him on its thick, woolly fur.

"You scared me. That was you causing all that noise out here, huh, boy?" I rubbed his belly as he turned on his back, slobbering in approval. His black coat smelled of dirt and wet grass. Tojo was a cute wolf, but far from a puppy. He was equal to my size without even standing on his hind legs.

"How long have you been out here? Mrs. Walters would be sick if she knew you were out running around in this weather. Now go, run on home," I said, and pointed toward Mrs. Walters' cabin, a few buildings down the road.

The path was dark and damp, but I was sure he knew the way. He replied by lying on the ground and pointing his big, blue pupils up at me. The whine of a hungry wolf.

"Don't look at me like that," I said, standing and turning my back on him. "I'm going inside; it's raining and cold." True to nature, his growl picked up once again. *He must really be hungry,* I thought.

"Fine! Ok, you big baby. I'll get you something to eat, then you go home. I won't have your mother blaming me if you get sick!" He howled, and from the way he sat patiently I can argue that he understood me as I hastened back inside, flicking a small switch that illuminated the kitchen.

I approached the cabinets where we stored most of our food. An animal Tojo's size was used to eating meat, and lots of it. In fact, I had walked him several times and knew Mrs. Walters kept a refrigerator full just for him. But Mother and I didn't have the means to feed such an animal.

"This will have to do," I said and grabbed a half-eaten loaf of bread, and a small silver can filled with salted dead tiny fish from the shelves. When I turned, the bread fell to the floor, the can of raw fish rolled to a stop at the table leg. My hands shot to my mouth, gaping at the girl who was standing in the center of the kitchen. She wore a white, cotton gown, plain, with no decorations or artwork that stopped just pass the knees. Her small calves and ankles, covered by a black-colored sludge that slogged its way down both legs. To thick to be blood, but still looked a part of her, like she was leaking.

"Who are you?" My words more fragile then a spiders web, and she was the spider, weaving a web of false reality. This isn't real.

She didn't answer, nor did she move, but hummed rather. A song, no, a song sounds much too cheerful, much too celebrative. This melody was daunting, low pitch, even for a child's voice as it loomed over you like a lullaby on a dark and cold night. The strangest part, it sounded vaguely familiar, a repressed memory. My feet froze in place while my mind hummed along. I couldn't look away. When she finally paused and met my gaze, our eyes connected with an invisible current that sent shocks through my body. The world around me grew still and silent, like it was only the two of us left alive on the entire island. She belted a scream so loud it forced my hands to my ears. The blaring, ear piercing sound only meant for me, ringing in my mind. I wanted to scream. I even tried, but my voice and limbs had lost function as my feet began lifting from the floor. Hovering just above the kitchen table, peering down at the girl in white, standing in her own puddle of black goo, her black and blue marbled stare focusing on me, With the twitch of her head my body shot across the room and slammed against the wall so hard the crash turned my sight into a blurred wave.

I whimpered and forced my eyelids to a cheek tingling close. If only my mother would walk in and see me fighting with a dead girl, floating helplessly in the air with silent screams, she would know I needed more than kickers.

You're not being paranoid.

I begged for her to stop, the ungodly hi pitch scream rattling in my brain like the last bean in a can. When she finally obliged, and silence overtook the home,

I peeked.

Awed and terrified by her levitation as she floated across the kitchen, halting inches from my face. If she puckered her lips, she would have kissed me. Closer I could see the fine details of her skin, an artist habit of observation, pale and cracking like old stones. She was cold, I could feel it. And she smelled of something awful, something beyond death, long gone and forgotten. The lights began flickering like the house was being electrocuted while we levitated eye to eye. The kitchen back door nearly pounded off its spring hinges from Tojo scratching claws, as he howled and barked outside.

The generator powered off again without warning.

She slowly stretched open her mouth, further than physically possible, as if preparing for the fatal blow. Out from the black hole between jaws and throat. Slithered a small snake, hissing its way out of her mouth, then coiling itself and launching at me with a full thrust. I collapsed back to the floor as it missed, then bolted down the hall for my bedroom.

The sounds of small feet pattering on the ceiling above me.

When I reached my room, I slammed the door shut, snatched up the thick cotton comforter, and curled on my bed.

The empty silence, no raindrops hitting the roof, no tree scraping the glass, no generator humming, or snoring mother.

I peeked out from underneath the blanket. *Thank you, lone streetlight*, I thought, as the orange glow persisted. My door remained closed; the journal still lay on the desk where I left it; the room was empty. I leaned over the edge of my cot, spotting my worn school clothes and boots smashed together in a pile under the bed.

My heart thumping, I peered toward the ceiling; there she was hovering above me, those gateways to the afterlife peering down. I thought to throw the covers back over my head, but I couldn't stop watching the snakes swarming and fighting one another as they slid in and out of her mouth, ears, and eyes. I screamed when she lunged towards me.

When I arose, it was morning, and mother was sitting on the edge of my cot, dressed for work and sobbing into a fistful of tissue.

"Sorry, honey, I didn't mean to startle you," she said, her eyes red and puffy, as though she had spent the entire night crying. "Are you in the mood for breakfast?" she asked comfortingly, as I numbly gazed at the room.

I thought to myself, that seemed too real to be a dream, rubbing the supposed nightmare from my eyes and squinting against the sun that shone through the window.

"Um, yeah… give me a minute. Let me get dressed," I said.

"Sure thing, honey," Mother said, pecking at the top of my head before she exited the room, stifling her tears.

I sat in bed a minute longer, my mind reliving that terrifying nightmare.

"It seemed so real," I said, staring at the old wooden desk that still bore my opened journal.

"I got to get dressed."

I tossed the blanket to the floor and took up the school uniform under my bed. The required clothing: brown trousers and a dark-blue sweatshirt with the name *Anastasia* in big white letters.

"God, I hope Mrs. Collins doesn't make me speak before class this time."

I strapped on my rain boots. It had been a long week of unwanted attention, but still I had my reasons for attending school. When I stepped over to the desk and snatched up my journal, I pondered by the light of the lamp.

"Hmm…" I mused, assessing the probabilities as I flipped off the switch and headed to the kitchen for breakfast. But it was my mother, asking questions about the can of meat and bread on the floor, that assured me most. That was no dream.

CHAPTER THREE

T HE HORSES' HOOVES CLOPPED AGAINST the pavement as the driver slowed their pace to a thudding trot. Malcamore felt an annoying nudge in his side, then peeked up at Samson, dressed in his finest gray suit, matching hat, and holding his wooden hand-carved cane.

"Mr. Malcamore!" Samson shouted, giving Malcamore another nudge. "Mr. Malcamore, we've arrived at the capital."

A bright light from streetlamps hanging from vines on every tree shone through its window. Malcamore sat up in his place.

"Would you stop poking me with that damn cane!" he shouted, drowsy with a dry taste of sleep. He squinted out at the bustling city of Quadrant 4. Islanders walking the roads, soldiers' trucks, traveling wagons, and city busses crossing at intersections. It had been a dreadful trip across the island, an entire day's journey when traveling by horse.

"Good… so we're at the king's home, I take it."

"Not yet, sir. We've reached the City," Samson said. Malcamore scowled; a trip by wagon was not what he would call ideal, but he had never been to the new king's home, nor had he received an award. Tonight, they invited him to experience both. Malcamore began slapping the pockets of his pants, searching for his case of hand-rolled smokes.

"How long was I out, Samson?"

"About half a day, young sir. You slept completely through Quadrants 2 and 3."

"Mission accomplished," he said with a modest laugh, then fished out a silver flask from the lining of his jacket.

"It would have been much wiser if we had chosen another form of transportation. But we're still on schedule. We should arrive at the estate soon, I would think," Samson said, handing Malcamore his matching tie from the wagon seat.

"Oh, you would say so," he scoffed, snatching it and throwing it around his neck in a huffing fit. "I won't have us draining the island's resources, Samson, but I am so glad we are on schedule."

"You don't sound pleased. Would you prefer me to have the driver turn us around?"

Malcamore, however, was still fighting with his tie in frustration, unraveling the knot, huffing at the rocking of the carriage.

"They're having an entire event for me, Samson. It's in my honor. How could I not show up? They even addressed me this letter," he said, lifting a small envelope with his name *Benjamin Malcamore* in red writing.

"Well, you are very honorable," Samson said, then turned wide-eyed at all the islanders and bright lights of the city glistening in the backdrop.

"And what are you gawking at? You've got the face of a schoolboy," Malcamore scoffed again.

"Everything just looks so bright and alive in this Quadrant. Sort of reminds me of how things used to be. I love it. You know..." Samson said, leaning forward. "I too have met King Theodore." A smile grew under the old man's mustache.

"You've been here? After the war, I mean."

"Why, yes, once... Sure I wasn't the biggest supporter of King Theodore at first, but I have been to his home."

"You've never mentioned this to me. I must hear this one. Go ahead," Malcamore encouraged, victorious in the fight with the tie. He relaxed until the driver's plea interrupted.

"Whoa!" William shouted, stopping Samson's story before it could begin.

"Whoa, now!" he said. Malcamore peered from the carriage window. The bigger horse of the two, named Bubba, a dark brown stallion, was kicking its leg and pulling its head in the opposite direction.

"Uh, Mr. Malcamore! Mr. Samson! We've run into an issue, if you don't mind looking!"

Malcamore, joined by Samson, gazed out. The activities in the once-cheerful city had halted. The busy roads turning quiet, islanders stopping, still as statues as they watched the lone four-wheeled wagon pass down the path to *Kings rd.*

"What do you make of this, old man? You said you've been here before," Malcamore whispered.

"I'm not sure. It seems, everyone's acting odd now, young sir."

"Odd is putting it mildly." Malcamore grunted, grabbing for the gun at his waist.

A few who were watching the wagon began walking alongside. One, dressed in a black robe with the islands symbol in the center, the usual attire of someone who spent his workdays preaching about the gods to the other Quadrants. Jumped on rails, Malcamore had installed a few years ago for Samsons handicap and pulled on the wagon's locked door handle.

"What are you doing?" Samson shouted, scooting to the other side of the wagon. The islander flicked a floppy tongue that splatted against the glass, leaving behind a sloppy wet print that oozed its way down. Another, dressed like a local mechanic, was running stride for stride and whispering words that strung together without pause.

"Get away from the wagon! Or lose a limb!" Malcamore shouted, hitting the window with the back of his gun. The islander let go and tumbled onto the dirt before springing back up to his feet.

"What in the name of Anastasia is going on?" Malcamore said.

"You know, young sir… I have heard that newcomers are more than rare now. It's forbidden, they say. Nobody may enter Quadrant Four without invitation," Samson said. Malcamore peered out at a sign on a corner that read *Path to Kings road*. He peered behind them at the islanders of Quadrant Four, stopping their pursuit, and watched from the paved road.

"Since the war, no one has dared step foot on this side of the island. No one," Samson said.

Malcamore took a few more steadying sips out of his silver flask, then leaned out of the wagon's window.

"Continue on! I won't have these freaks ruining my night! We have our invitation."

"Yes, Mr. Malcamore!" William shouted back, whipping at the reins.

Malcamore shifted his sight back to Samson as he dropped in his seat, guzzling down the remaining substance in his flask that burned its way down his stomach.

"Although, I might revise that if this approach keeps up."

"I agree. No award or celebration should be worth this trouble. And please tell me if I'm stepping over the line here."

"You're stepping over the line," Malcamore said, stretching out for what relief an islander his size could find in a basic traveler's wagon.

"That may be so, young sir, but do you think it's a great idea for you to be drinking so much before you get to the king's home?"

"It's a celebration, Samson, in my honor."

"I know, but... I would expect you would need to be... level-headed, for lack of a better word."

"Level-headed? You must be getting old, dear friend." He laughed, prancing his fingers through the air with a mocking grin. Samson frowned at the gesture.

"Relax, you old grump. I won't take another sip."

Travel had become much more enjoyable now that they were out of the city. No signs of irate islanders, only miles upon miles of lush meadows and grass-covered hills acting as bottoms for small mountains. Samson stared out at the view of slopes and the stars glimmering in the sky above them, while Malcamore spent his time re-studying the letter he had received from the king's court, stamped with the island's famous symbol, and a message inside that stated, *Your treason has been forgiven, we will award you the honor of joining the Brotherhood.*

Mr. Benjamin Malcamore and thank you for your service. The bottom of the page was Theodore's signature, signed in blood-colored letters. It was the first communication Malcamore had received since the war had ended.

"Why would the king choose to award me now?" he whispered, peering over the top of the letter at Samson.

Deprived of his hip flask, he fetched another hand-rolled smoke, struck a match, and exhaled another deep breath.

"How much longer, Samson? I'm becoming restless."

"We're arriving now," Samson said as the carriage slowed before coming to a full stop at a luxurious metal gate. Samson grabbed his cane and dismounted while Malcamore gazed at the long, daunting pathway to the king's home. Despite the exhausting ride and the strange greeting from the islanders, excitement was growing inside him.

"Wow," he whispered. He could hear music playing and guests chattering in the backdrop. The air smelled of fresh beef stew and burning wood.

"Is there a problem?" Malcamore asked, preparing to step out of the coach, beaten to the punch by an overly eager guard, who had already given the handle a hard pull.

"Sorry, Mr. Malcamore, but it's the rules. He won't show us his wrist," the guard said. "We require everyone to identify, orders from King Theodore himself."

"I absolutely will not!" Samson shouted. "We are the honored guests of this very dinner. Why should we have to identify?"

"Well, *we* are not the honored guests; *I* am the honored guest," Malcamore said. "And why in Anastasia are you creating a commotion about nothing, you grumpy old man? Show the soldier your wrist." Malcamore leaned out of the coach as he pulled up the sleeve of his suit, revealing his number and symbol.

The soldier pulled a black device from his pocket and flashed its intense blue light, causing his number and symbol to glow. He walked over to Samson and did the same, much to Samson's dismay.

"Thank you, Mr. Malcamore. Ok, they're clear!" the soldier shouted.

"Oh, you don't say," Samson said as he re-entered the wagon and the horses scampered down the graveled path.

Malcamore's uneasiness continued as the laughter from the party became clearer with every turn of the wheel as they traveled the last road, dark with tall, leafless, hugging trees above their heads.

"Everything all right out there?"

"Yeah! It's fine. Can't see a damn thing, though!" the driver said.

Malcamore forced down the slight lump in his throat.

"Are you, all right?"

"I'm great. Nerves, Samson. I'll be fine," he said, grabbing a handkerchief from his suit coat pocket to wipe the drips that had assembled at the top of his forehead.

"Now, about this time you visited the king," Malcamore said, refolding it to his pocket.

"Does the name Harold Wellington ring any bells?"

"Harold Wellington, Harold Wellington?" he said, tugging on a smoke in thought. "Ah! The author, right?"

"Correct, young sir! But not just any author—he was the finest poet I'd ever had the pleasure of meeting. Responsible for some of the best literature available on the island," Samson said.

"All right, and what's his part in this story?"

Samson curled his finger at Malcamore, who leaned in closer and dropped his voice to a whisper. "A book…"

Malcamore scowled. "A book?"

"Yes, a mandatory read. Everyone was calling it. All citizens on the island were to receive a copy after their testing, the new law."

"Mandatory read? New law? I've never heard of it."

"And neither would you. They never printed the book, thank God... or so I was told."

"Hmm... go on."

"From what I heard, maybe our king and his lords are not who we think."

"I work for them Samson, and he's your king."

"You're right and excuse me." Samson reached into the compartment of his gray suit, fetching his own hip flask, and swallowed a large gulp. Malcamore shot him a disapproving stare.

"And when we first met, I did not understand how you were part of the mob," Samson said, swallowing his drink. "You were always so kind, but Wellington, he was never the same after we returned from his visit, if you catch my drift. There was a distinct look in his eyes; he was sick. It was quite scary, young sir, quite scary. It's why I escaped from him with my wife, and then we found you. I still wasn't a hundred percent sure until that welcoming we just had. Something strange is definitely going on with this Quadrant."

Samson leaned back in his seat, and Malcamore did the same.

When the two first met, after the war 18 years ago, he had hidden Samson and his wife from a swarm of soldiers. He had stumbled upon them hiding in his fields, Samson bleeding from the leg.

Anyone suspected of still supporting the deceased King Pius III was in danger. But after the two swore their innocence, Malcamore granted him and his spouse permission to live in his home until things cooled down.

In the passing years, Samson's wife had come down with a severe illness that swept through the island like a plague. She died peacefully in her sleep soon after. Samson, heartbroken, asked Malcamore if he could continue to live with him. Malcamore full-heartily agreed, and the two had been inseparable ever since.

After a moment's pondering, Malcamore gasped. "So, you lied to me that day in my fields!"

The old coach jerked to a halt in front of a dimly lit palace made of stone and wood that sat amongst an open field of plush grass. They lined the driveway with a mixture of polished trucks and horse-driven wagons, much fancier than Malcamore's. The driver swung around in his chair and announced, "We have arrived at the king's estate!"

Samson studied the view outside, then switched back to Malcamore. "The time seems appropriate."

The driver opened the door to the carriage as Malcamore tossed out his cigarette to the grass.

"Before we go, are you sure Wellington never mentioned to you what he learned about King Theodore?"

"No, not a word. But if I'm being honest, whatever it was he learned cost him his life, I suppose," Samson said with a glare.

"Point taken, Samson. I'll be careful."

"Please do."

Malcamore stepped out of the coach, accompanied by Samson. They could see someone approaching so briskly that the back of his jacket flapped behind him in the wind.

"Mr. Melcamore!" he called as he extended his stubby hand in greeting.

"It's *Mal*camore. Lord Sanders, I presume? Glad to put a face to those letters. I hear plans of some big changes for our island are being prepared," Malcamore said, shaking his hand.

"Right! Malcamore, my apologies. Won't happen again, I swear; been doing a little too much celebrating myself. And yes, we have some very minor changes approaching. But don't let that worry you, son, nothing we can't handle," Sanders said. Sweat pouring down his cheeks as he swiped with the sleeve of his coat.

"Oh, and allow me to introduce my assistant, Samson, and my driver, William."

Lord Sanders gave a loud laugh. "Your assistant! Even I don't have an assistant, son."

"No surprises there," Samson muttered. The criticism too low for Lord Sanders to register. But Malcamore shot him another disapproving glance.

"Nice wagon you got here. Old school, I like it. Fine pair of beasts," Sanders said, nodding at the driver while he brushed Bubba with his palm.

"Thank you, sir. That's Coin, and that's Bubba, the big one there. I raised them both myself."

"Nice, very nice…and, Samson." He shifted his eyes to survey Malcamore's colleague, his stare now intent as he sought to concentrate. "Have we ever met before? You look familiar."

"Oh, no, sir, I should say not—I would have recalled."

"You fight in the war?"

"No, sir, just a humble servant all my life."

"Now that's depressing, son." An inappropriate laugh belted.

"You're King Theodore's new lord, correct?" Samson asked.

"You got it! And don't think I haven't heard about you boys sneaking around my island, taking all our booze and women." Sanders laughed at his own joke, slapping Samson on the back with a loud smack. Malcamore cringed.

"Well, I can't speak for Mr. Malcamore, but I would never! But I've read a lot about you in the papers."

"Well, don't do too much reading, Samson, is it? It'll rot your brain."

"Correct me if I'm mistaken, sir, but isn't the island the poorest it has ever been? Not to mention this year's Gathering." Samson said.

Lord Sanders's drunken banter turned serious as he stepped so close that Malcamore knew he could smell the liquor and stew on his breath. "Not for much longer," he whispered, his facial expression sinister for a pause, then cheerful.

"Now! Are you coming in or what?" He directed this question toward Malcamore. "We've got all night to talk politics. It's time we honor the islander himself."

Lord Sanders threw his arms around Malcamore, leaving Samson to follow as he escorted them inside the massive doors of King Theodore's home.

CHAPTER FOUR

EXHAUSTED AFTER BEING HELPED BACK aboard by survivors, Thomas lay curled on the flooded deck, softly stroking his wife's hair, who he found wedged between tables. She bawled into his soaked sweater, shaken and bruised.

"Now Charlie and Jacob are both gone? I can't take much more, my love. I think I'm dying, and it's so cold," Naomi whispered.

The earlier cries for help were silencing; the only sounds now were the slaps of water against the ship and random rumbles of thunder. His eyes grew heavy as they peered down at the dark ocean in mourning. He feared this time he had lost both his brother and his son for good. A ripple in a wave that thudded beneath them brought his mind back to the creature they had seen leaping out of the ocean.

"What... was that?" he said, staring down at the waves sloshing in repetition. It was down there, lurking. He was sure of it. The survivors who remained aboard and those who failed to retrieve a lifeboat returned to deck 3, hugging, bawling, and some crying as they embraced.

As the seconds passed, the tune of complaint turned to one of jubilation:

"Oh my God!"

"We're saved!"

"He did it! We're saved!"

Looking up, Thomas realized the cries were not of horror, but excitement. Then he too spotted the enchanted, glistening island appearing in the far distance, hovering over the black abyss. He scrunched his face in disbelief, wiping his eyes to confirm he was not dead.

"That can't be real," he said, narrow-eyed at the island floating just above the water, the waves currents rocking the massive ship closer to its shore. "Honey, look," Thomas said, standing.

Naomi gasped, and Thomas leaped into action, his voice just above a whisper.

"Ok, everyone, gather around," he ordered, clearing his throat and pushing the words louder over the growing excitement.

"Calm down, everyone, front and center, so I can take count," he said, tallying the heads one at a time, in tears at the absence of his brother and son.

"Now, we don't know if that island is safe or where it even came from. I think the women and children should stay here, while every able man joins me to make sure it's ok. We must be safe," Thomas said, stepping before the numbered far fewer than 6,000 who first boarded the ship two-and-a-half years ago: a rough thirty-three at the present, woman and children included. Their smiles left their battered faces as the silence of reality came over the group. "Well, don't all volunteer at once."

Frank Brusward appeared from the back of the crowd, the orange life jacket still cuffed around his neck.

"I'll go with you," Frank said.

"Me too," said Mrs. Elanor's grandson, Jack, pulling from her grasp and pushing his way to the front. A few other men stepped forward, able bodies such as Victor, Liam, A. J., and Elijah. Thomas led the small group of volunteers to the captain's closet on deck 6, where he kept weapons for such a time. A few Glock handguns, a pair of proof switch rifles, and one flare. Passing each out at random with its ammunition to men who could barely load them. At the front of the wheelhouse was a wooden helm, which he approached slowly, spinning the wheel that had all the restraints of a child's toy. Useless without power. Scanning the room that was filled with blank computer screens, motherboards once used for route planning, tracking winds, and monitoring hurricanes, now nothing but junk scraps with short-circuited wiring and broken glass. He gave the slick, wooden helm another few useless turns to the left, then to the right, then gazed out at *Lady Luck*'s speed as it cut through the waves. Surprised they were still afloat, and how fast it was heading for the island in the distance.

"Something is steering us," he said, staring out of the broken window.

Soon the ship came to a crashing stop at the foot of a vast peninsula, its bottom pressing against the bank. The atmosphere was warm, a welcoming feeling. Once the men had said goodbye to their families, they dropped a long, wooden emergency ramp overboard. Thomas's boots splashed down on damp sand. He took a deep, chest-expanding inhalation. Had they really done it, had they really found land? A breeze, carrying the smell of animal dung and vegetation, filled his nose as he turned to the cheering men, kissing the ground and thanking their lucky stars, then to the sand and the jungle in the distance. The trees hummed like a running generator or a barbed wire fence. It gave off a bright blue glistening that started at the roots, then spanned upward to the final tip of green and blue leaves.

"Fascinating," he muttered, then picked up a rock from where it lay. It sparkled like a stone he once found in a cave on vacation when he visited Tennessee as a child.

Then something in the dirt, much more disturbing, caught his eye.

"Look at that sky! Have you ever seen a sky like that, captain?" Frank asked with all the joy of a child on Christmas morning, walking up from behind and pointing up to the purple and green swirl that joined the appearing stars.

"I'm sorry about your brother, Tommy. He was a good man, he really was. But you've done it, damn it! He wouldn't have believed this, but you found land," Frank said, shaking Thomas by the shoulder.

"I still don't believe it myself," Thomas said, dropping the heated rock and dusting the wet dirt from his hands.

"Where do you think this place came from? It's so warm. It couldn't have possibly survived the ice rocks, or the floods, you think? And what's with those trees?"

A small bell rung from his pocket. Thomas reached in his pants and clicked the gold compass with a red dial, only pointing north. He stared at the ground.

"That thing that leaped out of the water, Frank, I couldn't make out what it was. Could you?"

"It all happened so fast, and I was trying to forget. It was dark and raining. How can anyone be sure what we saw? Maybe it was like a whale or something? Or some kind of undiscovered sea creature," Frank said.

Thomas looked up at Frank, then gestured down at the stone he'd just dropped. Next to the glistening rock was a 4ft webbed footprint in the sand.

CHAPTER FIVE

As MOTHER AND I FINISHED breakfast, I explained how I dropped the food last night when feeding Mrs. Walters's wolf Tojo. I didn't dare say anything about the girl; I didn't want to worry her further. Once done with our quiet daily breakfast, a meeting of questions like "How's the student's treating you in school?" I say fine and return a question about her work at the Drums. We washed up and headed for the old red truck parked on the front lawn.

Thuds and clacks came from under the hood while I stared out of the passenger window. *Who was that girl?* That was the only question in my mind worth pondering.

"Ok, that ought to do it," Mother said, closing the hood with a loud thud and snapping me out of my thoughts. It was her third attempt. She wedged a tiny bronze colored key into a slot next to the steering wheel and gave it a twist. The motor ignited with a ruffled boom, and a bright blue glow from the crystals powering the engine illuminated the ground beneath it.

"She's still got some fight in her," Mother said, smiling at me and trembling from the rumble.

We rarely drove, only if the weather in the Quadrant was rough, or when public transportation failed because of maintenance issues. I thought the truck was a bother more than an asset. Not only would its loud pipes bang as we traveled, making the idea of being inconspicuous impossible, but it was also pricey to maintain, with its constant usage of the island's crystals.

"A year's earnings to buy the damn thing and another year's earnings to keep it running," Father would say, coming into the house covered in soot after a long evening of replacing the charcoaled gems that had lost their power. I can still picture all his tools laid out across the front lawn on a big tarp, Father underneath, growling and murmuring to himself. Yet now, the old truck sped down the rocky roads of Quadrant Three. My mother, dressed for work in her matching scrubs, peered ahead, pushing her long, black hair from her face.

"I cannot believe they have the audacity to force you to attend that school."

"It's okay. I'm not even certain they're forcing me. It's therapeutic in a way."

"Any reporters been coming by?" Mother asked, in that tone where she knew she wouldn't like the answer.

"A few. They've been hanging around the halls. Principal Easterling thought it would be a good idea if I answered some questions for them. I didn't mind." I could tell by my mother's sickened reaction my words sent a creeping anger down her back.

"Rachel!" she shouted.

When I said, "It's fine," she frowned as if something awful had stunk up her nose.

"Questions? What questions should they have to keep asking an innocent girl, when they should ask that so-called King they put in charge all the questions? Puh! He has another thing coming if he thinks I'm going to just sit by."

As she continued her daily tirade, my mind snapped back to the little girl. Even in the comforting light of day, she still troubled me.

"She had to be real."

"What was that, honey?"

"Huh? Oh, it was nothing." I could sense Mother's stare.

"You know, we could keep on driving, drive until we're out of the Quadrant. I'll drive us off of this God-forsaken island if I have to."

Quietly, I turned my eyes to Mother's. I had hoped our last argument was the end of the discussion.

"And I would keep you safe. We would be ok; I will keep you safe. I can do it," she pleaded, glancing over, waiting to hear my response. "The Gathering is in two days," she pushed. "That's a good enough head start before anybody even noticed we were missing."

The red truck, with its scraped paint and hard, padded seats, pulled to the side of the road at a bland interchange. One turn could send us out of the Quadrant. It was that simple, it seemed.

"I'll give us a fighting chance." My mother's look was more desperate than I had ever seen. I couldn't find my words, staring out across the swamped fields and old wooden huts that lined the side of the road. Every second I tried to open my mouth, nothing would arise but a soundless whimper.

"Running from the Gathering is treason, Momma. They would kill us both."

"And that's a risk I'm willing to take!" she shouted.

43

"Where would we run? How would we live past the wall? We don't even know what's beyond Quadrant Three, never mind Anastasia."

"I don't care; we can find out. Or we could continue running from Quadrant to Quadrant until they're tired of chasing us."

"They'll never get tired of chasing us!" I shouted back, a little too loud for Mother's liking as she snapped a glare my way. "No one's ever escaped the Gathering, and I won't have us both living on the run because of me."

"I say we try," she said, blinking away a falling tear.

I wanted nothing more than to say, "hit the gas," and we would drive off into the sunset, leaving Quadrant Three and all its troubles behind. But I knew this was nothing but a dream. The bitter truth of it was that neither Mother nor I had any experience in crossing the island. There were murdering travelers, criminals on the run. A quick read of the daily paper could thoroughly inform you if you wanted to know more. Not to mention unforgiving animals not friendly like Tojo, who would see us as dinner if spotted at the wrong moment. The mob of soldiers, the king's guards, King Theodore himself, who, upon learning of our escape, would not stop hunting us until we both were dead. To put that risk on my mother or my friends, I would not allow. The number 18 was my burden to bear alone.

"Well, I'm leaving with you," Mother said after she had enough of the silence that came between us.

"And what about the drums, those children? Who would counsel them if you're not there?" I asked.

"You're my daughter! I love you more than my job, or anything else."

"Then don't ruin everyone's life over me! There has to be a better way." The words must have stung her like a hundred bugs, as she shook, then rested her head in her palm for a moment to calm herself.

"God, you are as stubborn as your father was," she hissed.

"I miss him too, Momma."

She put the old truck into gear as we putted down the graveled road and continued our drive to Anastasia High School.

As I gazed out of my window at the old, wooden shacks that transitioned to a long stretch of damp meadows, we came to another crawling stop a few miles down and parked in front of a wooden hut right outside the school.

"You want anything from out of here?" my mother asked. I looked up at the old, crooked shack that was barely standing, propped up by molding boards on its four corners. The tall grass surrounding it during the hotter time of year would project a stunning green. But at present, the clumps appeared brown and gloomy, slumping from all the rain. A grumpy, old man named Lewis—Lew, you knew him well enough—ran the shop. He had gotten the grand idea to turn his home into a shop long before I was born. When I was much younger, I enjoyed wandering in his former living room, browsing the shelves stacked with cans of fruit, medicine, hunting tools, and even toys at the right time of year.

"No, I'm fine."

"Ok, I need to run in here and grab a few things for work. I'll just be a second." Mother exited the truck and approached the old, wooden shop surrounded by damp grass. I looked up to the sky as gray clouds formed, blocking the beaming sunlight.

My mind was racing, not only about the strange girl, but about school. There would be a lot of talk about the approaching Gathering, I was sure. As surreal as it all seemed, I needed to say my last goodbyes, especially to my best friend. Surely, he wouldn't miss my last day.

"Hello… Hello, Lew. You in there?" I turn to Mother, watching her as she peeked through Lew's dusty windows.

"Hello… Lew?" Mother said, pounding her fist on the molded door.

"Hey, Mom. Mom!"

"Yeah?"

"I changed my mind." The truck door squeaked as I opened it, and my feet landed on graveled rocks and grass patches. I had my reasons for the change of mind: the face of the little girl in white appeared from inside Lew's shop. Mother hadn't mentioned a word about seeing her, which I took to mean that she couldn't.

"Geez, Rach, you almost gave me a heart attack. I don't think Lew's here," Mother said, attempting to follow my gaze when my boots splattered over a pool of wet — "Mom, is that… blood?" I asked, spotting the red trail that led to the fields behind the hut.

Before I knew it, I was chest-deep in wildly growing grass with wet tips poking at my school sweater.

My friends and I used to walk this route home every day after school, back when they still lived in the neighborhood.

I had entered a path in the trees, following the blood drops, when I picked up my mother's voice.

"Rachel! Get back in the truck," she shouted.

The blood stopped at the foot of a leafless tree, dripping from a small pile of bones. I looked at the triangle symbol tattooed on my wrist and saw that they structured the bones similarly. Someone had put this here. A crackle of dead tree limbs that had fallen a few feet away grabbed my attention. Looking up from my wrist, we locked eyes, me and something hideous, never seen, at least by me, and I'd walked nearly every inch of Quadrant Three. It had a body like a snake, but it crawled on all fours, hissing. A red, forked tongue in the air that clicked as it escaped from its mouth. I covered my scream, backing away as the little girl appeared between us, dressed in her torn, white gown that dropped just below the knees, and whispered, "Run."

I ran back the way I had come, with monstrous screeching sounds chasing me as I trampled through the thicket, being careful not to fall as I leaped over curling vines and tree stumps. I could hear its loud cries getting closer, feel its blood-thick breaths on my back. Finally, bursting out of the woods and into the damp meadows, I spot the truck tires kicking up dirt as it pushed through patches of tall grass. I glanced behind me, expecting to see that monster nipping at my heels, but surprised to find nothing there, and the screeches had faded to the sounds of banging pipes and a rumbling motor. *Those damn Kickers; you're losing your mind, Rachel.* Mother jumped out in one motion and with a loud warrior shout, grabbed a gun from the back and gave it a crystal-filled pump.

"I'm a shoot!" she screamed. Falling to the ground, I covered my head.

"Don't shoot," I yelled, peeking from my cover at her warrior-filled eyes, prepared for battle.

"What the hell? Rachel, what happened? What was chasing you?"

I slowly rose, slapping off wet grass and dirt from my school uniform. "Nice gun. Where d'you get it?"

"Never mind that. Why were you screaming?"

I limped back inside the rumbling truck and closed the door. Mother tossed the gun in the back, slammed the driver's door shut, and turned to face me. "You're bleeding," she said.

I glanced down at the blood splattered on my school pants. "It's nothing. I'm fine. Can we just go?"

"Let me see your leg, Rachel."

"It's not my blood, Momma. Look." I stretched my leg across the seat of the truck, rolling up the blood-splattered pants to my knee. "See, I'm fine. Now can we please just get out of here?" The tall, slumping grass surrounding the truck ruffled as I whipped my head every direction.

"No! First you need to talk to me, Rach. How can I know what's going on with you if you won't tell me?"

The thoughts of some innocent islander in the woods being devoured by that thing were taking priority in my mind. I couldn't even make out Mother's words. I had never seen anything so hideous. It all happened so fast.

"Something could have eaten Lew …"

The words sort of slipped from my mouth. I couldn't read if she believed me or not, but the shock on her face was a start.

"What?"

I didn't want her to think I was going crazy, although I wasn't sure that I wasn't.

"Yeah, this thing…with claws. It looked like a snake, a really big snake, and it made this clicking sound…" I shook as flashes of it reappeared in my memory. "It was eating, I'm sure of it. You didn't hear it?"

"No, I didn't hear anything… Where did it go?"

"When I looked back, it disappeared. We can talk about it more later, I promise. But can we please just leave?" I asked, pulling down my pants leg and jumping from the movement of the grass.

"Ok, later." Mother, without another question, put the truck in gear and drove us out of the meadows and back toward the main road. Rolling over the trail of blood, and passing Mr. Lewis' shop, the truck slammed to a halt at the sudden bang on the passenger window.

It was Mr. Lewis, slamming his wide-stretched palm against the glass, gesturing for me to lower it.

I did not.

"Hey, Katherine, sorry. I called back at you when you were at the door, but you must not have heard me. What's with all the screaming?" he asked, with his hands collapsed to his knees. I surveyed him from my seat. The plaid shirt and dirty red hair and rotten teeth were a normal appearance for Lew, but today he seemed different, offput and fidgeting. It was in his eyes.

"Yes, about that," Mother said. The door squeaked open, and she stepped out of the truck. I thought to stop her.

"I wanted to buy some cloths and material for work. I even banged at the door pretty hard. Then Rachel spotted blood and said this creature attacked her?"

Mr. Lewis, unflinching at my stare from behind the window glass, said, "Blood... Creature?" He looked up at the sky in thought, as if the answer were hiding in the clouds. "No, haven't seen no creatures. All kinds of snakes, though. They love to hide out in those fields when it's damp like this."

"You've got to put out some traps or something, Lew!" Mother shouted. "Rachel could have gotten hurt!"

"Yeah, you're probably right. I killed me a snake round 'bout six feet just the other day."

"Six feet?" Mother gasped.

"Yup. Gutted him and cooked him for dinner too, right out front. That explains the blood you saw. Seems to me they get more aggressive around this time of year," he said, looking at me.

"That was no snake," I whispered, then shouted, "There were piles of bones out in your woods!"

"Bones?" Lew said, his face wrinkling.

"Yeah, I thought it was from you. I thought that thing had eaten you."

"Hmm. Another mystery to me. Ain't nobody been here but my wife and me. You two were the first visitors of the day. I'll go out there and check it out though. Piles of bones out there. You sure?" A glob of spit left his mouth and landed on the dirt.

"I'm sure," I said.

"Well, if you do, please be careful. I didn't see that thing she was talking about, but I was ready for it," Mother said.

"Don't you worry your pretty little heart, Katherine. I'll be fine," Lew said with a laugh that ended in a wheezing cough. "Now come on. I'll let you inside so you can get what you need for work. Wouldn't want you coming all this way for nothing." I could see my mother's face questioning the offer when she followed Lew's steps.

"Hey, I'm coming in with you," I said before they reached the mold-covered door.

The dark hut smelled of tobacco and spoiled fruit. I beat away annoying buzzing flies with my hands, who were busy having a feast out of the old fruit basket on one shelf. Most of the shelves lining the living room were empty, except for some smokes and the medicine section. Mother studied a patch of white cloths and ointments; I could feel Lew's eyes planted on me from the other side of the room. When we approached the counter where Lew was standing, Mother laid two packs of cloths and three ointment bottles on the countertop.

"That a cost you seven coins."

While Mother ransacked her pockets, I spotted a pile of bloodied black robes sitting by the door. They had something written on them, but the letters were too far away for me to read.

Lew was watching me.

"Like I said, killed me a snake the other day," he said, then grinned. Relief came when I smelled fresh air and we finally exited the shop. I couldn't tell if I was being paranoid, but was happier outside.

"Thank you, Lew. I'll see you next time, ok?" Mother said as she waved goodbye, and I watched Lew stand guard in front of the old hut until we drove out of sight.

CHAPTER SIX

MALCAMORE AND SAMSON ENTERED THE dining hall and crowded party. The smell of burning sage from a crystal chandelier that hung from the ceiling, giving off a burgundy light. The laughter and conversation, including a violin-based band that played delightful music in an adjacent room, squeaked to a halt. He skimmed the now silent festivity; everyone dressed in black robes draped over their clothing, with a white mask, cutouts for the eyes, nose, and mouth.

"Why is everyone's face covered? I feel overdressed," Samson said, brushing down his gray-colored suit.

Malcamore shrugged, peering at one masked face after another. No one had mentioned any specific attire to him. "Just when I thought the night couldn't get any weirder." Malcamore said.

Lord Sanders drunkenly stretched both arms out wide as his voice sounded over the party. "Mel...Malcamore!" he said and nodded at the name, sure to get it right this time. "Has arrived, my fellow islanders!" The guests pulled back their masks from their faces, then clapped their hands together in a slow-forming applause. Malcamore half-waved and smiled crookedly as the chatter returned to normal volume and everyone re-masked once again. The string-based band struck up another tune, one Malcamore thought sounded too sad for the occasion.

He followed Lord Sanders's drunken bravado, stumbling through the dining hall, shoving aside conversations. After the last, "Out of my way!" and shove, he gestured to six large dining tables, draped with snowy-white cloths facing an elegant, curved staircase. "Seat for the man of honor," Lord Sanders said.

"Hello and thank you for your service."

"Yes, thank you for your service, Mr. Malcamore. This wouldn't have been possible without you."

"Yes, nice to meet you, sir, and thank you." One masked islander after another greeted him with the same formality, shaking Malcamore by the hand.

"Give him some space, you animals!" Lord Sanders said, stumbling into a seat at the table and clasping a mask to his face, with an aggressive pop of the string at the back of his head.

"Quite a crowd," Samson whispered. The maroon lighting from the chandelier dimmed darker to a shadowy haze and all those still standing rushed to their chairs in a hurry, padding their feet and scraping chairs into position as they filled the six dining tables to capacity.

"Guess we're starting already," Malcamore said as the rapping sound of high heels came from the second floor.

A woman appeared in a long, black, flowing dress. Her red shoes clacked as she approached the balcony that overlooked the party.

Hair, full and curly, dropping just below the shoulder, hid her face. They applauded and whistled as she leaned over the rail with a smile. Malcamore grinned at the sound of her voice.

"Ladies and gentlemen, welcome to the initiation of Mr. Benjamin Malcamore!" she shouted dramatically over the room as she clapped her hands together, gesturing for Malcamore to stand. He gave a smirk, stood, and waved to those in attendance at the other tables.

"Okay, okay, fellow islanders, settle down. I know we're all overly excited to hear from Mr. Malcamore. I'm sure he has a very interesting story to tell. But first..." She peeled the mask from her face, her smile turning mischievous.

"How about a few words from the man I am honored to call my husband? Our leader, King Bratust Theodore! First of his name." The islanders surged to their feet as the king exited a room and took abrupt steps to the balcony, waving at the crowd.

Malcamore had only met him once, but that was before he was king, when Malcamore was a boy and first wanted to join the mob. He looked much older now, but still as confident, wearing a long, black robe with his gray hair slicked to the back. "Thank you, Rose, for that lovely introduction. My beautiful wife, ladies and gentlemen. Isn't she amazing?" He gave her a kiss on the cheek as the crowd clapped its approval. Rose nodded politely and walked down the left side of the curved staircase, taking her seat at a table. Malcamore conveyed his suspicion at Samson, whose facial expression said the same.

The applause silenced at one swing of King Theodore's hand.

"Eighteen years ago, we won a war—a war for our freedom! For this beautiful island we call Anastasia!" The room fell more than silent as the king slowly peeled his mask from his face.

"It unites us in this journey, and united we will rule this island, if we truly wish to avoid extinction."

The crowd applauded as he basked, stroking his gray beard, slow and in wonderment. He pointed.

"There is a new day upon us. The island is in dying need of support from you and islanders like Benjamin Malcamore here. It's time we strive together to protect and build a better future for Anastasia. But we can only accomplish this together. Now, without further ado, Malcamore, please come up here and accept our invitation. We welcome you to the brotherhood, old friend."

As one, the crowd applauded again, and Samson even whistled with his fingers. Malcamore stood and made his way up to the protruding balcony. Once he was in position, the house went completely dark and a blinding blue crystal from above beamed down on his face, forcing him to block its blaze.

"Well, ok, um, thank you, King Theodore," he said, squinting out at the masked faces staring back at him through the dark. To maintain his focus, he planted his eyes on Samson's hat in the crowd and cleared his throat.

"And thank you to all in attendance for coming tonight. Many are more deserving of this honor than myself. I was only 18 when I joined the mob. I did not know what it would become. In those days, all we ever wanted was better conditions for our island." He gazed out, bowing his head in sadness.

"As you all know, many of us fought for the belief that we all should be free—free to live as we please, to come and go as we please, sharing the responsibilities of our island. It's true, I still believe Pius was going to lead us all to our deaths. Despite that, I've never been off the island. To see what's out there beyond the walls." He glanced back at King Theodore, who returned a forced smile. "It seems to me, the freedom we were fighting for then, is the same freedom we are still fighting for… today."

The bright light above him shut off completely, darkening the room to the sounds of scattered whispers.

"If I am being honest with you, fine islanders, there must be a better way for us to preserve the island. The Gatherings are—"

"Thank you, Mr. Malcamore, that will be enough," the king interrupted. Malcamore turned to him in shock.

"Thank you," he blurted, and walked back down the left side of the curved staircase, having to use its rail for support. Returning to his seat in the dark, there was no applause given this time by the watching masks. The burgundy chandelier returned to normal as King Theodore addressed the growing whispers.

"My islanders, listen to me," he said, clasping his hands together. "Everyone, Mr. Malcamore is Anastasia's first hero. And we will treat him with respect."

More murmurs filled the room.

"We are approaching a new era, my friends," the king shouted. "He's free to believe what he wants, and he's right. One day we all will explore beyond the walls, when the time comes," he said, staring directly at Malcamore, then the crowd. "Right? Right!" They muttered in agreement as a methodical applause slowly arose. "Now that the formalities and introductions are out of the way, let us enjoy the party and celebrate our freedom and prosperity!" And with that he quickly exited out of view, walking down the hall and disappearing behind a slamming door. Malcamore watched from his seat, wondering if his words had upset him. Did he go too far? He feared he had.

"Magnificent show," Samson said, leaning closer to Malcamore as the band continued its performance. The islanders stood from their seats, forming mini groups. Malcamore could feel the eyes behind the masks peering at him.

He chuckled. "It was a show indeed."

"You were inspiring, if you ask me, young sir."

"He didn't even let me finish my speech, Samson. I had so much more I wanted to say but thank you, anyway."

"No need. I think everyone knew what you were feeling."

"May I get you a drink, Mr. Malcamore?" A waitress in a short black skirt broke into the conversation. When she removed her mask, the two looked up in wonderment, Samson even dropping his mouth. She was stunning, dark brown hair that moved like silk, and she wore a black lace top, loose fitting, to put it mildly. Friendly smile tied it all together. The only thing, Malcamore pondered—she wasn't wearing any shoes. He sat up straight.

"Um, yes, I'll take an islander special on the rocks—no, make that two. First round on me, Samson."

"Oh, no, I won't have it. The first round on me."

"Gentleman," she interrupted, gently placing her hand on Malcamore's shoulder. "They informed me you two would pay for nothing all night. Drinks are on the house."

"Well, in that case, keep them coming," Malcamore said, giving her hand a couple pats. "Say, do you think you can bring us a couple of masks for ourselves? Feeling a little out of place here." With an eerie laugh, she turned, attracting his gaze until she was out of the room.

"Some things never change, do they, Benjamin?" a familiar voice spoke from above him.

He delayed turning, looking instead up at Samson, who had failed to notice that someone had approached. It seemed he, too, had been distracted by the waitress.

"Mask or not, I'd recognize that voice anywhere, Rosemary," Malcamore said, spinning in his seat.

"Who else would it be, you big slouch? Now, stand up and give me a hug."

Malcamore got to his feet, standing much taller than Rose as they shared a soft embrace. She smelled as good as the last time they hugged; he thought. Rose greeted Samson, who only returned a low sounding old man's grunt, and excused himself to explore the party, leaving the two alone. Rose removed her mask, readjusted her hair, and dimpled at Malcamore.

"So, tell me, Rose, how have you been?"

"Miserable, compared to you! The great Benjamin Malcamore. Everyone's calling you that, now that the cat's out of the bag, as they say. I myself didn't know, but I truly wonder how that felt."

"How what felt?"

"To kill King Pius, of course." She had said the words as if she had seen him do it herself. Malcamore didn't reply, only rocked back and forth a little, buying him time. "So, how did you do it? It couldn't have been easy. You were the one who killed Pius III, correct? Or have we gotten it wrong?"

"Don't believe everything you read, Rose," Malcamore said, grabbing the glass that she held in her hand and taking a sip.

"I suppose that is just what I heard," she said, smiling and snatching it back from him.

"The congratulations should be for you and your marriage. I guess we both got what we wanted, huh?"

"It's like I always say, Benjamin, great to have friends in powerful places."

Malcamore frowned. "I couldn't disagree with you more," he said, sharing another flirtatious smile with the server when she arrived with their drinks, leaning over him as she placed them on the table.

"Same old Benjamin, all right," Rose said, then masked quickly as the king walked down the staircase casually, puffing on a large cigar with his black robe trailing behind him on the floor.

"Mr. Malcamore!" he called. Malcamore, in mid-laugh with Rose, stopped to turn his attention to the king.

"I see you've met my wife," he said, taking Rose by the hand and giving it a delicate kiss, only his eyes and lips visible.

"Well, sir, Ms. Rose and I were… childhood friends, I suppose you could say."

"You don't say. She's never mentioned that to me." Ashes from his cigar crumbled to the floor. His stare was unreadable.

"Dance with me, Benjamin," Rose said, tugging on Malcamore's arm. "You don't mind, do you, honey?"

King Theodore glared at Malcamore. "No, you kids have fun… but I would like a chance to speak with you in my office, after the party settles down, if you don't mind."

Malcamore nodded as Rose pulled him onto a dance floor in the other room. The band struck up a new song as they danced.

"What's with the mask and robes?"

"It's a ritual, but you have bigger problems. They haven't been honest with you, Benjamin," she whispered.

"What do you mean?"

"It's about the king, you see. He and I—"

"Let me guess; you're not really married."

"What? Oh—yes, we're definitely married, and I love him very much. It's nothing like that."

"Ok, so, what is it then?"

After a gown-fluttering twirl, he stared into her eyes as she jerked him closer. Her skin was soft, her dress made of the rarest of fabrics and eyes were big and blue, clashing but still complementing her full red hair.

"Listen to me, Benjamin," she whispered. "Whatever it is my husband wishes for you to do, say yes. Do it so you can join the brotherhood."

"Just say yes. And why in Anastasia would I do that?" Rose tilted away, making a quick glance at the king who was still watching them dance from across the room, standing next to a growing pile of cigar ash.

"I can't explain that now, but they're not like us anymore, Benjamin. No one here is like us," she said, kissing him on the lips through the mask slit. She then returned to King Theodore's side, and they disappeared back up the steps. The band was still playing what sounded like a theme while he strolled back to his table, joined by an awaiting Samson, who noticed his puzzled face.

"Is everything all right?"

"Just fine, Samson." Malcamore swallowed his drink, then slammed the empty glass back down on the table. On cue, the waitress appeared once more with two more drinks. Malcamore, startled, grabbed the glasses.

"Oh, and what about our masks and robes?"

She laughed and smiled, going on with her work, not answering his question and still not wearing any shoes.

"You still love Rose, don't you?" Samson asked.

"Love her?!"

"Never mind, forget what I said. This is your party. How about we do a little celebrating ourselves?"

"Now you're talking," Malcamore said and lifted his glass. "To freedom!" he declared.

"To Anastasia," Samson said. Their glasses clinked and thus began a long night of celebrating.

CHAPTER SEVEN

THOMAS AND FRANK STARED DOWN, perplexed at the set of imprints in the sand.

"What do you think it could be?" Frank asked, hovering in observation above Thomas, who was hands and knees in dirt, eye level with one print.

"I'm not sure. Looks amphibian, reptilian maybe… Twice the size of any reptile I've ever seen, and that's saying a lot. But that's not the strange part." Thomas stood and took two large leaping strides across the dirt.

"The next pair is almost 10 feet away."

"What does that mean?" Frank asked.

"It's not only big, but it's fast. Very fast."

The two turned to a boy's shriek, resounding through the air. By the time he and Frank arrived, running across the beach, Jack, the youngest volunteer among them, was transfixed on the blue, glowing trees in the jungle.

"Something is that jungle, captain… We shouldn't be here," Jack whispered, his breaths erratic, his face pale like the blood had stopped flowing through his body. Thomas grabbed him by the cheek, studying his face.

"What happened, Jack? What's wrong? What did you see!"

"We shouldn't be here… We shouldn't be here… We shouldn't be here," he repeated without pause.

"The boy's got dementia!" Frank shouted.

"Snap out of it, boy!" Thomas gave him a light slap. Jack paused; his stare drifted on Thomas as a deafening, wet clicking surfaced like chirping crickets at nightfall.

"They're here," Jack said.

A loud screech from the jungle forced their hands to their ears.

Thomas, both ears covered, peered towards the water; the innocent-looking waves splashed against the sand like a shore on a Florida beach. He had heard that same cry during the storm. Stepping closer to the coastline, he squinted out at the full moon reflecting off the stretch of endless dark water. "Why… aren't the waters rising here?" he said, inching forward, one heavy breath at a time. He arrived at the edge of the peninsula, its sanded ground dropping off beneath him like a cliff in the Grand Canyon. The current of the waves splashed against his ankles, forcing all momentum towards the island. As far as his eyes could see. He scooped a handful of murky water that carried the smell of blood and salt. The drops slipped between his fingers.

At the last drop, glaring back up at him from under a rippling wave, was a pair of beady, slanted, yellow eyes.

"Where in hell are we?" Thomas said, his hand creeping to the Glock on his waist.

"Tommy!" Frank yelped, running up from behind.

"Jack ran off!"

"What do you mean, he ran off? He was just there," Thomas said, still peering at the monstrous eyes before they vanished back into the ocean.

"I mean, we turned our backs for a second and he ran into the jungle before we could stop him."

Thomas took slow, deliberate steps out of the cold water that dripped down from his pants leg. He turned to Frank's horrified expression and the men who were walking back for the ship.

"Hey! Stop!" Thomas shouted, limping across the sand, winded, when he finally arrived.

"Where is Jack?"

The seven other men groaned in unison, cringing from another deafening screech that blared.

"Captain... Thomas, we don't know what that sound is, but we sure as hell don't want to find out. So, we've changed our minds, and we're going back to the ship to protect the others. We have our own families to think about," Victor said. The once lawyer now self-proclaimed profit who argued he predicted the end of the world coming. He shifted the rifle he was carrying to his back. Thomas glared at each of them that all mumbled in agreement.

"We took our eyes off him for one second and the boy ran off. It's too dark out here to be babysitting and playing adventure, anyway. He'll find his way back," Victor said.

"I can barely see anything out here. And that noise, those prints in the sand," Frank whispered, his hand trembling on Thomas's shoulder.

Thomas glared back at *Lady Luck* anchored at the shore.

"You all were just so excited, now you want to leave a kid out here alone."

A scream.

"Jack!" Thomas yelled, limping as fast as he could. He was halfway to the maze of trees and hanging vines when he noticed none of the other men were following his action. He stopped.

"Ok, fine. We'll form two groups. Frank, you and Victor come with me, and the rest of you can go back to the ship and protect the others. Don't mention a word about Jack being missing. The last thing we need is Mrs. Elanor running off into the jungle. We'll find the boy and bring him back," Thomas said.

The others had no quarrels with the plan, although Frank's and Victor's faces said differently.

As they marched for the trees with the bluish-green glow at the end of the beach, Victor stepped forward.

"So, after we find Jack, we get back to the ship and leave this place. That should be the alternative plan."

"Leave? No, I didn't say that. We are not leaving. We couldn't if we wanted to. The engines, the power, the damn GPS, everything! All shot! And we don't have the personnel to fix it."

Victor grunted.

"What do you suggest we do then, Victor?"

"I suggest we try to fix whatever's wrong with the ship, then get the hell off this island. I'm happy you found land, Thomas, but my spirit is warning me about this place."

"Your spirit, huh? We have enough men here, and weapons, so we have a fighting chance. We'll die if we go back out on that water," Thomas said.

"Weapons! Fighting chance!" Victor laughed.

"Those men aren't soldiers. Those are doctors, deliverymen, and a few teachers, everyone's not military like you and Frank here.

Whatever's doing all that screeching will kill us, and that's the end, game over, no more humans."

"So, do what, stay out on the ocean until we starve to death, or maybe another storm kills the last of us? What about food? News flash Victor, you're not God or some kind of prophet, everything and everyone we've ever known is gone!"

"Listen! The both of you," Frank shouted over the argument. "Let's just find the kid and get back in one piece, okay? Then we'll take a vote on if we stay or go."

Thomas glared at Victor as he walked to the front of the formation and continued with a slow, determined pace, one sure boot in front of the other.

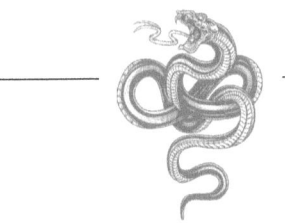

CHAPTER EIGHT

A WAILING HORN ALARM SOUNDED FROM the top of the large brick building as students scrambled across the grass. Standing at the entrance of the school was a pair of soldiers with identifier devices in hand, scanning each of the students' wrists as they entered the facility.

Still sitting in the rumbling truck with my mother; we shared another long hug, then I headed down the school walkway. The gray sky made the school seem gloomier than usual as I held out my wrist for identification. The soldiers standing guard shone a blue light on my number and symbol, granting me access to the school. I groaned, pulling back on the pair of brass doorhandles. The hallway emptied to the sounds of closing classroom doors.

My class, room 113, was brightly lit with the smell of Mrs. Collins's coffee brewing on her desk. A telltale sign for us students. Mrs. Collins would not officially lock her door until she'd had her first sip of morning brew, and this morning would be no different.

"You still have a few minutes," I whisper, laying my books on my desk in the back of the class.

With the alarm finally quieting, I had hoped to see Ashton sprinting down the schoolyard walkway, begging Mrs. Collins to let him in. He was good at that sort of thing, but the minutes ticked by uneventfully.

"Okay, students," Mrs. Collins said, her authoritative voice causing silence as she stepped into the middle of the room. She wore a cotton, black dress that fell to her ankles and her hair was wild and frizzy, like she had suffered strikes from lightning.

"Everybody, take your seats—yes, that means you, Matthew." She sipped from her mug and pointed to a student. He was a friend of mine, huddled with a group of boys. She arched her bushy eyebrow at him while peering through her glasses. Matthew danced to his seat, to the chuckle of the other students.

"With the Gathering approaching, and out of respect for Ms. Patterson," Mrs. Collins said, casting a glance over at me, "I will give her a chance to address the group if she chooses."

They turned in unison, long faces staring directly at me. After that ride to school, I was in no mood for any heartfelt speeches.

"It's fine, Rachel, if you don't wish to speak. In that case, we will continue our discussion from yesterday on Harvest seasons and their history."

This comment triggered a resounding groan, while I was excited about not having to talk about Gathering talk.

"Now, don't give me no lip and turn your history books to page 1,254."

The class fetched their books while I ripped out a scrap of paper from my pad; I scrawled on it, *Have you seen Ashton yet? I'm getting worried.* Crumpling the paper into a ball and waiting until Mrs.

Collins had turned to write on the chalkboard. I threw it across the room, accidentally hitting Jessie in the face. Startled, she looked over at me. "Read it," I mouthed.

Smoothing out the paper, Jessie wrote a message in response, waiting for another opportune moment to present itself before sending it back across the classroom. I fell out of my desk and it scraped the floor with a grinding noise.

"Yes, Ms. Patterson? Is everything okay?"

I stood with my hand, scooping the balled-up note. "No, ma'am. May I be excused? I'm having a kind of rough morning."

Mrs. Collins's eyes softened behind her glasses. "You may," she said, turning back to the board to continue with her lecture.

As I was walking down the halls, passing a group of girls who turned the corner, I recognized one of them; we went to the same summer camp every year when we were kids.

"Uh oh, dead girl walking," she said, causing the others to laugh. Once famously nicknamed "fatty patty" and now she was the one with the inappropriate jokes.

"Won't be missing you neither," I muttered as they passed, and I turned down another long hallway. It was quiet besides the faint sounds of teachers in their rooms giving lectures.

I approached the girl's bathroom before pushing open the door. I paused and checked behind me. I don't know why I checked, but the day had my nerves on edge. *You're being paranoid again.*

Calming myself, I flicked a switch on the wall, triggering crystals that lit up the bathroom with a blue glow. I stared at my reflection through the cracked mirror that hung above the sink. After a few cold splashes of water, I reached into my pocket and pulled out the scrap of paper to read what Jessie had written.

71

No one's seen Ashton in days now, but I'm sure he's ok. I cannot believe you keep coming to this school, Rachel.

I threw the paper to the floor. The Gathering was approaching, and nothing was going as I'd hoped. Locking myself in one stall that lined the girl's bathroom, I examined my wrist, the 18 tattooed to my skin. The blue crystals that illuminated the bathroom flickered, then shut off completely.

"Not again," I wailed, tugging on the handle of the stall, then pulled harder when it wouldn't unlock. A rotten, spoiled smell filled the bathroom and caused me to gag, wheezing and gasping at the floor. I spotted the pair of dead feet standing outside the stall. Then her head peaked underneath, her hair scraping the floor. The silver lock slowly unlatched before breaking off and rattling to the ground. The door eased open as I stared out at the empty blackness that filled the bathroom. She appeared.

"Let me show you!" she shouted, her voice deep with death as she reached for my face. At the touch, my body went limp; the air escaped from my lungs and black goo began oozing from my mouth.

"I can't breathe," I cried, sliding to the floor, grabbing at my neck. I attempted to crawl away on my stomach, gasping for breaths, puking up the black sludge. "Why are you doing this to me?" I whimpered, crawling through the spinning room. The little girl stood over my body like death itself, staring down as I choked away my last breaths into unconsciousness.

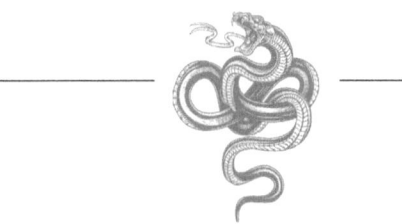

CHAPTER NINE

MALCAMORE SLAMMED ANOTHER EMPTY GLASS onto the table.

"Anastasiaaa, Anastasiaaa.
My island, I shall cherish thee,
from quad one through quad four.
Every inch I'll adore,
and be all that I can beeee."

Celebrative shouts followed as Malcamore and others sang the island's ritual in a drunken stupor. Even the king's Lord Sanders belted it out from where he lay on the floor. Malcamore gave a drunken shout of, "Fine playing, sirs! Just fine!" then collapsed his head to the table as a voice spoke from above him.

"A minute of your time, Mr. Malcamore, please. Would you mind answering a few questions?" Malcamore peeked up from his folded arms at the boyish face hovering over his shoulder. His shirt was buttoned to the neck and his hat was pushed down to the brim of his nose. His stance was wobbly from too much drinking, Malcamore assumed.

"I'm not doing any interviews tonight, son! And aren't you too young to be at a party like this?"

"So, you're aware what type of party this is, then?"

"I said no questions!" he shouted, raising his spinning head and shoving the boy aside.

"You'll know soon enough," the boy said as Malcamore re-lifted from the table at the words. His sight landed on a drunken Samson. Maybe it was time they headed home. As he prepared to stand, the waitress approached him with another drink. She collapsed onto his lap, forcing him back to a seat.

"You're not getting tired on me, are you?" she whispered, her voice soft and seductive. Malcamore, who could barely keep his head up straight, took a sip out of the glass and placed it on the table.

"They call me Tootie," she said.

"Tootie, it is getting late… I was thinking about heading home soon."

"Late? The fun is just getting started." She leaned in so close that her breath felt warming. She whispered a few enchanted words, then gave his hair a slight sniff and rub. Malcamore's head was spinning like a wheel when a loud crash came from the other side of the room.

Samson, whose drunken steps had lost their balance, knocked a decoration to the floor.

"Samson, are you alright, old man?"

"I'm fine, young sir," he moaned, crawling back to the table, his cane in one hand while his other draped over a server's shoulder. Malcamore turned back to Tootie on his lap and assured her he was interested in what she had whispered. But first he wanted to find a bathroom and drain the snake. A modest attempt to be funny, although her laugh was very unusual and loud. Not that funny, he thought.

Walking up to the overlooking balcony, the lack of resistance surprised him. No one had even mumbled a word to stop him as he reached the last step and peered down the hallway to his left, then his right. It was the largest house he'd ever visited—much larger than King Pius's old home.

After two unsuccessful attempts at finding the bathroom—one door led to a closet, filled with nothing but fancy coats and linen for the beds—he opened the second and the light from the hallway half filled the room, revealing pictures and small artifacts that lined the wall, and a rather large clay statue that sat on the floor. It was of a creature with claws and fangs protruding from its opened mouth. Malcamore pondered at the sculpture. He had never seen such a gory beast in his life. He took one step in the room for further investigations when a loud whoosh and rapid clicking came from the ceiling. He peered upward as the haunting sound continued. Following his intuition, he softly shut the door.

Behind door number three was a large and soft-looking bed covered with a red linen that sagged to the polished floors. A small table next to it and a large window overlooked the islands' hills. At first, he reacted with the normal mistaken shock, almost closing it shut. But he paused, turned to see if someone was watching, and edged into the dark room.

What Rose had said was still troubling his mind. What did she mean when she inferred *they're not like us? Who's not like us?* He wondered. He didn't know if it was the nerves or the alcohol he'd been consuming all night, but he wanted more information. Electing not to turn on the lights, the first place he searched was the nightstand by the bed. Drunkenly, he fumbled through the drawer with loud ruffles filled with random documents deemed important. Some even baring the king's blooded signature. One stated, *Quadrant One: population of 2717, system stabling, jurisdiction East border wall. LC average 55.8. and rising.*

He refolded the paper and tossed the information aside, his eyes focused on another at the bottom of the pile. It was ancient-looking. He sat on the edge of the bed and unfolded the map of Anastasia. A faint voice began speaking outside the room. He froze, waiting as it traveled down the hall. Once it faded, with gentler movements, he gathered the other papers and crammed them back in the drawer.

He paced while examining the map in thought, his fingers tracing the line of connecting red x's covering the paper. Flipping it over, the words on the back stated, *Our New Life Awaits.*

"They've been outside of the wall?" He gasped with his hand to his mouth.

"Or something outside of the wall has been here..." He wiped the sweat from his brow, studying the coordinates. Each started from a different Quadrant, and each dotted line led to groups of blood-colored x's way beyond the walls.

"Who are you searching for?"

The opening of the door startled him as he refolded the map to his pocket. An angry voice, then a bright blue light illuminated the entire room. It revealed Malcamore, though he hadn't been spotted.

An ease came at the sight of her tossing her mask to the bed, then embarrassment as she began undressing. Malcamore felt uncomfortable.

"I don't mean to scare you. I was only looking for the bathroom," he said, stepping forward. Frightened, Rose whipped around, now wearing nothing but her undergarments.

"Benjamin! What the hell are you doing in my room?" she hissed.

"Like I said, I was looking for the bathroom… and I got lost."

"You got lost. Well, it's pretty obvious this isn't the bathroom. And if my husband had found you in here, he would have had you killed."

"And not kill me himself? Some king he turned out to be," he scoffed, stepping closer to Rose.

"What are you doing, Benjamin? You're drunk, aren't you?"

"So if I am? It was my party," he said, reaching for her hand, then pulling her in closer.

"It was a small celebration for our island, Benjamin, that was all. Get over yourself," Rose said, pulling from his grasp, flopping down on the plush bed, swinging one leg over the other. "There's a guest room down the hall. Can't have you driving all the way back to Quadrant One in your condition. I'm sure Samson is quite drunk as well; you both need to go sleep it off."

"You mean in that room with that thing lying dead on the floor?" Malcamore said.

Rose pondered for a second, then burst into laughter. "That *thing* is a one-of-a-kind sculpture, and it cost us a fortune. There's a bed in there for our special guest, it's actually really nice."

"I'll take my chances on the road, or…" He plopped down with a couple cushioned bounces. "I could sleep in here with you."

She smiled a little in thought until loud knocking came from the door.

"Shit, you might need to hide… That could be Theodore," she said.

"I'm not hiding! We're not doing anything wrong."

"Hide, now! He would kill us both if he knew you were in here." She tossed her clothes back on and scurried across the room.

"I will not hide."

The loud bangs continued as Rose scoffed and peeked out the crack. It was a servant.

"What is it?"

"Um, M-M-Ms. Rose, the king, sent me to l-l-look for that man, Mr. Malcamore. You haven't seen him, have you? He w-w-wishes to speak with him."

Malcamore, now fully stretched out on the bed, peeked up at Rose, who spun her sight back to the servant.

"No, I have not seen him, thank you, but I suggest you search the banquet. He may still be at the party."

"I did, madam, but I can't find him anywhere."

"And why would you come here? Go search again," she said sharply, slamming the door back shut.

"See what you've done? You think that's coincidence? Theodore sent him, I'm sure of it."

"You're being fearful, Rose. Besides, Samson and I were preparing to leave."

"No! You must go see him. It must be important, Benjamin, if he insists on speaking with you. He's your king. Now, please let's go. I'll walk you to his office."

"Alright, alright… I'll go, but first I really need to use your restroom," he said, attempting to sober his demeanor as he stood.

CHAPTER TEN

THE CRYSTALS INSIDE THE TREES hummed, shining a dim blue light over the scene as they marched through the jungle. It was a welcome warmth from when they first arrived on the island. The weather while they were on the water had been getting too cold to bare, and the oxygen had been thinning. But now closer to the trees, it felt like they were being cooked from the inside out. The sweat dripped from Thomas's brow as he peered upward at the high-pitched beastly laughter coming from above, shaking tree limbs and falling leaves.

"Look," Thomas said, pointing at the troops of chimpanzees swinging from limb to limb. Not your normal spotted animals in a hike through the amazon or local zoo. These were different. Their fur glistened like the glowing crystals inside the tree, with white running strikes of gray streaking down their backs and to the tips of their tails. Their eyes were so crystal-blue; when a pair focused on him, it was chilling, otherworldly, even. Their lunges and leaps caused hanging sticks tied at the roots, creating a triangle-shaped artifact, to rattle against one another.

"Those are handmade, right? It has to be," Frank said, staring up at the hundreds of small triangle-shaped objects dangling from branches.

"You just remember to keep your eyes peeled," Thomas said.

The three began shouting Jack's name, forcing through prickly shrubs and swinging vines, the air humid and murky, like a hike through the jungle at the worst time of year. The insects were nagging and oversized; Thomas pondered on how the wildlife came to exist. Random eyes that would spot them, then scurry away into bushes. The chimpanzees still followed from above, swinging from limb to limb, acting as tour guides.

"What did you say?" Frank hissed.

"I didn't say nothing," Victor said.

"There!" Thomas spotted Jack through the split of trees standing next to a glowing oak with roots that busted through dirt and curled across the ground.

"I found him!"

"Will you stop whispering? Damn it, stop!" Frank hissed.

"I told you before I didn't say a word. What are you hearing?" Victor asked. Frank began shaking his head and slamming his palm to his skull. Thomas turned from them and pushed through a patch of hanging vines.

"Jack, come on, buddy. Let's get you back to the ship," Thomas said. His hand grazed the oak, and he snatched it away from the heat protruding from the bark. He grabbed Jack by the chin and studied his face. His pupils burned black, shriveled like fried olives or dried-out raisins, his skin boiling.

"I can't see…" Jack whimpered. He picked Jack up and tossed him over his shoulder and met up with Frank and Victor, who were still fighting.

"I got Jack. Let's get back to the ship."

"Frank here lost his mind…" Victor said, making small circles at his own head with the tip of his index finger.

"I have not, I'm fine."

"Tell him what you told me about hearing voices."

Frank looked wide-eyed at Thomas, sweat dripping from his forehead and down his cheek. "It's nothing, I'll be ok. As you said, let's hurry back to the ship, it's like an oven in here."

Thomas nodded, and they all hastened back through the glowing jungle.

A blaring screech rang out like a monster's cry, overpowering the frantic limb shaking coming from the monkeys.

They stopped. Each of them scanned the jungle but couldn't decide where it came from. A gust of wind joined the blue-eyed chimpanzees above their heads, rattling the hanging artifacts until one fell to the foot of Thomas. He scooped it up.

"Tommy!" Frank called.

Thomas spun to Frank's frightened face, then back to the artifact in hand. His first assumption was wrong; they were not hanging sticks at all. But bones. Human bones, it seemed.

Another screech blared.

"Anybody got eyes on it?" Thomas said, dropping the bone to the ground.

The answer to his question came as an agonizing scream. Frank, snatched by his legs, and dragged high into a glowing tree. His nails clawed at the dirt, reaching in desperation for passing limbs that snapped at his grab.

The chimpanzees squawked louder.

Thomas gave chase, then vomited at the fluorescent sight amongst the hedges. A hideous creature, a snake's head and body attached to two pairs of sharp claws that were ripping apart Frank and his frame of 6'1, 210 pounds like he was a sheet of loose-leaf paper. Frank's brief cries of agony silenced to the crackle of his bones and blood splatters.

With young Jack draped over his shoulder, Thomas ran behind Victor, who left at Frank's first scream. He thought to leave him behind as well when Victor's foot got tangled in a cluster of roots. He dropped his gun and fell to the turf, tumbling to a stop against a glowing oak.

"Get up!" Thomas shouted, grabbing Victor by the arm.

A wet clicking sent his gaze upwards.

"Victor, get up now," Thomas whispered, slowly backing away as Jack began to cry. Creeping down the side of the glowing tree was another monstrous snake. This one all of 9 feet, beady, yellow eyes, armored skin, and a body that curled when it moved, hissing a red, forked tongue from its mouth.

Victor lunged to his feet as the snake-like serpent spat out a black sludge that sprayed over his face. Victor screamed. Thomas unloaded shots from his Glock at the armored flesh. It roared, a fang-revealing screech, then darted back up the tree quicker than a blink.

The two ran across the white sand, young Jack still draped over Thomas's shoulder. When they arrived back at the ship, breathless with fear, the entire crew of survivors were waiting and watching from the main lounging deck.

"It seems someone didn't follow instructions," Thomas breathed. Mrs. Elanor ran up to him, crying into her purple bandana. She snatched Jack from his arms in hysteria and disappeared inside.

"You still thinking about staying?" Victor whispered, wiping and spitting the black sludge from his face.

"Like I said before, we don't have a choice. We wouldn't last another week on the water. We're stuck here."

"We won't last through the night here. I don't know, we found this place, maybe there's another place, a safer one."

"Another place?" Thomas said in disbelief, hugging his wife Naomi, who dragged to him with a loving squeeze.

"What happened out there? We could hear the screams. Are you ok?" Naomi asked, still clinging to Thomas, brushing down his graying hair.

"I'm fine, my love… but we lost Frank… Frank's dead."

She gasped. "No… His wife…this will devastate her."

"I know."

"I thought we had lost you too when you didn't come back with the others. What happened?" she asked softly.

"There's something in that jungle, Naomi, something evil. It ate Frank," he said as more blaring screeches began ringing out from the trees in the background, the sound jolting everybody's attention.

"I don't like it here," Naomi said, leaning in closer to Thomas.

"During the storm, that thing leaped out of the water. I don't want to sound crazy but, maybe it pushed us here, you know, some kind of feeding ground, and those are its babies," Thomas mused. She gave a mouth-covering gasp.

"It's just a guess, I don't know. I could be wrong, but it's all…" He shook. "That thing ripped Frank apart in seconds, Naomi. Seconds,"

"What happened to Frank?" shouted a doctor by the name of Steers, who was listening to the conversation.

"Where is Frank? What happened to Frank? Is he dead? Is Frank dead? Have we lost him too now?"

"Calm down, Rob," Thomas said, wiping a tear from Naomi and turning to face Dr. Robert Steers, who stood swaddled in an old blanket. "And, yes, my friend Frank Brusward's dead, may God bless his soul."

The people whimpered and cried as the news spread about Frank. Many liked him, but this also showed that their nightmare was far from over but just beginning. When the news reached Sidney, his wife, her loud, painful scream silenced all talking as she ran to the other side of the ship in tears.

"I think we should go back out to the water. At least nothing could hunt us in the water," Dr. Steers said.

"That's what I've been telling him," Victor chimed.

"We must stick together, whatever we decide. But this ship isn't fit to go back out there. It will sink, and we don't have the staff or technology to fix it. I guarantee you, we will drown or starve to death. Now that jungle has signs of human life and even food. We have weapons, so I think it's our best chance. I'll keep a lookout for tonight and we will discuss this further in the morning," he shouted as they abandoned his plea, disappearing into their individual corners of the ship.

Naomi came over and placed her hands on his as they stood at the edge of the rail, listening to the screeching cries.

CHAPTER ELEVEN

A THICK, WHITE FOG COVERED THE beautiful glowing garden being trampled by a mob. They held torches and weapons in hand as they made their way to King Pius's III home, hidden in the middle of the woods. Elizabeth, the king's youngest daughter, watching the stars from the rooftop, spotted the approaching flames.

"Oh no," she gasped, leaning over the roof's edges, peering down at the mob of islanders with torches and weapons in hand. There had been rumors spreading throughout Anastasia. Islanders turning on the royal family. Her father had spoken of a plan for them to escape in case of an emergency. But tonight, he remained locked in his chamber, strategizing ideas with his court.

Elizabeth reentered the home through the window of the attic, her small feet pitter-pattering down the halls.

"Father! Father!" she screamed.

The maid's laughter echoed from the kitchen downstairs.

"Nobody knows they're here." She banged with her fist in desperation at her father's door. "Father, we must leave! The mob is here!"

When no answer came, she leaned her ear against the wooden surface. From within, a heated argument with his newfound apprentice was unfolding.

"So, you all feel this way then, even you!" King Pius III shouted. Another voice returned a shout. She couldn't make out his words, but the voice was familiar.

"I took you in, treated you like a son, and this is how you repay me. You do not know what you have done to our island, do you? Well…get on with it, do what you must!" King Pius III said. A loud, agonizing scream followed, and the door almost broke off its hinges from the pounds of Elizabeth's shoulder. She had never heard her father in such pain.

"See who's at the door!"

Elizabeth spun to the shouts of triumph from the mob as they reached the home. She hastened for her older sister's room, bursting through the entry. "Annabelle… Annabelle!" A raucous bang came from downstairs. She turned, eyes searching for the best place to hide. First was the gigantic bed with long, draping sheets that sat at the center of the room. Next was the treasure chest in the far corner. Then she fixed her sight on to the spacious closet. She decided it would do and softly shut its doors behind her.

"Ok think, Lizzy, what do I do, what do I do…" she whispered. More victorious yells came from the mob of islanders as they barged down the halls. Elizabeth dropped to her knees and began weeping. Screams from those who had failed to escape crescendo to blaring gun shots.

The palace fell quiet as a graveyard except for echoing boots and deep, gruff voices. The groundkeepers. A baby's cry belted from the other side of the room, snatching Elizabeth back to the present.

"What was that…" Elizabeth peeked out of the hiding spot and focused on the small baby's crib that stood next to the bed. She gasped.

"The baby. Where is Annabelle?"

After a silent prayer, she scurried across the room to its aid. "Shh… Shh, everything is going to be okay," she whispered.

Gently, she took a small blue blanket and swaddled it snugly. "I have to find us a way out of here." Quickening her steps to the doorway, she peered out, peeking down the staircase at three soldiers standing guard at the front door. A voice exiting out of her father's room forced her progression as she gripped the baby tighter in her arms. "You must stay silent for me, okay, little one?" She took slow steps down the curved, wooden staircase. Her eyes never left the soldiers, who were now amid abandoning their posts and heading out the front door. As soon as it shut behind them, Elizabeth abandoned caution and ran, heading for the hall that led to the kitchen. A dead body, lying in a puddle of his own blood at the entry, stopped her in her tracks. His name was Yori. He was one of her father's best guards, part of the family for as long as she could remember. She cried as she continued her pace, clutching the swaddled newborn.

The silhouette of a islander standing next to the glass-framed window stopped her escape. Her heart raced, knowing she was running out of options. To make matters worse, the child fussed with another loud cry. "Shh, shh!" Elizabeth pleaded, patting the baby back in a motherly fashion. The shadowy figure by the window turned their direction as a firm call came from behind.

"Hey, stay right there!" a soldier said. She spun and ran past before he could reach, and sprinted for the front door. It swung open as more soldiers from the mob re-entered the home.

Elizabeth pounded back up the stairs, catching sight of her father's apprentice standing near his room. He made no move to stop her, but returned a look of shame. Gasping, Elizabeth ran for Annabelle's room once again, slamming the bedroom door behind her and locking it shut.

"God, no!" she screamed. Laying the crying baby on the bed, she used all her strength to drag the massive chest where her big sister Annabelle would store expensive clothing into the closet before grabbing the child and shutting the door behind them.

"Shh, Auntie Lizzy is here," she whispered. The door burst open, slapping against the wall. "Where'd you go, you little brat?"

"What's all this racket?" The other voice came from who was standing guard outside her father's chambers. She knew that boy. It was Benjamin.

"The king's daughter, we saw her run this way!" the soldier yelled back. Elizabeth, peeking through the closet slits, could see Benjamin joining the search.

"You're sure she came this way?" he asked. She watched, patting the baby and holding her breath.

The soldier's boots echoed through the room as she laid her niece in the chest and used the clothes inside to make a soft nest of sorts. It was a long shot, but it was her only hope. "You'll be safe in here," she whispered and kissed her on the cheek. She shut the chest that half muffled the cries while a hard pair of boots knocking against the floor made their way to the closet.

The knob slowly turned.

Elizabeth wiped at salted tears. When the door cracked open, she pushed through with a high-pitched scream, surprising the soldiers as she sprinted past, heading for the stairs. The soldiers followed without a moment's hesitation.

"Stop her!"

She burst through the front door and darted into the woods outside. Thorns and tree limbs tore at her gown, ripping the delicate fabric and piercing her skin.

Elizabeth continued to race, leaping over roots and pushing through thickets until exhaustion finally overtook her. Gasping, she rested with her back pressed against a tree, peering out at the burning torches not too far behind. A thick, white fog laid over the night like a blanket. Reality was setting in.

The mob had won, her father was dead, and no matter what happened next, her life from this day forward would never be the same, nor would Anastasia.

A clicking sounded from above.

Shielded by the hanging branches and leaves, she failed to notice the creature crawling closer. Its forked tongue licked at the air as it slithered through the towering branches. It flopped to the ground with a ruffle of fallen leaves.

Elizabeth's eyes jerked open and scanned the dark. She ran farther into the woods, farther into the blinding fog. Alone and afraid, she wept, crooning a song to herself her mother would sing at night whenever she couldn't sleep.

The guards in search ran towards the loud scream, their torches finding the shape of Elizabeth in the fog. They stared, transfixed, some even horrified. The creature slowly wrapped and coiled itself around her body, its claws preparing to tear at her skin. Elizabeth

whimpered as it squeezed tighter, wringing the air from her lungs. In a flash, it dragged her limp body up into the trees.

CHAPTER TWELVE

A MASKED ISLANDER FACING A WALL gave a squeaky hum, the melody clunky and off pitch, then paused to say words that spewed out like a child's playful ramble. "He's going to join; you're definitely going to join. I know it's not the time. But why wouldn't you join, everyone wants to."

Malcamore approached the sink to wash his hands. The masked islander in a black robe stood to his left, talking to himself, or to Malcamore, he wasn't sure. The water drizzled to a stop; Malcamore could feel the stranger's eyes staring while his childlike voice continued with its banter.

"You're joining us, right? I mean, why wouldn't you? You would be crazy not to join the brotherhood. They don't let anyone in, you know."

"I'm sorry, sir, are you talking to me?" Malcamore asked, wiping his hands on his suit.

"I would hate to see what happens to you if you didn't." He hummed.

"Did you just threaten me? I don't take threats lightly."

"They'll eat your flesh if you don't" The masked islander stormed out of the bathroom, leaving Malcamore behind in puzzlement. When he exited, he decided not to share the experience with Rose, who was waiting for him in the hall. He wanted to gather more information on what exactly the Brotherhood was for himself.

"Remember what I told you," Rose said, pushing on the double door that shut with a resounding thud.

Malcamore skimmed the dismal room. A chandelier hung from the ceiling, though not illuminating, and two soft, cushioned seats sat in front of the king's desk. The moonlight shone through a window that started at the floor and finished at the ceiling, falling on a portrait of King Theodore.

"Mr. Malcamore!" he called from the shadows. "Take a seat."

His two palms gestured in front of him. Malcamore sat in one chair as the king's face slowly became visible.

"Welcome to my office. What do you think?"

"I like it. It's…big."

"Sorry for the lighting in here. I have a terrible headache from all that drinking. That party got a little wild, didn't it?"

Malcamore laughed. "Yes, sir, it did."

The king leaned back in his seat once again, studying Malcamore. After a moment of silence, he propped his feet up on his desk.

"I will level with you, Benjamin… Can I call you Benjamin?"

"Of course, my king."

"Good. Now, I have a… let's say, a minor problem on my hands, and I would like you to fix this problem for me." King Theodore stood. His long, black robe followed as he sat in the open seat next to Malcamore.

"Depends on the problem, sir."

"Well, as you know, Benjamin, the Gathering for this year is around the corner."

Malcamore nodded.

"Well, I'm not sure if you've heard, but this year, we have a certain situation in Quadrant Three. A young lady by the name of Rachel Patterson. You've heard of her, yes?"

"You're speaking about the girl with the 18."

"That's the one!" King Theodore said. "The damn papers have not been kind on their reports of this year's Gatherings. I've heard small talks of an uprising over this girl, and I want you to make sure she gets her butt on that bus! And that nothing gets out of hand. Do you understand, Benjamin?" he said, unblinking, his voice light but face serious.

Samson had mentioned Rachel a few days ago at their home. Ever since then, the ungodly truth gnawed at him like vermin. *Gathering Sentences Young Teen to Death*, read the headline; he knew then.

"I'm not sure, my king. I don't think I want to get involved. I've seen enough Gatherings—the crying families, the chaos."

King Theodore smiled behind his stare. "Of course, I understand. Trust me, I realize no one could enjoy these Gatherings, but it's what we have to do… Come now, Benjamin, an ex-soldier like yourself… you truly must understand the balance needed." He gestured to the number and symbol on Malcamore's wrist.

"What's your number, Benjamin?"

"76, sir."

"76. That isn't so bad. Strong islander like yourself got a long life ahead of you, I would guess."

"That's the plan," Malcamore said.

"Now… look at my number, son." King Theodore slid up the sleeves of his robe. The number 99 was carved into his wrist.

After a quick glance, Malcamore looked back up. "That's a nice number, sir, it is your system after all, but no one can live forever."

"Benjamin, that's where you're wrong," the king said, retrieving another cigar and lighting it with a struck match.

"Now, Benjamin," he said, stepping to the tall window with the beautiful view of the island and its massive stone wall in the backdrop. The moonlight that shone through the glass landed on his face. "That was some speech you gave out there about freedom. Let me be the first to say I think we were dead wrong for what we did to you after the war. Accusing you of treason. Forcing you into hiding like that."

"I wasn't hiding, sir." Malcamore grunted.

"Oh, trust me, I know you weren't. At the end of the day, you killed king Pius III, and that's what was best for the island. I applaud that kind of bravery; I don't shun it."

"The war was eighteen years ago, my king?"

"Ah! Who cares about how she escaped? The last thing we need is another war, but the child must go to her Gathering. No exceptions, it's the law. Interview the islanders, close some portfolios, and relax the rest of the way. I'm asking you to…oversee things there. Simple."

"To be clear, is this your way of still accusing me? Asking me to help you capture this poor girl. To do God knows what?"

The king laughed. "You'll find out about the Gathering when it's your turn. And I'm not requesting anything, Benjamin… I'm ordering it."

Malcamore fought to keep his patience. Suddenly, it all made sense why they summoned him. He nodded behind his clenched jaw as he rose to his feet.

"Excellent!" The king's expression was jovial once again.

"Then it's settled. You will head to Quadrant Three to oversee the Gathering there. I'm putting you in charge of last interviews, Ms. Patterson's especially."

Malcamore murmured as he stormed out of the office, feeling the king's eyes glaring at his back.

Running down the hall of the luxurious home and down the curved staircase, he spotted Samson speaking with Tootie.

"Samson! Get the driver, it's time we go."

"Just a moment, young sir. I ordered us two bowls of stew."

"Well, get it for the road, Samson. We must leave."

"Excuse me, Miss? Can I get those stews to go, please?"

"Sure thing, handsome." Tootie winked.

"See, young sir, we can take it to go."

"Have you seen Rose, Samson?"

"No, not since you danced with her. Is everything okay? You look like you've seen a ghost."

"I'll tell you all about it in the wagon. Ready the driver, I'll wait for the food."

Samson rushed outside the home to the sounds of his tapping cane.

"How could I be so stupid?" Malcamore whispered.

"Here you are," Tootie said, handing Malcamore two bowls of steaming stew.

"Raincheck on that invitation, sweetheart."

"It's fine, cutie." She kissed him on the cheek and smiled. "Oh, I could eat you up... One day, perhaps."

With an uncomfortable feeling intensifying, he left, pondering down the front steps of the home.

"Benjamin!"

A voice made him skid to a stop, spilling drops of stew to the ground. There was Rose, smoking, looking unbothered.

"Your husband is... some kind of guy," Malcamore said through his teeth.

"Let me guess. He give you the whole 99 routine?" Rose laughed.

"I'm happy you're enjoying yourself, Rose, but I'm not amused."

"Listen, Benjie," she said, making her way down the steps. "If this is about the Gathering this year, it's special and it has to happen. I wish things were different, too, but there's more to it than you know." She reached out, running her fingers through his hair.

Benjie? He hadn't heard that name in years.

"What did you mean when you said they're not like us?"

She stopped her stroking hands and backed away, smoke pouring out in a stream from her mouth. "I can't explain that now. You haven't joined yet."

Malcamore narrowed his eyes in suspicion. It was clear they were hiding something.

By now, Samson and the driver were waiting at the bottom of the steps.

"Goodbye, Rose," he said. He turned and got into the coach, watching her as the wagon slowly rolled away. The door behind her burst open as the Lord of Quadrant Three rushed out.

"Mr. Malcamore!" he yelled. "Mr. Malcamore!" Gasping, he glanced over at Rose, who took another long drag on her cigarette.

"They're supposed to be my escort!" he shouted.

Rose ignored him, flicking the smoke away and stalking back into her estate home.

Malcamore turned from the window as they progressed down the rocky path. "*Love* her?" he asked, his mouth twisting into a self-mocking smile.

"It happens, young sir. Life and love. It twists and turns, often getting the better of us. All one can do is sit back, enjoy the ride."

"Hm."

"So, where to now?"

"Quadrant Three."

Samson's jaw dropped to his chest.

"I know, but we have orders. I also have a few questions for the girl myself." Malcamore leaned out the window. "To Quadrant Three, William!"

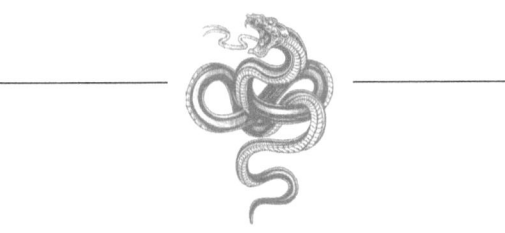

CHAPTER THIRTEEN

"THOMAS!" NAOMI CALLED IN A despairing voice. His eyes sprung open from where he slept, and there, floating over the bloody sunlit waves, was a wooden lifeboat bobbing in the water, preparing to crash against the sand.

"Is that a boat?" Thomas yelled, leaping to his feet as he ran across the deck. His action caused everyone to awaken, passing by Victor, who lethargically rose, coughing and wheezing into his hand.

Thomas ran down the emergency ramp, hoping it would be his son or maybe even Charlie as he limped across the warming sand, standing at the island's cliff edge with the last piece of underwater dirt beneath his bare feet. At first touch, he peeked inside and gasped at the sight of the punk rock t-shirt. A band called 3Ls famously stood for Last Life to Live. An internet sensation that went viral for singing about the ice rocks plummeting for Earth. Thomas dragged the lifeboat the rest of the way. There were no shouts of joy, but a stench that reeked of death. The first boat of many to arrive, he assumed.

"Dr. Steers!" Thomas screamed. "Help me! Get them off the boat!"

Standing to his right, Steers followed the order, helping Thomas pull the boat the rest of the way. There were three bodies inside, so scraggly their bones were protruding, and their skin looked pale and burned at the same time. They laid the three across the sand and, rolling to his back in the 3Ls t-shirt, was his son, Jacob.

"Son, are you alive?" Thomas whispered, kneeling, pushing past Jacob's wild beard and checking for a pulse.

Jacob wheezed and gave a dry, crackling smile.

"I…thought for sure I was…dead. Am I dead?" Jacob asked.

"Not sure yet, we just might be," Thomas said.

"Do you have any water? Bryson and Eli, we were just talking about cold water this morning. Eli mentioned seeing a frozen bird flying over us. I saw it too. It smelled like a chicken. You was there, and Mom was there, Grandpa was there, but you didn't think about it at all, did you?" He coughed.

"The air was so thin, it felt like a cold air bath, you could smell it, taste it." He coughed.

"We were dying of thirst by the morning," Jacob rambled, words dry and crumbling like old crackers.

"Water! Bring him some water!" Thomas screamed to Steers, who was hunched over the other two bodies.

"Thomas, they didn't make it," Dr. Steers said.

Thomas peered over at Bryson and Eli lying back up on the sand.

"I think they're dead, son." Jacob attempted to sit up straight before collapsing onto his back.

"H-H-ow, did we end up here?" He puffed.

Thomas thought for a moment, then glared out at the beautiful view of beaming sunlight and ocean waves crashing against the shore.

100

Then pondered the monster in the storm. Dr. Steers arrived with a canteen of fresh water. Thomas cradled the back of Jacob's head and assisted him in a sip.

"How's Mom and Uncle Charlie? Are they ok?" Jacob asked, collapsing back to the dirt.

"Your mother's fine, but—your uncle didn't make it," Thomas said.

Jacob closed his eyes. "We're all good as dead anyway, what does it matter."

Thomas re-capped the canteen and stood, peering over at Bryson and Eli as oversized flies swarmed. They were surely dead, dehydration most likely the cause. A cold night, and two close to the sun in the morning. The island temperatures, however, felt more controlled. "Let's get you fed and some more fresh water, then I'll tell you everything I know so far."

Clouds of smoke floated in the sky and broken boards and logs crackled under roaring flames. A risk, yes, but they all were starving and finally had somewhere they could build a fire. The remaining survivors, Victor and his two daughters, Dr. Steers, Sidney, the widow of Frank Brusward, who was weeping into Naomi's hug, Thomas, and Jacob, amongst a few others, all gathered around a burning chicken, the last of reserved rations, taken from the kitchen unable to be cooked until now, plucked clean and roasted in the flames while forming clouds covered the sun.

Thomas and Jacob sat amongst the sand, facing the trees that were humming a blueish glow.

"Terrible what happened to Uncle Charlie. Frank, too. I know you guys were close," Jacob said.

"Hmm."

"You know what keeps racking my brain about this place? It's not the glowing trees or how did the weird-looking animals get here or even those snake monsters you told me about."

"Ok, then what is it?"

"Hear me out. The entire world! Destroyed by two giant ice rocks that ended up flooding the entire freaking planet! Who knows how high in the air we could be right now? My guess would be roughly 20,000 feet, maybe more judging by the air on the water. America, China, Russia, all beneath our feet, hell for all we know we might be the last humans alive. But none of that explains how this place got here. Where did it come from? There're only two options that I can think of... both impossible. It either somehow floated up or..."

"Or it was already in the sky," Thomas said, standing and dusting off the dirt from his battered pants. "You're forgetting another option, son, the one where we're all dead and this is hell, and we just don't know it yet. I haven't fully ruled that one out either," Thomas said, squinting out at a small child with glistening blue skin that appeared amongst the trees.

"Wow, the island in the sky," Jacob said in astonishment.

"Do you see that, boy?" Thomas asked.

"What boy?" He turned Jacob's chin manually.

"That boy." The two stared out at the half-clothed child, a woolen cloth draped around his waist and whose skin was radiant. Thomas stepped forward a bit, and the boy turned and ran back into the jungle.

"Hey! Stop!" Thomas shouted, running across the sand. He stopped before he entered the labyrinth of trees and vines to face his son.

"Wait, let's not go in there, not alone."

"There are people here?" Jacob panted.

"I don't think that's people," Thomas said, gazing at where the boy disappeared.

"Last night… We need to go check on Jack. Poor kid lost his sight and got scared out of his mind by those things. I didn't see him or Mrs. Elanor by the fire."

"Hell, I'm scared right now," Jacob said.

"Everyone! Finish up with the food, meeting on *Lady Luck* right now!" Thomas shouted, hand cupped around his mouth, walking across the sand and heading for the ship. As they boarded, they spotted Victor walking down the emergency ramp, coughing into his hand. His face had grown whiter, with red veins shooting across his cheeks.

"Victor, we are about to have a meeting, are you alright?" Thomas asked, stopping to study Victor, who looked like a walking zombie.

"I'll be fine," Victor snapped, still coughing as he passed.

"Please tell the others to hurry; we have an emergency."

Victor only grunted.

"What's happened to him?" Jacob asked.

"I'm not sure," Thomas said, pulling open the door of deck 1 that led to the cabins inside. The hall was dark and cramped as they shuffled down to a cabin with a bronze plated 5 on the door. Thomas gave three hard knocks and waited; the turning of locks came next, and then a pair of brown eyes peeked out from the cracked doorway.

"What do you want now?" Mrs. Elanor said.

"Good afternoon, Mrs. Elanor. We would like to speak with Jack if that's ok. Oh, and I wanted to tell you we are about to have a meeting. I have some fascinating news. Not to mention there's a warm fire and food being cooked—"

"No, thank you. We're not hungry at the moment, and he's still not feeling well. He hasn't got his sight back, not since last night. What the hell even happened out there? He won't tell me anything."

"We will only be a second, Mrs. Elanor, I promise."

The door slammed shut in his face. Thomas turned to Jacob.

"You're not very popular with your crew, I see," Jacob said, as the door squeaked open.

"Make it quick."

Thomas's boots thudded as he entered the dark room, finding Jack snuggled tight in the bed, staring up at the ceiling. He peeked to see if his eyes had turned back to normal. They had not.

"Jack, can you hear me?" Thomas asked.

"Yeah, I hear ya, it's the seeing ya part."

"Mrs. Elanor, do you mind giving us a minute alone?"

"I do mind," she said, from where she sat next to Jack on the bed, patting his covered feet.

"Grandma, let me talk to the captain for a bit," Jack whispered.

Mrs. Elanor glared at Thomas as she got up from the bed and exited the room, shutting the door behind her.

"Captain… Can you do me a favor and open that window for me? It's so stuffy in here; I could use a little fresh air."

Thomas walked over to the round window cut in the corner. He gave the small screws on its sides a couple of twists, and a gust of salted wind whooshed through the cabin room.

He paced the floor, then took a seat at the edge of Jack's bed, sighed twice, patting the boy's foot like his grandmother just had.

"You did good, kid, you know that. You were really brave to even try to go out on an undiscovered island. That took guts, which many older, bigger men among us don't have."

Jack forced a dry smile.

"Do you remember when I saw you by that tree? Was there something inside of it that caught your attention?" Thomas asked.

"No, it wasn't like that. It was more like I could see it in my mind." Jack's words trailed off as he turned in his bed to face the wall.

"The crystals inside the tree, they have some sort of power. And ever since…" Jack paused.

"Ever since what?" Thomas asked.

"I keep hearing voices in my head. All night they kept whispering I can't make out the words; it sounds like gibberish and they have these hissing voices, laughing like it was taunting me."

"Do you think it's those creatures? The ones who ate Frank?" Jacob asked, from where he was leaning against the door.

"Maybe."

"Can you hear them right now?" Thomas asked.

"Yes." Jack answered and readjusted himself in the bed.

"We saw a boy… out there in the jungle. A few moments ago, my son and I. Did you see anyone last night?"

Jack swung his head, then pulled the covers over his face. "No, and I can't see much of nothing now neither. You're an excellent captain, and I trust you, so whatever you decide, I'm with you," Jack said.

"That means a lot to me. Get some rest and don't forget to tell your grandmother to get you something to eat before it's all gone." Thomas stood and he and Jacob exited the room, softly shutting the door, and headed down the cramped hallway with molded carpet floors.

"Poor kid."

"Yeah, poor all of us if he's right. I've seen those things and what they're capable of."

"You think that's what's whispering to him? Those things that got Frank?"

"That's what he said, I was there. Frank complained about hearing voices too. It has to be something not of this world. Whatever lives here."

"What about the boy?"

Thomas paused in thought and spun back for cabin five.

"Ah, give the kid a break, Dad, he looks exhausted," Jacob said as Thomas didn't even bother knocking at the door.

Jacob fell to his bottom as Thomas grabbed his weapon from the holster and fired a shot into the creature that was standing tall with protruding claws over Jack. It gave an angered hiss, then squirmed back out of the open window with a loud screech. The tapping of its sharp claws moved up the side of the ship and then to the main deck above them. Thomas looked at Jack, who was screaming under his blanket, then to Jacob, who was quivering on the floor.

"What's going on?" Naomi called, bursting into the room with Mrs. Elanor at her side.

"Why are you shooting?"

"Something's here! Get back in your rooms!" Thomas shouted. Mrs. Elanor pushed her way through the group and into the room with Jack. Thomas and Jacob ran outside to the upper deck 1, where the snake-like creature was standing, staring at them behind its evil yellow eyes. It stood up tall in its defense, perching on its webbed feet, coiling its body like a snake preparing to strike. Then it leaped into the water with a diving splash.

They both ran to the rails.

"What the hell was that?"

"That...is what ate Frank?"

"That's what ate Frank! And it's going to eat us too if we stay here. The others are right, we got to fix the ship and get off this island, it's not safe here."

"There's more than one of them," Thomas said to Jacob, who dropped his bottom lip. Thomas glared out at the water. *The others. Where were the others?* he thought, peering out at the dying fire on the beach.

"They're gone!" Thomas screamed as he ran across the deck and down the emergency ramp. His boots kicked up sand as he and Jacob sprinted to the made fire pit.

"Hey! Come back!" Thomas shouted into the jungle, spotting the foot tracks that led into the trees. Then at Naomi, who was walking across the sand.

"What happened?" she asked.

"They're gone…Everyone is…gone."

CHAPTER FOURTEEN

A FAINT HUM SOUNDED OVER THE bathroom as the lights illuminated it once more. My eyes slowly opened as I sat up. The little girl disappeared, along with all the black sludge. Not wanting to waste another moment, I took the opportunity and sprinted out the bathroom.

Bursting through the exit, I slammed into a familiar friend.

"Ashton!" I said, pulling him into a desperate hug. Then I pushed back and studied his clothes. He was wearing a black jacket and matching pants, his hat so low over his face, I could barely recognize him, and he smelled like he had been drinking.

"I was afraid you weren't coming… And what are you wearing. How'd you get them to let you in school dressed like that?" I asked, but could not care less, I was just so happy to see him.

"This is my spy gear. you like?" he said, posing with his finger as a gun. I forced a smile. But right now wasn't the time for games.

"What were you running from?" he asked, peering at the girls' bathroom behind me. I was too afraid to look back.

"It's… Hey, no one's seen you all week. What have you been up too? There's been something strange going on around here."

"What do you mean, strange?" His eyes squinted under the brim of his hat. I hesitated at first, then the truth belted from my lips in one long run-on sentence. I told him about the nightmares, the little girl, and the monster in the woods as we walked the school halls.

"It attacked you?" he asked in shock at the part about the monsters.

"Yes! I don't know what it was. It sort of looked like a snake, but they were huge, and they had these claws." I shivered, like I do whenever I think back on it.

"So they are real," he mumbled.

"What do you mean? What do you know about them?"

Ashton dazed off in thought, and his look turned more serious. "Listen… I know you're scared, Rach, but you won't have to be for long. I've been working on a plan all week. Trust me. There won't be a Gathering this year," he said, staring with a mischievous look. I had seen that face on him before, and it could only mean bad news.

"What are you saying? You know what kind of trouble you can get into if someone were to even hear you talking like that. Don't do anything stupid." I whispered, in case someone was listening.

"Get the crew together and meet me at the library during lunch. I have something I want to show you all."

"What is it?"

"Just meet me there, okay?" We hugged, a friend's hug, and he hurried in the opposite direction.

I finished the walk alone and pushed open the door to classroom 113.

"Nice of you to return, Ms. Patterson," Mrs. Collins said, standing at the chalkboard. I hadn't realized how much time had passed, noticing the two-hour difference of the clock on the wall. She ordered me to return to my desk as she continued her lecture. I tried my best to tune her out as the topic had changed to a class discussion about the tests, and how one could reach a good score. Most students had little brothers or sister test days coming up. I pulled out my black journal, sketching graphic pictures of the little girl who had been haunting me. The vision was still fuzzy, like a dream you want to remember but can't.

"Who here can tell me exactly what our life span numbers represent?" Mrs. Collins asked in the background. A student shouted the answer.

"*ILC.*"

"Precisely. Our *Islanders Life Contributions*," Mrs. Collins said, writing the phrase and its meaning in big, bold, chalked letters.

What did it matter? I began thinking. The Gatherings were the only life my generation knew. The rules were so simple, even the small children understood them. On your thirteenth birthday, they tested you in three departments: mental, physical, and spiritual. Based on your scores, they gave you what they called a life span number. Because of the spike in population on the island, and the lack of crystals, drastic measures must be taken, or at least that's what we're told. Once you reached the age of that number, they sentenced you to your Gathering, where a grand new life awaited you—a chance to start over and try it all out again. They commanded every person to test under a certain age after the Last War had ended and the death of King Pius III, a law enforced without reform. Somewhere between the numbers of 40 and 60, selected for the poorer class, and 70 and higher for the other end of the spectrum, although I never knew anyone on that end of the spectrum.

As luck would have it, I received the shortest lifespan given to anyone thus far–the number 18. It was only five years from the day of my testing. Now that I was 18, with every passing second, I felt less and less alive.

I tapped my chewed pencil against the desk,

"Are you okay?" Jessie asked, glimpsing at the daunting sketches in my journal. She had crept over in the middle of class and slid into the vacant seat beside me. Startled, I slammed the book shut.

"Yeah, I'm okay. Hey, Ashton wants all of us to meet up with him during lunch. Meet me by my locker after class."

"Here we go. Wonder what the hell that boy is planning this time," Jessie said. It wasn't news to her that Ashton had an ambitious scheme to stop the Gathering; he'd been trying every year since I returned from the testing facilities with my 18.

"You know how he gets," I whispered back.

Seeing Mrs. Collins dusting the chalk off her hands, Jessie only acknowledged my idea to meet at the lockers and hurried back to her desk.

The hours passed until the alarm sounded, the first half of school had ended, and it was time for lunch. The smell of fresh baked bread and beef seeped through the walls while students rushed out the door like hungry wolves. I gathered my things and prepared to exit the class.

"Ms. Patterson!" Mrs. Collins called, stopping me before I could leave.

"Yes, ma'am?"

"Ahcumu-ta-rahu."

"Achumi a-what?" I asked.

"It's pronounced Achumu-ta-rahu."

"What does that mean?"

"It's an ancient saying our ancestors practiced. It means 'Blessing in disguise.' And that's what your number 18 is. A blessing in disguise."

"Thanks, Mrs. Collins. I'll, uh, keep that in mind," I said.

I figured it was a teacher's way of trying to comfort me.

"Go on now, get you some lunch. I heard they're serving something rather special today."

I waved goodbye and left the class. When I reached my locker, Jessie was waiting, standing amongst the crowd.

"Okay, so what is it Ashton wants to meet about now? And why is it so necessary we have to miss lunch for it? I'm starving."

"I don't know. I saw him coming back from the restroom, he said for all of us to meet him at the library during lunch."

"Phillip missing lunch. Guess we'll see how that goes,"

I laughed because she was right; the others and especially Phillip, wouldn't be too happy about this emergency meeting during lunch. "You get the crew together; I'm going to catch up with Ashton at the library."

Jessie gave me a playful shove. "Trying to get some alone time with Ashton, huh… Little Rachel wants to… you know… before her Gathering. I don't blame you."

"Jessie!"

"Don't say 'Jessie!' like that, I know what's going on."

"Just do it, Jess." I laughed and closed my locker.

Once out the back doors of the school, I headed down the concrete walkway. Most students of Anastasia High usually avoided this section of the campus. A long, curvy trail covered with dead leaves and dead grass on each side. Concealed at the back of the school grounds stood our old library. The building itself was eerie:

massive high walls and round windows covered by wooden boards. A caution taken when the weather got bad, but it would seem no one had gotten around to taking them down. A row of molding stone pillars held up the structure, and leafless trees on dying grass were the cherry on top.

It was only fitting that the librarian was a strange, old woman named Ms. Anna. The quiet type who seemed to float when she walked. Not literally, but her small feet barely made a sound when she entered the room. She was quite tall for her age, and her voice was scratchy like you wanted to give her a glass of water. Everyone was convinced she was an evil witch who practiced spells in her office. But this was only a rumor. I was no stranger to the library, though I too thought Ms. Anna to be quite odd, there was no denying that.

The chills of wind whisked under my school sweater as I drew back on the bronze-colored door handles. "Why would he want to meet here, of all places?" I muttered, scanning the dimly lit library for Ashton.

The sky peeked through cracks of boarded windows; hanging on walls were rows of glowing crystals with plastic covers, lighting up the room in a reddish haze. My rain boots squeaked against the floor as I reached the empty librarian's desk that sat at the front of the room. A name plate and stacks of books were present, but otherwise, no Ms. Anna.

"Figures." I continued my search through the rows of book-filled shelves that lined the library aisles. I scanned the book collections— from history to philosophy and even horror stories, my favorite since I was a living one. *The Man in the Shadows parts 1-4,* by Christopher Ferguson, *The Moon Rock,* by Cinthia Calastore, *Nightmares* by John Casey. I grabbed this last one and examined the cover. It was black with a flapping, blue-winged butterfly trapped in a cage, and a pair of evil-looking eyes lurking in the back. I skimmed through the first few pages.

If you're reading this then it's too late and I'm already dead. They have trapped me down in this cellar for thirty days... I think... One loses track of time when you don't get to see the sun. I only know when it's night by his presence. He comes down here reeking of island booze and blood and demanding I should obey him if I want to eat. You would obey him too if you were me. I'm sure he's killed before. I bet my life on it, which isn't worth much now at the moment. If you were wondering how I got down here? How did I let some old fool and his friends trap me? How did I write this book? All feasible questions that I promise you I will answer personally. But first I need you to do something for me... something simple. Just whisper the name...

"Rachel..." I dropped the book to the floor as Ashton popped out from behind the bookshelf.

"Hey...don't get us caught, ok? Come on—I don't want Ms. Anna to know we're here," he whispered.

"Sorry, I got distracted," I said in relief, placing the book back on the shelf. "Where were you?" I asked, following him to the very back of the library. A section I never visited, never wanted to. There was not much lighting, even fewer hanging crystals and boarded windows. We crossed stacks of dusty books piled all over the floor. "Where are we going?"

Ashton ignored me, stepping over one small hill after another.

At the end of the cluttered aisle were two doors. One marked *private*, and the other, *Ms. Anna's office*. Ashton crouched low to the ground, signaling for me to do the same, placing his index finger over his lips. We crept, watching her bouncing shadow flailing on the wall beside us.

A loud scream belted, and we froze at the sounds of her raspy voice. The shout grew louder and louder until she was almost screaming. For sure she had discovered us. Neither Ashton nor I dared to move as I clung to the back of his jacket. I wasn't sure Ms. Anna wasn't a witch, nor did I want to find out today.

But after a long pause without seeing her charge out the door on those long, lanky legs, we sighed and proceeded; she was only singing to herself.

CHAPTER FIFTEEN

BURNING STICKS CRACKLED IN THE fire. The thick, white clouds from the smoke floated up towards flashes of lightning. They had stopped to make camp and would meet with Rachel Patterson in the morning. Malcamore figured it would be troublesome trying to find a room at this hour—far simpler to stop where they were and get some rest. Quadrant Three was infamous for its unfriendly township anyway, and rooms that may have been available were even worse than sleeping outside.

William, the driver, had no quarrels with Malcamore's decision to slumber outdoors, currently wrapped snuggly in a sleeping bag and giving out a ground-shaking snore with random whispers and laughs.

The three huddled around the flames, trying their best to stay warm from the chilly wind.

"Samson," Malcamore called, busy twirling his knife and studying the map he had stolen from the king's home. "What do you think about the world outside the walls?"

Samson sat up from his sleeping bag. "Well… I really don't think about it much nowadays. Anastasia's been my only concern. When I was a much younger islander, I used to think about it a lot, what's outside the walls, the world beyond our own. But then I met my wife, started working. You know how it is."

"Hm. I still think about it every day," Malcamore said as he refolded the map. "Head to the wagon if you don't mind, old friend, and retrieve that stew you ordered. I'll get us some more wood for the fire."

"Yes, young sir. Though I don't understand why we couldn't go into town. Maybe find a room available for travelers? It's cold out tonight, and I think it even looks like rain." Samson shivered as he looked up at the lightning strikes.

"Stop your whining, Samson. Besides, fresh air may do us some good," Malcamore said.

"And what's this about the girl with the 18? Why are they making us oversee her Gathering?"

The answer flashed in Malcamore's mind. "Like I told you before, Samson, I must meet her first before I can be sure."

"Sure of what?"

"What's with all these questions?" Malcamore snapped, standing. "The food, remember."

Giving his pants a beating with the palms of his hands, he headed for the thicket.

"Yes, young sir. The food—I'll go retrieve it," Samson shouted to Malcamore, who disappeared into the gloomy woods.

It was essential they have enough to burn through the night, as Malcamore didn't want any surprises from wild animals that might lurk in the dark.

Engulfed with thoughts about the girl with the 18, he hacked away at the limbs of a tree with his knife. Boiling with anger, he walked farther and did the same to another. He was carrying an arm full of broken limbs when his ears caught the humming.

A sweet child's hum.

Soothing alongside the night's fog. He lost interest in the sticks, dropping the branches to the ground.

"Who's there?" he called shakily. A chilly breeze joined the soft hum.

"That song," he whispered. "Hey! Is someone out there?"

A thick, growing fog blanketed the darkness. Flames from the camp were no longer visible.

He knew this song. He had heard it many times before.

"Where are you?" he said, peering out at the darker parts of the forest. The sound of every crackling stick causing him to flinch with shaking legs, and eyes bouncing from one tree to the next.

The hazy fog formed a cloud at the root of a tree. Upon arrival, he stood in fear, his worst nightmare standing before him.

"Elizabeth?" His voice emerged, gasping from the massive snakes that circled her body from where she lay on the dirt. Each hissed and lunged out at his feet while Elizabeth crooned the sweet melody until her black pupils met his.

"Elizabeth…?" Malcamore whimpered. His trembling hands reached out to remove the snakes as her soft voice turned demonically deep.

"It's all your fault!" she shouted. The cold ground collapsed beneath Malcamore's feet in an instant. He screamed, falling deep into a dark, muddy pit. He clawed at the dirt with his hands and feet, clinging to whatever surface they could find. A boom of thunder sounded, and the rain poured down in buckets.

"Young sir!" Samson shouted into the backdrop.

"Samson! I'm over here. I've fallen into a…trap of some sort," Malcamore called out from the pit, the moist clay collapsing on top of his head.

A patch of dead leaves shuffled above the sinking hole as his sight shot upwards to the rain pouring on his face. He expected to see Samson, who could assist him in escaping. Malcamore froze. Elizabeth. Her black, soulless eyes now peered down at him from above.

"Samson!" he shouted in a terrified scream, sliding deeper into the pit.

Elizabeth's face turned upward, then back down on Malcamore.

"Samson, I'm down here!" Malcamore called, large chunks of clay and mud falling from his slipping hands. With her focus back on him, Elizabeth crawled her way into the hole with small gray hands and feet.

His eyelids were closed by the time she reached him. When it fell silent, he hoped she disappeared, then felt her slick, black hair graze his ear. Her voice was sweet and child-like, the way he remembered it to be.

"A life for a life, Benjamin," Elizabeth said.

"Take my cane!" Samson's voice broke into the scene. When he opened his eyes again, Samson was standing above the hole and stretching out his cane. Malcamore had never been so happy to see that mustache and climbed his way back to the surface, covered in mud and huffing.

"A little girl…" he said, crawling back towards the pit and staring down the hole that was slowly filling with water.

Elizabeth had vanished.

"There was a little girl here, Samson. I swear it," he said, pleading in disbelief. "Just a second ago, Elizabeth was here and there were snakes… Tons of them!"

Samson crawled across the dirt to assist. He, too, stared down into the dark, empty pit. "Seems like some kind of hunter's trap, young sir. A sink hole, false ground, I would guess. We must be on the cuffs of someone's property. But who's Elizabeth?" Samson said.

"Ah, no, you don't understand. This wasn't some normal little girl. She was humming this song... The song was like..." He hummed a little in dismay, attempting to copy the melody.

Whether Samson believed him, he only nodded. "Let's get back to the wagon. The rain came sooner than we expected." They helped one another off the turf as they began walking towards the dead campfire. "It's been a long night, young sir."

"You're right, it has. We should get some sleep," Malcamore said, glimpsing back at the woods for a sight of Elizabeth.

When the sun was on the horizon, Samson and the driver William began readying the horses.

"Mr. Malcamore, are you awake?" Samson asked, re-entering the wagon. "I suggest we get a move on if we want to be in Quadrant Three city by noon."

"I'm not asleep, Samson," Malcamore said, though he remained curled in his seat. "I couldn't sleep a wink after last night. Are we ready to depart?"

"Yes, everything's ready to go."

"All right, let's get a move on then. We should stop in town before we see the girl. I need to freshen up, Samson, maybe even buy some new clothes. I smell like hell after falling into that hole last night," Malcamore said as the wagon made its way down the road.

CHAPTER SIXTEEN

Drops of rain fell onto the upper deck, causing streams of water to slip through cracks in the captain's cabin. The remaining survivors—Thomas, Naomi, their son Jacob, Mrs. Elanor and her grandson, Jack—huddled together. No one else had returned.

"How many days have we been here now?" Naomi whispered in exhaustion.

"This is our second night, my love."

"Geez, it already feels like we've been here a week." Naomi sighed.

"I see your week and raise you a year."

"I'm starving… has anyone got anything to eat?" Jack whimpered over the rumbling thunder. His burned sockets peered up at Mrs. Elanor, rocking and crooning "Hush, Little Baby" in the bed.

Thomas, on the floor with arms wrapped around Naomi, slowly rose with a groan. He tiptoed across the cramped room where Jacob was in a fetal position in the corner.

"Hand me my bag, son."

Jacob reached next to him, sliding his father the heavy duffel bag.

"I have little here, but it's better than nothing." He felt through the space, calling out the items inside. "Five bottles of fresh water, two packs of Ritz crackers, a couple of old sandwiches, rope, and an extra flare gun. The rest is just clothes and stuff."

"Let me see that flare," Jacob said. Thomas slid the small orange gun across the floor to a stop at Jacob's feet.

"Be careful with that, it's loaded."

"In case I want to kill myself."

"That's it?" Mrs. Elanor moaned. "That's all the food we have, some crackers and old sandwiches?"

"I'm afraid so, or at least that's edible. The kitchen may have a few things."

"I barely got a chance to have any chicken," Jacob said.

She shook her head in grief and continued her hum, rocking Jack back and forth. Thomas grabbed a pack of crackers from his bag. He opened the wrapping, taking care not to waste a crumb. He handed Jack his first portion of four pieces, then did the same for the others. They all took small bites as they chewed.

The rain was still dripping through the cracks while Thomas searched his mind for something to say. Something to drown out the silence and rain pouring outside.

"I miss sports," he injected.

Jack's head swung from Mrs. Elanor's clutch.

Naomi in mid-chew from a tiny bite of her cracker. "What?" she asked.

"Sports. You know, like football, basketball. I miss them..."

"You, of all people, miss sports?" Naomi said.

"Yeah, I never really cared for 'em too much back in the old days. Thought it was rather pointless. Grown men hollering like hyenas over a child's game. But…I miss sports now. I think about it more than I ever have before. I try to remember who won the last finals and who were the greatest champions of all time, stuff like that. Stuff I should remember." He laughed a little.

"My father… My father loved, and I mean *loved* the Chicago Cubs. We weren't even from Chicago, I never understood it. Charlie and I both hated baseball." He laughed to himself again in remembrance of a different time. Back to the perceived normal where he and his father and Charlie would gather around the living room television during opening season. He could still smell the pork chops on the grill, hear the twisting fizzle of his dad's beer top as he leaned back in that old recliner, remote in hand. The room fell silent to nothing but the storm ramping up outside. The heavy raindrops crashed against the waters and the round window that hung in the corner over Jacob.

"I miss music," Naomi whispered. "Some nights, when it's really quiet and I'm really still, I can hear music playing in my head. Sometimes whole symphonies. It really sounds beautiful…"

"I miss pizza," Jack added, his voice muffled by the grip of Mrs. Elanor's clutch. They all laughed a little, even Mrs. Elanor.

"I think I might have a little something to eat in my room," she said, rising from the bed, then halted at a shout from Thomas.

"No!" he hissed. "We must stay together. Besides, something could be out there."

"It could just as well come get us in here, can't it? Jack, honey, I'll just be a second. I think I got some chips and a few other items I had been saving for a time like this. But I think it'll go good with your crackers, Thomas. I figure we might as well eat it."

"I'll go with you," Jacob said, standing.

She gave Jack a soft kiss on the head.

When she opened the door, Mrs. Elanor snatched into the darkness with a loud scream. Sounds of rapid clicking and screeches blared from the halls. Jack shouted and attempted to run after her, but he fell when grabbed by Naomi, who was yelling for Thomas to shut the door. Thomas crawled across the room and slammed it shut, grabbing the gun from the floor.

The screeches and screams fell quiet to tatting claws and wet snarls. Jack wept into Naomi's arms, and Jacob quickly moved from under the window.

"Please don't open that door again, baby. Please, please don't open it," Naomi whispered, with tears rolling down her cheeks.

Thomas stared at the entry. He had enough. With his gun poised, his hand slowly reached for the knob. A blaring alarm rang over the island, causing Thomas to turn his sight to the window. The sharp claws of the creatures tapped against the walls like nails on drumming fingers. Then the sound moved above their heads. The alarm continued to wail as Thomas walked to the window and glared out at the glowing jungle in the backdrop.

"Someone's here and they know it," Thomas whispered. "We can't stay on this ship… Those things, whatever they are, will pick us off one by one if we don't leave soon. If we can survive the night, I say first thing in the morning, we make our way across the island. It's our only hope." The faint alarm quieted, and Thomas stared out of the window at the dozens of creatures galloping across the sand.

"I'm in. Let's do it. What other choice do we have? I'm ready to be off this ship, anyway. I never want to see another ship for the rest of my life. Something's ringing an alarm out there. Maybe they're stranded here and signaling for any survivors," Jacob said.

"Yeah, that's what I'm thinking too. That boy in the jungle, maybe the others were saved."

"They're not normal," Jack whispered.

"Who isn't?" Thomas asked.

"Those crystals, the ones glowing in those trees, the ones that blinded me. It controls this island. I could sense it. If somebody lives here, they couldn't possibly be normal."

Jack cried harder into Naomi's chest as she stroked his brown hair and hummed as his grandmother had.

"We don't have another choice, we must go." The clicking returned to the hallway as they all quieted once again. Thomas took a slow, determined step with the gun raised.

"Get away from the door," Jack whispered.

Thomas wiped at a drop of sweat and took another step.

"I can hear them talking in my head," Jacob shouted, bawling and covering his ears. "Get away from the door, captain!"

A loud screech came, and the door jolted open. Staring at him from the darkness were the evil, yellow eyes. It smelled of blood, and its black snake-like skin glistened in the lightning strike.

Naomi screamed as it hissed out a massive, red, forked tongue, then took a step inside the room, dipping its head through the doorway. Jacob fired a flare shot that stuck into its skull. It gave a roaring cry as the bright red fire burned at its face, then hissed out a gook that sprayed across the room. Thomas slammed the door shut again in a hurry, and Jacob dragged the bed and pushed it against the door. Panting, Thomas gazed at his son. "If we make it to morning," he whispered. Jacob nodded as he slid down, gasping for breath.

CHAPTER SEVENTEEN

"C'MON, THROUGH HERE," ASHTON SAID, leading through the door marked *Private*. The room was so dark my eyes took a minute to readjust as I peered down the iron stairwell spiraling below us.

"You want to go down there?" My words echoed down the stone walls.

"Yeah," Ashton said, still leading the way. We descended one step at a time. I followed slowly, grasping the shaking rail for support.

"What is this place?" I asked, making sure of my footing.

As we approached the bottom of the iron steps, my feet landed on wobbly wood floors, and a tall wooden door marked *SR* stood before me. Ashton pulled out the set of gold keys once again and shoved one into the keyhole.

"Damn it," he said, giving the knob a few hard turns and repeating the process. "It was working the other day, I swear..." He reached inside his pocket again, this time pulling out a small knife.

"Look out for Ms. Anna for us, will you? This might take a bit."

I turned, looking back up the way we came at the dark, spiraling stairs I never knew existed. "Well, at least hurry!" I whispered, thinking I'd heard the creaking above us. After Ashton jammed and pried his knife, *SR* sprung open.

"Got it!" he shouted.

I continued my watch while Ashton searched the room to the sounds of fumbling tables and crashes.

"Sorry, can't see a damn thing in here. Just come in and close the door, it'll be fine."

I entered, watching.

Ashton was busy running from wall to wall, patting down every corner. "This place is an old study room, I think."

"How do you know about it?"

"Found it!" He flipped a small switch that caused a red light to glow on the ceiling.

"I followed Ms. Anna down here one day after school. That freaking lady really gives me the creeps. I've been tracking her and a few others all week. But Ms. Anna is always acting so weird. I knew she had to have some information on the Gatherings."

"You could have just asked her."

"Now where's the fun in that?" Ashton said with a smile. I figured he had been up to something as I observed him dragging and moving desks out of the way, then knocking on distinct parts of the floor with his fist.

"Now what are you doing?" I asked, stepping closer.

"When I followed Ms. Anna, I saw her hide something under one of these floorboards. Give me a hand, will you?" he said, tugging on a stained, misplaced board. Together, we pulled on the outer edge with our nails. Ashton even wedged his knife in between the appearing slit, and he pried it open with a loud pop, then stuck his arm into the small hole in the floor.

"What's in there?"

"Just a second… I almost got it" He jerked his empty hand back, looking at me in shock.

"What happened?" I asked. He shook his head and reached into the mystery gap again, this time pulling out an old, dusty, red book. It had gold trimming and a small gold strap and lock.

"Aha!" he exclaimed, placing the board back over the hole in the floor, and laid the book down between us.

"Recognize that?" Ashton said, gesturing to the cover. The island's infamous triangle symbol with two monsters coiling around it.

"That's them!" I said, reaching for the book and skimming through a few pages. I frowned at some disturbing drawings inside, the pictures of islanders falling into a deep pit.

"What's wrong with the words?" I asked, spinning the book upside down as the letters became legible.

"Some of its written upside down, some right side up, some backwards. But you have to decipher what goes where, it's actually pretty complicated. Hey, those creatures you mentioned, did they look like this?"

"Yeah… but much bigger in person," I said, handing him back the book. "So, what do we do now?"

"Now we wait." Ashton placed the book on one of the four tables that lined the room, hopping up to a seat. "Where's the rest of the guys, anyway?" he asked.

"They'll be here. I told Jessie to get them because I wanted a chance to talk with you first… alone." I could see him blush under his hat.

"Well, that's fine, I guess. Phillip knows how to get down here. I told him too."

"It's just… with the Gathering so close, I wanted to say something I should've said a long time ago, before it's too late."

"Like what?"

"We've been best friends our entire lives, Ashton. And we've never said I love you so… I love you." I wasn't embarrassed to say it. Ashton, however, was.

"No, I guess we haven't," he said, leaping off the table. "Well, I love you too, Rach… a lot. Don't worry—nothing bad is going to happen to you. I won't let it… I'll protect you, I promise." We held each other, this time not a friend's hug. Tighter than we'd ever hugged before.

"I told you I knew where they were!" Phillip said as he and the rest of the crew burst through the door. Ashton and I sprung apart.

"Keep it down!" Ashton hissed

"We were waiting on you guys," I said, trying not to sound upset about their timing.

"Uh-huh, sure you were," Phillip said, sitting on one table.

"Ms. Anna didn't see any of you, right?" Ashton asked Phillip, who returned a frown.

"Of course not, this isn't amateur hour."

"Hey, Rachel," Lola said, greeting me with a wave as she and Jessie crept into the room. I smiled and waved back.

"You guys want us to come back? I mean, it is lunch and I'm starving," Matthew said as he softly closed the door behind him.

"No, I want you guys here. All of you. I have something I want to show you." We gathered around the circular table as Ashton retrieved the red book with the gold strap. "Do any of you know what this is?"

No one spoke, but we all shared the same look of suspicion at one another.

"Neither did I…at first. Before I found it."

"And by found, you mean you stole," Jessie said. I nudged her with my hand.

"What? I want to know what we're getting ourselves into down here."

"Fine, yes, I stole it. May I continue now?" Ashton said with exaggerated politeness.

"You may," Jessie answered, just as primly.

"Like I was saying, this book that I'm going to 'obtain,'" he said, looking over at Jessie, "is one that contains some dark secrets about our island."

"What secrets?" Lola asked. Ashton dropped the tone of his voice.

"About Anastasia, about a species coming to kill us all."

"Ahh, wait. Let me stop you right there," Phillip interrupted. "Is this another conspiracy speech? Cause if it is, I'm out."

"Yeah, me too," Matthew said.

"Mrs. Collins spent half the morning giving a lecture about our ILC and the tests. From the harvesting to our ancestors. You would know if you showed up sometimes. Besides, how can you tell what's in this book, anyway? Most of its written in gibberish." Matthew had grabbed the book and was now flipping through the pages; I thought most of the same.

"Not gibberish! The words are backwards, and some parts are upside down," Ashton said.

"But why would somebody go through the trouble to write a book like that?" Lola asked, snatching the book from Matthew and examining it for herself.

"I'm not sure, but I don't think we're the only ones living on this island. Those monsters you see on the cover, they have a name for them in here. They call them Fiends. There's a reason we're not allowed outside of the walls, you know. Haven't you ever wondered what's beyond the wall?" he said as the book made its way back into his possession.

"I've spent days researching the information in this book, and, guys, let me tell you, it suggests some strange shit is going on here."

"Okay, enough with the suspense, Ashton. Spit it out," Jessie said.

Ashton cleared his throat like a teacher addressing the class and prepared to read. "For it to make any sense, take it one line at a time," he repeated.

"*What you are preparing to embark on is forbidden knowledge.* He spun the book.

The secrets of a brotherhood intertwined with all knowledge from far before. We are the keepers of time. If you are reading this book without being a keeper of time, I declare you cursed." He spun the book.

"*Death to you and anyone who shares your name.*"

"Well, I'm out!" Matthew shouted, stepping toward the exit.

"Stop, Matthew, let him finish," Lola said, grabbing him by the arm. Matthew reluctantly returned to the table as Ashton continued.

"*If you are a keeper of time, you may proceed.*" Ashton turned the page. "*These are the laws. As it is written, so it shall be. Verse One: The unknown world will be created, not born. Verse Two: We must protect Anastasia from all who may seek her. By whom, no one shall ask. Verse Three: Their ages of darkness will feed our youth. Their world is no more. Verse Four: We shall make sacrifices alike. But Immortality for all that share the bond.*"

"Okay, I've heard enough, Ashton," Jessie said, interrupting the reading. "What the hell is this even talking about? If I wanted to hear garbage like this, I could go into the city and listen to one of the drunk, homeless people outside the Drums."

"Guys, don't you see?" Ashton said, slamming the book shut. "This book is hinting at the fact that we're all being controlled. Their ages of darkness will feed our youth. The Gathering isn't some kind of new life. They're killing us!"

"What! How did you conclude we're being controlled from that garbage? Besides, they only call it a new life so that the people who are about to die won't freak out about it, everyone knows that. Sorry, Rach, I didn't mean—" Jessie said.

"It's ok," I answered. Her mouth was always saying things it shouldn't. "But who are *they*, you think? And what's Ms. Anna doing with a book like this?"

"Right, Rachel! Who are they? And correction—Ms. Anna *had* a book like this." Ashton picked up the book once again and skimmed quickly through the pages before placing it back on the table, pointing to a passage. "Look right here. I thought this one was the worst."

And the end fell from the sky upon them, bringing death upon us. Death to all those who are called… Humans.

"You guys don't think that sounds important?"

"Ok, but what's a human? I thought you said they called them Fiends," Jessie said.

"Yeah, and what does this have to do with Rachel?" Lola asked.

"I think it's both. It also talks about our blood and their blood, and how our seeds are their seeds and stuff like that. It gets weird and disturbing actually, I haven't decoded all of it yet."

"Why can't we just ask Ms. Anna what it means?" Phillip said.

"Oh, yeah, sure: 'Hey, creepy librarian lady. Yes, some friends and I stole that hidden book of time under your floor, in that room marked private, and we were wondering if you could tell us what it means.' No way, Phillip," Ashton said.

"The book and this room both freak me out." Jessie shivered; I shared her sentiments.

"Rachel, tell them about what happened on your way to school this morning." I shot Ashton an angry look. I wasn't ready to share that information with the group just yet. Each of them stared at me in question.

"What?" Jessie asked. "What happened on your way to school, Rach?"

I sighed. "I've been seeing this strange girl all morning… It started a few nights ago but got even worse last night in my home, and she had these snakes around her."

"Was it a dream?" Lola asked, hiding under the collar of her school sweater.

"No, and then these creatures in the woods, over by old man Lew's shop, attacked me. He said they were snakes, but there's no way they could have been snakes."

"What do you think it was?" Jessie asked.

"I'm not sure… It looked just like those monsters on the cover."

"Fiends," Ashton said.

"Those things. I don't have a clue about who the little girl is…"

"I hate snakes," Lola whispered.

"Yeah, but these were way creepier. Not like regular snakes. These… These were different. Evil-looking, and they had claws."

"Claws!" Jessie shrieked.

"Maybe they're working with the Humans," Lola said.

"So, what's your brilliant plan?" asked Matthew.

"The plan is, we go to the papers with this book. We can start a petition and get everyone on board. Travel Quadrant to Quadrant, telling everyone about the danger the island might be in. We don't know how high this goes! We start with Quadrant Three, then Two and One, and we storm Quadrant Four and take back our island!"

Matthew shook his head. "Yeah, I'm out. Look, I love you, Rachel, and I will definitely miss you, but this is crazy. Six kids from the city taking on who or whatever it is ruling the island because of a book? Going against the king, mind you. Just thinking this way is cause for treason. I got a family to think about. My little brother's testing is coming up. I can't risk putting him in harm's way."

"He's right, Rach, it all sounds way too risky and dangerous," Lola added.

"Guys, we can do this! This is our proof right here! Do the math. We knew there was some reason for Rachel's 18. This could be the answer."

My eyes darted to the floor; I could hear a hissing coming from under the boards.

"You guys hear that?" I whispered as they continued their argument.

"This is not about Rachel's 18 and you know it. This is about you not being able to let go of the fact that we can't stop it!"

"You guys, do you hear that?" I matched their volume, causing them all to quiet. "Listen!"

It was Jessie who spoke first. "Yeah, I hear that."

The hissing had grown louder, and a loud thud banged against the floorboards, rocking the table at the legs.

"It's coming from the floor."

"What was that?" Jessie shrieked at another loud thud, this one coming from right beneath us. I glanced to the loose board where we found the book, spotting the head of a snake trying to push his way through.

"Guys, I think we should leave now," Matthew said, stepping slowly toward the exit.

The door to the secret room swung open, and a tall figure loomed over him. He let out a yell of fright.

"What are you kids doing down here?" Ms. Anna screamed in her high, raspy voice.

We froze—all but Ashton, who I saw shove the red book inside the back of his trousers, using his shirt to cover it before anyone else could notice.

"This room is private property!" Mrs. Anna continued shrilly over the sounds of banging floorboards. "Who gave you permission to be down here? This is trespassing!" She gasped. "You've even angered my babies!" she shrieked, referring to the loud thuds still drumming underneath us, pushing past and running to the aid of her pet snakes.

We all stood, too afraid to speak. It was Matthew who ran first, followed by Phillip and the rest of us escaping out the old study room.

"Don't let me catch you down here again!" we heard her scream as we raced back up the iron stairwell and scrambled through the library halls. Once outside, only then did we stop to catch our breaths.

"Ashton, you can't be serious," Phillip gasped, still panting. "You're talking about monsters here—actual monsters. It's just a stupid book; monsters aren't running around, secretly ruling the island." He grabbed his book bag off the ground from where he had dumped it. "Sorry, Rach, I am. I wish we could do more."

"It's okay, Phillip," I said. I had expected none of this and could not fault my friends for being scared.

"You guys," Phillip finished, "we only got about twenty minutes of lunch left. If we hurry now, we can still make it."

The rest of the crew followed, all but me and Ashton, who stood alone on the pathway.

"You don't think I'm crazy, do you, Rach?" Ashton asked, staring at the ground.

"No, I think that book of yours is crazy. But you're just trying to help, and I think that's sweet. Let's go, we may as well eat, I'll get you an extra lunch tray."

"Um, can we do this another time?" He scratched the back of his head, avoiding my stare.

"Another time? Ashton, it's my last day at school."

"I'm sorry. I'll be back in time to walk you home, promise. I just have a few more things to sort out."

We shared one last hug, and I watched my best friend leave once again. I felt as if he was avoiding me.

As I re-entered Property High alone, the sight of Principal Easterling rushing down the hall towards me wasn't exciting.

"Ms. Patterson!" he called.

"Yes, Mr. Easterling?"

"They informed me that a special guest is on his way to see you now. If you don't mind, would you follow me to my office?

It wasn't a request, so I nodded and followed the principal, though my stomach was giving angry growls. Maybe skipping lunch hadn't been such an excellent idea.

Mr. Easterling opened his office door and gestured for me to have a seat.

"So, who is this mysterious person coming to see me?" I asked.

"I'm told his name is Benjamin Malcamore."

CHAPTER EIGHTEEN

THE SCHOOL BELL BLASTED AS Malcamore and Samson walked down the halls of Property High. They came face to face with a door labeled *Principal's office*. Malcamore stopped Samson before he could knock and leaned against the door.

"When is your guest coming, Mr. Easterling? Lunch is already over, and I'm starving."

"I'm not sure. They told me they buzzed him in at the gate. I don't understand what's taking him so long."

Malcamore okayed, and Samson gave the door three loud raps.

"About time, that must be him," Principal Easterling said, swinging it open.

Samson stepped through first, tapping his cane to the ground.

"Hello, sir! Entering is Mr. Benjamin Malcamore!" Samson said, standing at attention as Malcamore entered the room.

"That will be enough, Samson," Malcamore said.

He could feel Rachel's eyes studying him from her chair on the other side of the office. They had stopped in town to freshen up.

His suit was new, and he even carried a large bag with the island's infamous symbol on the front.

"Oh! Well, welcome, both of you. I'm Principal Easterling, and this young lady here—"

"Rachel Patterson," Malcamore interrupted, approaching Rachel and extending his hand. "I've heard a lot about you."

Rachel looked at him with questioning eyes. "Yes, I'm Rachel Patterson."

Malcamore smiled, giving her hand a pat and turning to his friend. "Samson!"

"Yes, young sir?"

"Why don't you have Principal Easterling here give you a tour of the school? I would like to have a few words alone with Ms. Patterson, if that would be okay with you," he said, glancing at Rachel again.

"Sure, I guess."

"Mr. Easterling, would you be so kind as to show my colleague around?" Malcamore said.

"Of course," Principal Easterling said, escorting Samson out of the room. "And your name—Samson, is it?"

"Yes, sir, correct,"

"And what is your first name?"

"It's Samson, sir."

"So, your name is Samson Samson?"

Their voices faded, leaving Rachel and Malcamore alone.

Malcamore slammed his bag on the table, causing Rachel to wince. His first choice was one of these—a small black device known as an identifier.

"May I see your wrist, Ms. Patterson?" he asked.

"Yes, sir," Rachel breathed, revealing her number 18 and symbol.

Malcamore shone a blue light on the number, and her name and Quadrant appeared on the small device's screen. Setting this aside, he laid a small, black recorder onto the table, looking up at her as he did so. "You don't mind, do you?"

"No, sir, I'm used to reporters coming by."

"Oh, I'm not with the paper," Malcamore said. "I was in the mob. I'm a… retired general, you could say. They asked me to close your portfolio personally. Might you have any idea why?"

"No, sir, I guess it makes sense—the Gathering and all…" Rachel's words trailed off.

"Yes, the Gathering." Malcamore pressed a button on the recorder as it let out a static-filled hum. "My name is Benjamin Malcamore," he intoned, "and I am here with… state your name, please, for the record."

"Rachel Patterson."

"Thank you, Ms. Patterson. I will ask you a few questions concerning your departure for your Gathering. Do you understand? Please state yes or no."

"Yes," Rachel replied.

"Very well…" Malcamore fumbled through some loose papers from the bag. Dropping a few to the ground and banging his head on the table when he stood. He took three deep breaths to calm himself, then handed them to Rachel. "Just a formality," he assured. "We're required to deliver them to every islander being Gathered, and whose portfolio is being closed."

Rachel narrowed her eyes; he could feel she sensed his nervousness.

"Sorry, nerves get the best of me sometimes."

"Me too," Rachel said.

After clearing his throat, he said, "It says here that you are the daughter of Katherine and John Patterson, is that correct?"

"Yes."

"No siblings?"

"That's right, I'm an only child," Rachel said.

"I see. And Quadrant Three is your original home?"

She paused, looking up at Malcamore. His eyes were steady once again.

"Answer the question please, Ms. Patterson. We're almost done here."

"Yes," she said with defiance.

"And are you of the age for Gathering, assigned to you by the laws of your king, King Theodore?"

"Yes."

"State your age for the record, please."

"18."

"Are you ready for your new life that awaits you?"

"Yes, whatever that means."

"Let the records show that I, Benjamin Malcamore, have cleared Ms. Rachel Patterson for her Gathering, and that her portfolio is now complete." Malcamore stopped the recorder, noticing the tears slipping down her face.

"It's okay, Ms. Patterson, I understand." He reached inside the pocket of his suit and brought out a handkerchief. She blew her nose and offered the handkerchief back, but Malcamore declined.

"Thank you," she said, still sniffling, fighting to hold back more tears that threatened to fall.

After a few moments, when Rachel had regained some control, Malcamore leaned forward with a glare. "Ms. Patterson, I have a few more questions. Off the record, if that's okay."

"Yes, sir," Rachel said.

"Can you tell me a little more about your parents?"

"Um, yeah, sure." Rachel took a breath, composing herself. "My mom's a nurse. She works at the shelters in the city–they call them the Drums."

"I'm aware. They have one in every Quadrant now. Well, everyone other than Quadrant Four. But please, continue. What about your father?"

"My father was in the mob, like you."

"Is that so?"

"Yeah."

"Hmm. Then I take it he's no longer serving?"

Rachel looked up in sadness. "No, sir, he died a couple years ago in a work accident."

"I'm sorry to hear that. How did he… die, if you don't mind?" Malcamore said.

"No, its fine. He worked for a digging company in the caves. They would mine for crystals sunup until sundown some days. He was always working. One day, someone from his job just… showed up at our home, with the worst news of my life. And the next thing I knew, my daddy…"

She began weeping again. "The walls of the cave, they collapsed, and four men died. One of them was my daddy; his job was dangerous, but it was the only way we could afford our home."

"He sounds like he was an honorable islander."

"He was, sir," Rachel said.

"I'm sorry for your loss, Ms. Patterson. But with you having such a low number, were you not offered any of your father's remaining time? The law states that with a sudden death in the family, the remaining years may transfer to another immediate family member."

"No, sir. And excuse my language, but that law is some bullshit." She whispered the last word. "We tried, but they kept sending back rejection letter after rejection letter, all saying the Gathering, there's a new life that awaits me. I tried so hard on my testing day! And 18, that's what I got. 18! Contribution to Anastasia, my ass!" She pounded the table in front of her.

"I apologize, Mrs. Patterson; I won't bother you with any more of these questions."

"Wait… that's it?" Rachel asked.

"That is all," Malcamore said, standing and shaking her hand again. "I'm very sorry for everything, but I must leave," he said, tossing the identifier and recorder back into the bag.

"So, what happens next?"

"I'll be in touch." After another firm handshake, he quickly exited the office.

At the close of the door, he ran down the school hallways, searching for Samson and spotting him on a stroll with Principal Easterling.

"Samson! There you are. Let's go!"

"Right now? He was just about to let me give a speech to some kids about the benefits of a powerful education."

"Later. We have much more important business. Thank you for your kindness, Mr. Asherling," Malcamore said, sparing the principal a glance.

"It's Easterling."

"Well, thank you again, Mr. Easterling. But we must go. Come along, Samson."

"Thanks again, Mr. Easterling. I will return later to give that speech!" Samson called as Malcamore all but dragged him from the school.

"Ready the driver," he said as soon as they were out of earshot. "We have very little time if we wish to make the Gathering." He hurried, almost jogging.

"Again? Slow down, young sir. What's going on? Where do we have to be?"

Malcamore readied the horses himself as Samson awakened William, who was sleeping at the helm. "Quadrant One. I have to speak with someone there; she's the only one who can help."

"Then we're finally returning home! Excellent! I have a few things I need to take care of myself," Samson said in excitement.

"No, we're not going home just yet. I must visit a friend who lives in the city. A very, particular individual. You'll see when we get there, but I bet she can help."

"Why? Help with what?"

"The girl!" Malcamore shouted. "I know the girl!"

"Of course, you know her. I told you about her in the papers, remember?"

"Yes, I wasn't sure before, but I know that girl, and she's not who she thinks she is. If we're to help her, we *must* get to Quadrant One. Do you understand?" He glared at Samson.

"Help her? How can we possibly help her? And who *is* she? Young sir, you're not making any sense."

"You'll understand soon enough. Now let's go."

CHAPTER NINETEEN

"YOU GOTTA CALL THEM BACK, baby. Just pick up the phone and at least hear what they have to say… Here, toss me your phone, I'll do it for you," Naomi said, rising to her knee, his military t-shirt stopping just above her naked thigh. Thomas grunted and tossed, watching anxiously as she swiped through the missed calls on the latest iPhone.

"It's ringing." She gasped, removing the phone from her ear and pressing the number one.

"It asked if this was Thomas Edwards." Her facial expression slowly changed from a smile to unreadable as the voice on the other end spoke. He couldn't resist running closer and sitting next to her on the bed.

"What did they say?"

"It's a recording."

"Put it on speaker."

"And most of all we here at United States Government, thank you, Thomas Edwards, for your service in the Navy Military branch.

We salute you and may God be with you, a special message from your first woman President. Elected year 2032, Mrs. Silvia Clines. Thank you." The phone call ended on its own.

A cold, salted taste of water filled his lungs as he collapsed through the bedroom floor, sinking deeper into stinging-cold water. He gawked at underwater highways and bridges as he sank. Cars, tall buildings, and neighborhoods once called home. He sank deeper, whooshing faster through the water from something tugging at his ankle. He shot his sight down to the yellow-eyed snake dragging him by the claw. Thomas screamed with water-filled shouts, squirming and swinging his arms for the surface. When the creature finally released him, swimming away in the black, he floated alone in the emptiness. The water was dark, skin throbbing cold. It spanned for what seemed infinite; like an astronaut floating in outer space. He gaped. Then swallowed a mouth full of salted water as a 200-foot monster whisked towards him with an opened mouth, belting a terrifying screech.

It was the third bucket of water that snapped open Thomas's eyes from where he lay on the floor in the captain's chamber. Startled, he sat up straight. He reached for his gun as he scanned the room. His family was gone. Above him was something that only looked human, but with glowing skin, dressed in a dirty, green wool with blue eyes peering downward. Thomas jumped to his feet.

"Where the hell is my family?" he shouted, wiping the water from his face.

The blue-like being tilted his head in question.

"Kanya statda Tyeyu"

"What did you say?" Thomas said.

"Tye yu Tye yu!"

"I don't understand what you are saying."

"Naomi!" Thomas screamed.

"Thomas! We're out here!" Thomas burst out of the captain's chamber and onto the upper deck 1. Stunned to a stop by the three islanders standing out on the beach, holding his family hostage at weapon point with large, metallic guns glowing from the crystals inside.

"Tye yu Tye yu!" the being said from behind, shoving Thomas with the others.

"Ok, ok, I'm going." He gave each of them a hug, wrapping his arms around Naomi.

"I've failed—"

"Shh. Don't you dare say that."

The glowing beings marched them across the sand and into the humming jungle.

Thomas pleaded the trees were swarming with monsters, but they only met his pleas with shouts of the unknown language and a shove from a warm gun. As they marched through the humid terrain, the crystals glowing inside the trees caused boils to appear on their skin and sweat to drip profusely. Thomas peered at the sluggishness in Naomi, who was holding Jack's hand.

"Are you ok?" he whispered.

Naomi gave an aching moan and grimaced. "I'm tired, I guess, it's really warm. I can barely breathe," she said, still clinging to Jack, who hadn't spoken a word. Her dry lips puckered against Thomas's cheek as she patted his scars. "You're always so brave, and I'm with you to the end." She smiled.

"Tye yu! Beba! Keponya!" the being shouted, forcing them apart.

They continued pushing through vines to the shouts of screaming monkeys and clacking artifacts above their heads. Drenched in sweat,

Thomas gazed upward at the hidden wall that rose for miles in the air, with trees that towered over its edge.

"You got to be kidding me," Naomi said.

"They have a wall. A wall?" Jacob whispered. Thomas studied the massive square-shaped stones that formed the barrier. There were deep marks and scratches that trailed to the top. While the islanders were busy in a discussion, Thomas leaned into Naomi's ear.

"I still have my gun," he whispered.

"No, you're just going to upset them; let's see where they take us," she hissed.

"And what if they kill us and eat us?"

"I don't think they will."

"We can't be sure. Son, do you still have that flare?"

"Yeah, I do."

"Let me see it," Thomas whispered. Jack cautiously slid Thomas the flare behind his back. "Ok, everybody, when I say run, we run."

"What about me?" Jack whimpered.

"Don't worry, Jack, I'll carry you." With a stern eye on the islanders, Thomas waited for the right moment to strike.

"Opaya! Gaen! T!" one of them shouted. A loud rumble came from the wall, and the massive cement blocks separated like sliding doors. It revealed the grass meadows, caves, and overlapping hills on the other side. Thomas stared out at the scenery; it was beautiful, like a painting.

"Tye! Yu! Tye Yu!" they shouted. Thomas wiped the puddle of sweat from his forehead and turned to the humming tree next to him. The crystals inside beamed like an oven light. He pointed the flare gun and fired the last of the two shots available. The oak exploded into roaring blue and green flames that forced all standing near it to the turf. With his ears ringing and half his face feeling as if he kissed the sun, he scrambled to his feet with the help of Jacob and Naomi. Thomas grabbed Jack by the hand as they ran through the opened gate, leaving behind the shouts of beings who were more worried about saving the crystals inside the tree. The four sprinted through tall grass and farmed fields before busting out of high meadows that revealed a length of overlapping hills and caves in the backdrop.

"Did we lose them? I can't believe that worked," Naomi said in exhaustion.

"They cared more about those crystals than us. They'll be searching; let's see if we can find somewhere safe to hide before nightfall."

An animal appeared from behind a grass-covered hill. It looked like a doe but had wild, glowing eyes and fur, like the chimps. It started drinking from a water hole a few ticks down the path. It stopped and stared up at them, took a few more sips, then galloped away into the valley.

They ran for the water, Thomas helping Jack, then drinking in gulps at a time himself. It was fresh. He covered the sun's evening glare with the palm of his hand. "Those caves, how about we make it there and we can camp for the night? We won't be too far from the fresh water, and maybe we can even find something to eat. In the morning we'll come up with a plan."

"Whatever that animal was, it looked pretty good enough to eat, if you ask me," Jacob said. A blaring alarm belted over the island.

"Let's get going," Thomas said, and they hurried for the caves in the distance.

CHAPTER TWENTY

ONCE SCHOOL HAD ENDED, MOST students took their chance to vanish, although a few remembered to slow their end-of-school momentum and say their goodbyes with a hug or a share of a quick memory. I strolled the hallway, admiring every detail of the school. I had grown fond of this place, learned a lot about life in these halls over the years; I was definitely going to miss them.

I exited the cafeteria after a sad goodbye with the lunch ladies, whose hugs smelled of fresh bread and beef. They even let me pick at the leftovers from lunch. I stopped by a panting Mr. Easterling, sweating a lot for just a sprint down the hall. He wanted to have a brief chat and let me know his thoughts on the meaning of the Gatherings, bawling up his fist and swearing a time or two as he spoke. I appreciated the straightforward sentiment and even the awkward, sweaty hug that followed.

Afterward, I could hear the rumbling motor of the old, red truck before even reaching the doors of the school. *Such a hideous sound,*

I thought, nearing the vehicle. Then laughed at the sight of Ashton, running at full speed and sliding to a stop at my mother's window just as I reached the truck.

"Hey, Mrs. Patterson," he said, still attempting to catch his breath.

"Hello, Ashton, how are you?" Mother said, narrow-eyed behind the space in the driver's window.

"I'm doing alright. I was wondering if it would be okay if I walked Rachel home this evening," he said, glancing over at me as I prepared to open the door.

Mother's gaze turned to me, then flicked back to Ashton. "Sure, I guess that would be fine…Rachel?" Mother said, looking with the unapproving nod. "Both of you, keep curfew in mind, and please don't get in any trouble."

"Yes, ma'am."

I shut the door and the sounds of its pipes putted and roared down the street.

"She should look into getting that machine fixed," Ashton said.

I laughed a little at the joke. "You're late. Now, let's walk."

Just as we were exiting school grounds, Ashton suddenly stopped and gazed out at the public buses a few feet away. Many were taking students back into the city, while other kids, like myself, were walking home towards the neighborhoods. "I've got a better idea. How 'bout we go hang out? Just for a bit. Don't worry, I'll have you back way before curfew."

For all that I wanted to go with him, I didn't want to cause any trouble in the city and risk making things tougher on my mother.

"Well…" I hesitated, looking over to the long line of students and traveling islanders.

"Please!" Ashton begged. I sighed, giving into his pleading.

"But you better behave." My words hung on the tip of my pointed finger.

"Ah, say no more, my lady." He bowed. "Follow me," he said with a new skip in his step as we headed for the bus stop outside the school.

Ashton and I stood cramped on the bus as it jolted down the dirt roads of Quadrant Three. He was disappearing behind the bodies of two much larger islanders, sweating and burping amongst other things. I laughed at his disgruntled face.

The bus came to a screeching halt, its doors on both sides sliding open with a loud ding. "City limits!" the driver yelled, and all the passengers made a dive for the exits, including me and Ashton.

"So, where to?" I asked, intrigued despite earlier hesitation, cooped up in the house every day after school. It was time I get some fresh air.

The streets were bustling and hectic; Gathering times always seemed to make the Quadrants busier than usual. This was the city market, an extensive display of storefronts where islanders bargained away some of their most prized possessions. Food to entertainment could be purchased, amongst other things, if you were willing to risk being out past curfew. They called that the red hour, only for adults. Some shops and store fronts were more familiar, while other mobile stores were travelers passing through.

"I say we wing it," Ashton suggested as we strolled down the crowded market's main pathway. "Energy crystals! Get your blue crystals here!" a creepy sales attendant yelled as we passed by. He was standing before a small wagon that he was using for display. He wore a battered purple robe that seemed inappropriate and a bit revealing. His hair was dirty, and his face, well…unpleasant.

"Darling, blue crystals here. Only cost you ten coins a pound, but I'd be willing to bargain, if you have something of value," he said, stopping me as we passed.

"I'm fine, thank you," I said politely, but the purple-robed man insisted.

"Ah, come now," he wheedled. "I'll even go as low as five for a beautiful young lady like yourself." He grasped me by the hand with his clammy palms.

"She said she's fine!" Ashton interrupted.

Not missing a beat, he turned to him, grinning to show his rotten teeth. "Okay, sir, how about *you* then?" He snatched up a bowl of the blue energy crystals from the shelf behind him, shaking them inside like a bowl of marbles.

Ashton sighed and examined them, grabbing a handful. "These don't even look real."

"Of course, they're real!" he said, stepping closer to Ashton and pulling out a small magnifying glass from his pocket. "Here, inspect."

"No, I think we're both okay." Ashton took a deliberate step back, bringing me with him.

"Puh!" the sales attendant said, scowling, snatching the bowl from Ashton's grip and turning away. "Crystals! Get your crystals! Only twenty coins a pound!"

"Was it something I said?" Ashton asked, looking at me.

We continued our saunter down the busy market way.

"Jewelry and dresses! I have jewelry, dresses, and trinkets!" a lady called from her store. "Sir! Young man! You must be interested?" she said to Ashton, who returned a frown. She clicked her tongue.

"Come see, come see what I have, and hello there." She waved; every finger covered in rings. She wore a beautiful ray of a colored scarf that wrapped around her hair. I had approached from the beckoning, but a dangling stone that hung from the display had caught my eye.

"Hello. You have some beautiful things," I said, admiring the hanging trinkets.

"Thank you, young lady. Can I interest you in something? I have some beautiful dresses, just in from the Capital."

"No, thank you, but how much for this one? It's beautiful." I gestured to the shining green stone. "I've never seen a crystal like this."

"That there is an original sandstone. Plucked from the sand outside the walls, they're supposed to bring a wonderful fortune. Only a few remain… but it seems I have a nice collection of them. Ten coins and it's yours."

When my hand went into my pocket, I realized I hadn't prepared to visit the city and had no money with me at all.

She read my expression and turned to Ashton instead. "No worries, no worries. How much do you have, sir?"

Ashton pulled some coins from his own pocket, counting them on his palm. "Ten is all I have, Rach."

"Tell you what I'll do," she said, stepping out from behind her counter. "If you can tell me one secret, and if it's an excellent one, I'll let you have this for free." She stared at Ashton as she spoke.

"Me?" he asked, caught off-guard by the offer, as was I.

"Yes, you. One secret," she repeated.

Ashton thought for a moment, then leaned closer and whispered in her ear. I couldn't hear any of the words, but to my surprise, she turned to me with a smile and handed me the stone.

"I'm an islander of my word," she stated, grabbing the green, hanging stone and handing it to me. I looked at Ashton in astonishment as she bade us farewell and continued her calls.

"What did you say to her?"

"Can't tell you. It's a secret." He winked.

As we walked, we reached a busy intersection where a sizable crowd was gathering. We looked up at the enormous, bright-yellow tent unfolding on the corner. Four islanders hammered away while another held a sign labeled *Theatrics Show starting soon*.

Before I could express interest, one holding a loudspeaker stepped before us.

"*The Tale of the Great Magician*, starring Timothy Bartholomeus, will begin shortly. Get your tickets here! Only one coin per person. Only 50 seats available," he announced, his voice carrying across the crowded market.

Ashton and I looked at one another, nodding in agreement. He paid the one-coin entry fee for each of us, and we made our way through the quickly growing crowd. The tent reeked of animal dung as we found two open seats and prepared for a show. Fully crowded, a light beamed down, eliminating the tent's darkness, and the show began. In classic Quadrant Three theatrics, they accidentally set a crew member to fire within the first five minutes. The host of the show, who never broke character, extinguished him.

Once the entertainment had finally ended, a drama filled story about a magician on a quest to prove magic was real. The sun was fading away as we exited the large, yellow tent, bursting into laughter.

"No, but a true magician knows no magic!" I quoted, waving my hands in the air, mimicking the actor's moves, and clutching my stomach.

"Oh my God, that part was the worst." Ashton groaned. "Is it wrong that I want my coin back?" he added, still grinning.

"I bet you do. I'm so sorry, I'll pay you back," I said, about to suggest we head for the bus that had arrived at the end of the street. An old islander woman, hunched over, clutching her cane, stared at me from amongst the crowd. She was unmoving, unbothered by the hundreds that filled the marketplace. I tried to look away with a slight laugh at another joke from Ashton. But my eyes still found hers, watching me and me alone.

She pointed.

"Hey, aren't you the girl with the 18?" a small boy asked, tugging on my sweatshirt from behind.

"Hey, kid, give her a break," Ashton said, trying to nudge the little boy away.

"You *are* her, right? It's you! You're all everyone talks about." His voice had risen to a shout.

"It's her! The girl with the 18!" he shouted again and again.

I didn't pay the boy much mind; I still focused my eyes on the elderly woman in the crowd, neither of us turning away.

"Rach, you okay?" Ashton asked, concerned, as a mob slowly formed around us.

"The kid's right. It is her!" someone shouted from the growing ruckus.

"Let's go," Ashton said, grabbing me by the arm, forcing our way through the throng of islanders.

"I'm sorry, I have no comment," I whispered while they followed behind, shouting their support. The soldiers I noticed nearby were readying their weapons in caution.

"Thank you, but please, I'm just trying to get home," I said several times as we continued to fight our way through.

When we approached the arriving bus, a pair of old, wrinkled hands grabbed me by the arm. I jumped at the touch.

"The Fiends desire you, child…" she whispered in a chilling, slow, and grave tone. Time seemed to freeze. The surrounding chaos faded, then went black.

"Your death is imminent, child. But there's still so much for you to learn. A life for a life." Her last words grew legs and crawled down my back. She released her grasp, and Ashton tugged me onto the bus with the sliding doors dinging to a close.

The bus ride back was silent, mostly. We were the only passengers other than a married couple who had spent half the journey discussing their plans for supper, and a lone islander who sat asleep in the back. The bus came to a halt at the stop nearest my neighborhood.

"Last trip," the driver said as the doors slid open. Ashton and I both rose from our seats, thanking him as we exited. The wind swirled and gusted as we walked down the dimly lit road, guided by the lone streetlight that was beaming over the neighborhood. We turned down Sector road.

"I miss living out here," Ashton said. They were the first words either of us had spoken to each other since getting on the bus.

"Yeah, I miss you living out here, too. It's been too quiet."

"I bet. All those families they forced to move away. You were one of the lucky ones."

"Yeah… lucky," I said, holding my wrist in the air.

"You know what I mean. Living in the Drums, it sucks. The guards, you get no privacy, no sleep… and the food! Don't get me started on the food."

"My mom tells me stories about it all the time."

162

Ashton swung his head. "Trust me, it's even worse when you live there."

"I have an idea!" I said, trying to brighten the mood. "Maybe you and the crew can move in with my mom after I'm gone. Keep an eye on her for me, keep her company."

His eyes softened at the gesture, then a smile crept onto his face. "I'd love to, Rach, but after all this is over, I'm getting out of Quadrant Three for good."

"Where would you go?"

"Anywhere but here. Who knows, might even try to leave Anastasia altogether somehow. If something's coming here, that means there's another world somewhere, I guess?"

It wasn't the first time he'd talked about escaping Anastasia. Everyone had thought about it, but no one had ever gotten past the walls. I feared there would be nothing I could say to convince him otherwise this time.

When we reached my home, the intense smell of boiling food hit my nostrils as I slammed the door shut.

My stomach gave a roar.

"Mom, I'm home!" I called as he dumped his bags by the door and walked into the kitchen.

"Rachel! And I see you've still got Ashton with you," Mother said, stirring a steaming iron pot on the stove.

"I was wondering if he could stay for dinner?"

"If that's ok with you, Mrs. Patterson."

"I don't see why not," Mother said, grabbing two bowls from the cabinets and pouring us a large spoon full of fish stew. "I was just finishing up."

The flickering streetlight shone down on the neighborhood while the delicious brew warmed my belly. The sight of a few neighbors rushing home before curfew was a bit of entertainment as I slurped down the last of the bowl.

"What do you think she meant? A life for a life?" Ashton asked.

"I'm not sure, but it might have something to do with the girl I've been seeing."

"What about the Fiends? She mentioned them by name; how would she know them?"

"Maybe it's both?"

The springs on the front door squeaked as the light spilled over the yard. "It's getting late, Ashton," Mother said, stepping out onto the front porch. On cue, an old military truck puttered passed our home.

"You're not thinking about sending him home this time of night," I said.

Mom glared a mother's glare. "Why do I feel I've been set up?" She sighed. "But I suppose you're right. I'll go look in the closet for some extra blankets. You sleep in the living room, Ashton." She disappeared back into the house as Ashton swung to face me from his seat on the steps.

"I don't have to stay the night, Rachel, I'll be fine."

"Shh, I wasn't ready for you to go yet. Besides, it *is* late," I whispered back.

A flash of lightning and loud thunder rumbled.

"Looks like the rain's coming back," Mother said as she made her way back to the porch, armed with blankets and a pillow. "Too late for you to be heading home now. I'll stop by in the morning and explain this to your mother. I'm sure it will worry her sick."

"Thanks, Mrs. Patterson. And she'll be fine. She understands it's a lot going on right now."

Mother finally caught my eye and head gestures, raised an eyebrow, then gave an exaggerated yawn. "Guess I will head to my room and get some rest, a long day at work today. You two be good, okay?" she said, then walked down the creaking floors of the old cabin halls.

Back inside, I plopped down on the sofa. Ashton grabbed his bag he'd left by the door and began fumbling through his compartments. "I want to show you something, Rach." He pulled out the dusty red book.

"Not this thing again." I sighed, exhausted by it all.

"Just hear me out, okay? I know you don't believe me, but it's worse than we thought."

"I can't believe you still have that thing. Ms. Anna will kill you! You can't just steal people's things—"

"Something else lives here, Rachel," he interrupted.

"What do you mean?"

"Anastasia. Something was here before us, I'm sure of it now."

"Something like what?"

"Those Fiends… like that lady said. And the ones you saw earlier today. But since the death of King Pius III, I also think they've been controlling us too. Do you ever wonder what actually started the war with King Pius?"

"It was over how he was wasting the island's crystals… right?"

"They did not build the wall to keep us in, Rach, they built it to keep those Fiends out."

I couldn't find the words to protest his argument, but it was when he pointed at a drawing in the book that I felt my hairs stand up straight.

"Here… look, the last known drawing of King Pius III and his family."

Outside, the wind howled, and the storm worsened, causing the lights to flicker then go dark.

"What happened?" Ashton asked, looking around the room.

"It's just the stupid generator, it's always going out when it storms. Hey, maybe we should have bought those crystals from that guy, huh?" I said, laughing a little. "Hold on, I'll run to my room and grab some candles. I keep a few in my desk drawer."

I fumbled my way in the darkness through the cabin, surprised Mother hadn't burst through the door in a pajama-wearing frantic. I figured she was already asleep and dead tired from work. Retrieving some candles from my drawer, I peered upwards to the corner where I first saw the girl. *You 're being paranoid, Rachel.*

Returning to Ashton, I made a flat surface for the nightlight using a plate from the kitchen and sat it between us. "There. See? Much better," I said, while the fluttering fire illuminated the living room. "Okay, you were saying?"

Ashton was intensely focused, only breaking to flip through pages of the red book. "It seems they killed king Pius III because he wouldn't join them—"

"Wait, stop right there!" I said at the turn of the page. I recognized a drawing in the book. "That's her!" I gasped, running to the table where I placed my diary. I returned, searching for the sketches I had drawn earlier that day. Holding it in comparison, closer to the flickering candle, the books fell from my trembling hands.

"That's her? Are you sure?" Ashton asked.

"Who does that book say she is?" I whispered with my hands covering my mouth.

Ashton grabbed the book from the floor and began flipping through the pages, returning to the drawing of the mysterious girl and her family. "It says here..." he said, squinting, "her name is... Elizabeth Pius. The youngest daughter of King Pius III."

"It says that?" I grabbed the book and read aloud, "...*eman sih erahs ohw esoht dna Suip Gnik fo sgniward nwonk tsal.*" I shook, remembering to read the words backwards and flipped the book.

Last known drawings of King Pius and those who share his name.

"And see, look here at the bottom, it has their names and deaths," Ashton said.

I flipped through the book. "*Elizabeth age twelve.*"

In my mind, I could hear the mob bursting through Elizabeth's home, chasing her through the palace. The vision coming to me like a repressed memory. How terrifying it must have been.

"Does it say anything else?" Ashton asked.

I continued to read backwards.

"The king had five children, all of them now deceased." I slammed the book shut and examined the dusty, beaten, red cover.

"Harold Wellington, who is that?" I asked, referring to the name signed at the bottom of the book, an author's signature.

"I'm not sure, I've never heard of him," Ashton said.

"You've got to return this, Ashton, you could get in big trouble if someone found you with this, I think."

He only sighed.

"What if she finds out you took it?"

"I'm not going back to that school, Rachel."

I collapsed my head into my palm, a look I'd seen on my mother at least a hundred times. I was puzzled by it all, but none of this would stop my Gathering. If the little girl was the daughter of King Pius III, why was she haunting me?

The rain poured heavily outside; I could hear the tree tapping in my room. My eyes bounced around as the dark presence had returned, I could feel it. She was here.

"So, what next?" I asked, turning my focus to the book. "What happened after that?"

"There is no next. That's all it says," Ashton replied.

"After the pictures of King Pius III, it goes blank?"

"I guess so… See? Just empty pages." he said, flipping through the white, empty sheets that followed the final drawing.

He leaned toward me, talking. I could still see his lips moving but it was as if someone had turned off his voice. I screamed at the small snake that slithered across the floor towards me. Then dozens of them, sliding through the cracks of the cabin walls. One drew closer as it slithered over my leg, I booted it aside in a fright as more poured into our home. The swarm overtook Ashton's body completely, while more pushed through the ceiling and flopped down on my head.

Appearing from the shadows was Elizabeth in her white gown, hovering above me, while the snakes acted as shackles, pinning me to the floor.

"Come!" Elizabeth demanded in an otherworldly scream. A forceful wind blasted open our front door with a loud bang.

I cried, straining to free myself. A Fiend stood on the brink of my living room. Its skin was reptilian, standing tall on its hind legs, evil, yellow eyes glaring at me as it rocked. In a blink, another joined it, then another, one by one, until dozens filled my living room. Each of them hissing and clicking from their tongues.

I gasped for desperate breaths as the snakes, acting as chains, slid up my arm and poured into my opened mouth.

"Rachel!" Ashton broke through my shouts of terror, his hands on my cheeks, snapping me out of the trance. "Are you ok? You just started screaming!"

I pored over the room. No snakes or Fiends in sight. Elizabeth neither.

"I'm not. I'm not ok," I whispered.

Ashton comforted me with a soft embrace, trying to calm my pounding heartbeat.

"All I asked was if something related you to the royal family. Then you started screaming."

Mother came running into the living room, dressed in her robe pajamas.

"Is everything alright in here?" she asked frantically. She rushed towards me and squeezed the little air I had left.

"Rachel?" she whimpered.

"Everything is fine, Mom, go back to sleep." I turned to face Ashton, who was wide-eyed and as worried for me as Mother.

"That was enough excitement for me, today. It's late." My hands couldn't stop trembling as I reached out to hug him.

"I'm sorry, I didn't mean to…"

"No, it's fine, I need a second," I said, standing on noodled legs.

"I understand."

"Night, Rach."

"Goodnight, Ashton." He leaned over and kissed me on the lips, our first kiss. Not exactly how I would have planned it. I smiled softly, wiping away a fallen tear, and headed down the dark hall for bed.

CHAPTER TWENTY-ONE

WITH THE MOON SETTING IN over Quadrant One, the coach wagon slowed at a four-way stop. A sign read, *Brossel RD Keep Straight. Section B*, with a black painted arrow pointing to the left, the remainder of its white letterings scraped away. Bubba and Coin huffed as Malcamore glared out at the abandoned storefronts and graveled streets. The path was dimly lit from the crystals that hung off the side of shingled rooftops. Most of this part of the city was ravaged and gutted. Quadrant One—home sweet home. It was not as populated as the other Quadrants on the island. Its conditions were unsuitable for living, the decree of most islanders who found it much simpler to live off their own means near the outskirts, rather than in town by the poorly funded markets.

"This will do, William. We'll be back in a blink!" Malcamore called out to the driver. A flame sizzled at the tip of a hand-rolled cigarette as he exhaled a thin line of smoke and exited the coach.

Malcamore and Samson strolled down the section of B boulevard, to the lone sounds of Samson's cane striking the cold, hard ground.

Bakers rd. Malcamore stared up at the signpost in study before the sound of shattering glass came from a storefront.

Two children appeared, little islander boys roughly around the age of 10, sprinted out of an abandoned building. The punier of the two wore a mask of a monster with yellow eyes and sagging skin. The much larger and rounder boy's cheeks poked out like a rodent hiding a cluster of acorns in his mouth. He blew out long strains of spit with his arms stretched out like wings.

"Eat the monster. Eat the monster!" the frail boy screamed. The other laughed as he chased him back. Both kids were unapologetic about crashing into Malcamore and Samson, making them a part of their game and using them as shields before scurrying down the dark streets.

"Damn brutlums, and I wonder where their parents are, letting them run rampant through the streets at this hour, it's way past curfew.

"If they even have parents," Malcamore said.

"Entire island's gone mad, I swear. Where are we even headed, young sir? We never come to the city."

"To the house of a friend, like I told you. I knew her back when I was in the war. She's a little...different, Samson, so don't judge her."

"Judge? I wouldn't even think of it. You should know me better than that." Then the sounds of Samson's tapping cane stopped. "But different how, might I ask?"

"You'll see for yourself soon enough, we're almost there. It's just a little more way. I think we go down this street and take a left, or is it right? No, it's left, I'm sure of it. And at the end of that street is—"

"Can I help you fellas?"

A screeching voice, spewing from an old blind man rocking in his chair at a storefront. The small writing in black paint above the

172

door said *Custom Shoes*. But spotting from the window inside were nothing but broken-down shelves and spiderwebs that cluttered the wall. The islander slowly stood, his brown robe heavying over his trembling legs. He limped towards them, frail with a blank and white stare, as if God had forgotten to give him pupils.

"You don't mind, do you? It's how I see," he said, stretching out his wrinkled hands to the face of Malcamore. He rubbed across his eyes, then his ears, nose, and chin. Malcamore thought the wrinkled fingers were more like bones than fleshed-out hands. He walked over to Samson afterward and did the same.

"Father and son, I'm guessing," he prattled.

"You could say that," Malcamore said.

"What street you looking for?" the blind man asked, sliding back down into his seat in the creaking rocking chair. He pointed to his wrinkled bald head with his finger. "I got it all up here."

"Flog… or is it Fueg…?"

"Fladance, you mean. Yeah, you're on the right path. It's down that street, like you were saying. Fladance's a dead-end street though, not much to see down there." He laughed a little, then winced as if it was painful. "Only way out is back the way you came."

"Yeah, that's the one. Thank you, kind sir. Told you, Samson. We're almost there."

"What you want to go down that street for?" the blind man asked. "Just a bunch of witch doctors down that way. You ain't sick, are ya?"

"No sir, not sick. Just searching for an old friend."

"An old witch friend, ya mean," he said, rocking solemnly in his chair.

Malcamore ignored that last bit as he and Samson continued down the path. They were a few steps away when the old man began whistling a song to himself. It was the same melody he had heard Elizabeth humming in the woods.

Malcamore spun back around to the storefront.

The blind man rose to his feet. His movements much quicker this time as he stared behind white pupils, then hurried into the building, slamming the door shut. Malcamore stopped as the sounds of Samson's cane tapped from behind.

"It's fine, Samson. Like I said, it's just this way," Malcamore said, crushing his smoke to the ground.

There, at the dead end of Fladance Street, stood a small wooden cottage with black smoke pouring out from its rooftop, with a hazy orange glow coming from inside.

Malcamore brushed down the perceived dirt on his jacket and hair. "This is it."

"Right you are, young sir. Now, just give it a knock because it's cold. And I would be lying if I didn't say the blind man back there didn't scare the shit out of me."

Malcamore tried peeking through the cabin's window, then looked back at the way they'd come. For the first time, the idea to visit his friend seemed ludicrous. He hadn't spoken to this person in years. Then he was going to show up unannounced and ask for such a favor? After what happened before?

"What are you waiting for? We've been standing out here for at least three minutes now. Are we going in or not?"

"I'm not stalling, Samson, if that's what you're thinking. I'm collecting my thoughts. What if she's not even here? She could have moved or maybe went to the markets buying food before the curfew." His words were lower than a murmur.

Samson looked at the desolate city surrounding them.

"The market? I doubt it."

"Ah, what do you know, Samson?"

"I know you're nervous."

Malcamore laughed too loud at this suggestion as the old, wooden door swung open with a screech, revealing a beautiful islander standing on the threshold. Her dreadlocks were thick and hung down to the small of her back, and her big, brown eyes glistened as she smiled. Her black gown, made of soft fabric, dropped loosely to her ankle.

"Cause a real woman always makes ya nervous."

Malcamore cleared his throat as Samson smiled from ear to ear. "Cassandra! I've missed you," Malcamore said.

"Sure, ya did," Cassandra said, opening the door and inviting them in. "Come in before someone else sees ya. And bring ya friend Samson, too."

"How does she know my name?" Samson asked in a whisper as they entered the home.

"Close my door please, Samson."

The old wooden door slowly thudded shut.

"And take off your shoes. I don't like dirt on my floor. It's bad luck, Benjamin, you know that," she chided, poking at the fireplace in the corner with an iron stick. They both removed their shoes and placed them at the entrance. The smell and heat from the crackling wood filled the home, giving it a warm and cozy sense. It was obvious Samson appreciated this the most, shouting that his old bones couldn't bear the cold much longer as he approached the fire next to Cassandra.

Red and brown beads that hung from the ceiling rattled against one another, catching Malcamore's attention as he was placing down his shoes. A little strange, he thought, but not as strange as the life-sized doll sitting in a chair at the kitchen table. It didn't move, or anything paranormal like that. Thank God Malcamore gathered. But it did, however, look too real. Too alive for his liking. It had frizzy, purple hair with a matching color blouse, and tiny, matching color shoes.

"Lovely home you have here, madam, and thank you mostly for having it so warm in here. I try to tell Malcamore I'm not as young as I used to be," Samson said, with his hands hovering over the flames.

"Ah, thank you, Samson. I do my best. And Benjamin can be a bit bullheaded. Trust me, I know," Casandra said, Malcamore grunted.

"Would you like me to put on some hot tea for you guys?"

Samson gazed at her in mystery. "It's like you're reading my mind."

Cassandra led the them into the kitchen and poured water into a copper-colored pot, then tossed a struck match into a pile of logs surrounded by stone rocks. Hanging the pot over the roaring flames, she turned to face them, laughing at how wide-eyed he was at the doll sitting up straight at the table.

"Oh, don't mind her. That's Penelope. She just likes to be seen. So, Benjamin, how was the award ceremony?" she asked, pouring a substance that he only hoped to be tea into the steaming pot.

"You heard about that?" Malcamore said.

"I heard?" Cassandra clicked her tongue like the words insulted her. "Of course, I heard. I'm not living under a rock. They wrote a story about you in the papers, don't ya know? The great Benjamin Malcamore, the king's killer. I didn't know whether to laugh or cry when I read the damn thing. A little birdie told me about the ceremony, though."

"Yeah, well, it was all politics, nothing more," Malcamore huffed.

"You never were a fan of the game, were you, Benjamin? So strange they'd honor you so long after the war, and on this year no less." The copper teapot let out a soft whistle as she placed two silver mugs on the table in front of Penelope. She grabbed a green mitten from the counter and poured the steaming brew into the cups. "It's hot, gentlemen. Might want to give it a second to cool."

Malcamore nodded and forced a smile. He still hadn't taken his eyes off the doll. Her black marbles watched him from where she sat at the other end of the table.

"I said the same, but I have my ideas why," Malcamore said.

"Oh, I bet you do. Here ya go, sweetheart. Be careful, it's still a little hot," she said, handing Samson his cup first, then walking around the table and giving Malcamore one. They thanked her as she stared at them both, unblinking until they had taken their first sip. Striking a match, she lit a smoke that appeared from out of her dreadlocks and focused her eyes on Malcamore behind the haze as he slurped down large sips of warm tea.

"I know you're here about the girl. Am I right?"

Samson nearly choked, coughing into his fist with apologies.

"You okay there, Samson?"

"I'm fine, sorry... it's boiling," he said, looking over at Malcamore.

Cassandra walked to the table and took a seat next to Penelope, inhaling long drags of her smoke as she studied the two. "I told ya this would happen, didn't I? I can't help you, Benjamin. There's nothing you can do this time."

"I saw the king's daughter in the woods; she whispered something to me... A life for a life, Cassandra," Malcamore said.

Cassandra smiled mischievously, as if he had spoken magic words. "A life for a life you say?"

"Does *he* know?" Pointing her black-painted fingernail to Samson, she clicked her tongue again as Malcamore shook his head.

"Shame on you, Benjamin."

"Do I know what, young sir?"

"Hush, Samson," Malcamore hissed.

"Take a seat, both of you, and bring your cups." She stood from her chair and grabbed the copper pot, refilling their mugs as they sat at the table. Setting the pot back over the dying fire, she flopped back in her seat.

"Hm, what to do, what to do?" she said solemnly, smashing her smoke out on the wood surface. Her face lit up with sudden excitement.

"I got it! We'll just ask her for ourselves what to do."

"Who?" Malcamore asked, his voice shaking. The words were harder than usual to push out.

"You know who I speak of, Benjamin. You said you've seen her. Strange times we live in today. Has that tea kicked in yet, fellas?"

They didn't respond.

"You can see and hear me perfectly fine. You'll just remain nice and still for me. Do you understand?"

He tried to let out a word, but it was as if his brain forgot how to function. Cassandra was right, he could still see and hear perfectly fine. He strained to look at Samson, who was only staring at Penelope.

"Good, looks like we're ready to begin then. Penelope, dear, will you get my ball for me out of the other room?"

At the words, the doll's hands pushed against the table with a loud grind, her doll feet and purple doll shoes collapsed to the floor. Cassandra watched casually as Malcamore and Samson whimpered.

"Hush your mouths. Do you want my help or not?" Loud crashes and a door slamming shut came from the other room, then the small tapping feet returned to the kitchen. Penelope reappeared, holding a small, crystalized ball that sat perfectly on top of a beautiful wood-carved stand. She stretched out her plastic arms and placed the ball at the center of the table, and returned to her seat.

"I thought I said no shoes on my floor," Cassandra said.

"Sorry, Momma," Penelope said.

Malcamore thought Samson had fainted, or he had fainted and just woken up rather quickly as his head slumped to his chin, then jerked back into its upright position.

"No need for fear, Samson," Cassandra said with a screeching laugh.

The crystal ball filled with clouds of smoke and the flames that warmed the home extinguished throughout the cabin, leaving them sitting in darkness. Cassandra began rubbing the smoke-filled ball, chanting in a language only she and Penelope seemed to understand.

"Peysha Cape Yaposha," she said as the smoke thickened. She repeated the words, and Penelope joined the chant.

"Yes, there is something among us, not of our world, something... evil," Cassandra said while Penelope still chanted.

"There's evil present, and it wants something. It wants, it wants." Cassandra's eyes rolled to the back of her head and her neck jerked back and forth. "Rachel Patterson." She hissed, her eyes now red-veined and yellow. At the mention of the name, a stench of death filled the room. Suddenly, Elizabeth appeared and was now standing on top of the wooden table where they gathered, her menacing stare on Benjamin Malcamore.

"Penelope, now!" Cassandra shouted. Penelope gave a roaring inhale that caused the legs of the table to shake. With a piercing scream, Elizabeth's spirit shot into the body of Penelope. The doll swallowed like a child forcing down her vegetables. After a moment of silence, she belted out a loud agonizing scream, then spoke quickly, without pause.

"Benjamin Malcamore must pay for his sin by death. The gods blessed the royal family and Anastasia will fall. The End is nigh. It has been spoken." Penelope gazed across the table with her black marbled eyes. She tilted her head, then shrieked. Her small doll feet padded across the table, knocking the mugs to the floor until she stood before him.

Malcamore's intestines were doing somersaults inside his stomach. His right eye shifted to Samson, who this time had passed out with his chin collapsed to his chest. Malcamore whimpered.

"I'm sorry."

Penelope tilted her doll head, her silky purple hair dangling over her shoulder. She began coughing dramatically, like a sick child. Gagging while her small doll hands pulled at her throat. Penelope fell to her knees, crawling towards Malcamore. She lifted her head, her mouth stretching open and revealing the yellow eyes of a small snake squirming inside her. She blasted a scream so loud the walls of the once cozy cabin shook.

Then, in an instant, before Cassandra, who was still chanting in the background, could call out to stop her, before another tear rolled down the cheek of Malcamore, her doll body collapsed to the table with marble eyes staring up at him. She was now lifeless, the way a doll should be.

Cassandra pushed back and slowly stood, retrieving her like a caring mother. She disappeared out of the dark kitchen, Penelope slumped in one hand, the crystal ball in the other.

After walking the home and relighting the flames to bring back the orange glow, she sat back at the table.

"How ya feeling? You got your life back yet, or are ya still out of it?" she asked, snapping her fingers at their faces.

"I'm fine," Malcamore grunted. Turning to Samson, who was snoring in a deep sleep. "What'd you do to Samson?"

"He'll be ok. Those words have that effect on the weary. He should wake up any moment."

Samson jolted up in his seat, spinning his sight like he had awakened from a horrible nightmare. "Where the hell am I? What's going on?" He looked over at Malcamore, then Cassandra, and jumped out of his chair.

"You... you... what did you do to me? What was in that tea?"

Cassandra clicked her tongue with a laugh. "It was tea, sweet Samson, and you fell asleep. I'm sure your old bones could use the rest, am I right?" Samson stared at the empty seat where Penelope was sitting.

"Where's that thing? That doll thing? Penelope, you called her. Where is she?" he asked in a frightened panic, too scared to even return to his chair.

"I put her away for now, Samson. She's just a doll, no need to be afraid of a little old doll, is there? Now," she said, fixing her eyes on Malcamore, "the girl with the 18, yes?"

"Yes, Cassandra. Is there any way you can help?"

"I'm not sure. You knew they would kill her when they found her, and there's nothing you can do about that now. I'm surprised they let her live as long as they did."

"We must stop this Gathering!" he shouted in a sudden rage, banging his fist on the table.

Cassandra snapped towards him, clicking her tongue. "You kill our king, but desperately wish to spare the life of his granddaughter?

I wonder why." She narrowed her eyes, glaring at him from behind the lit match at the tip of her smoke.

"No need, I think I know," she said. "Even if it were possible, as I told you once before, saving her life will only cost you your own."

"But how, Cassandra?" Malcamore asked.

"Young sir!" Samson shouted from the corner of the room, grabbing his cane and slowly making his way for the exit.

"Hush, Samson."

"Very well." Cassandra stood and scampered to the shelves on the walls. They were lined with small crystal bottles in a range of colors; Malcamore had thought they were forms of tea and ointments, but he was wrong. Studying these, she plucked two from the collection and turned to face Malcamore, who was slowly rising to his feet. "Are you familiar with the story about the two lovers?"

"No, what is that?" he asked through his teeth, the effects of the tea still present.

"It's an old folktale our ancestors told about a couple who were madly in love. My grandmother used to read me the story when I was a little islander girl, and I won't bore you with the details, but the two came up with an idea to run away together."

"And what was the idea?"

"To fake the death of the girl with a potion, only for her to be rescued by her lover much later. It didn't work, of course. The timing was off, and they both died in each other's arms. It's quite good actually, read it sometime." She hoisted a red crystal valve in the air. "This, Benjamin, is poison. A deadly poison, that's it," she said, holding up the other. "And this one is the antidote to such poison. The only antidote I have, mind you. If you were to swallow the red one, you will die in a matter of seconds. You will have less

182

than one hour to follow it with this blue one here if you wish for that individual to live again, that is. Take them. Give the red one to the child, and you, Benjamin, keep the blue one. You'll come up with something, I'm sure."

"Thank you, Cassandra, I knew you could help me." Malcamore reached for the vials as Cassandra jerked back.

"*But...*" she paused, her eyes meeting his desperate reach, "if you do this, Benjamin, you will die..."

He thought for a second, then grabbed both bottles from Cassandra's hands.

"I would suggest you hurry or there won't be a child for you to save."

"Thank you, you've done too much for me already," he said in a hurrying manner, walking to the door and tucking his feet back into his boots. Malcamore leaned in and kissed Cassandra softly on the cheek. "I really have missed you, and you've gotten good with the whole witch thing. Quite good."

"I'm sure I'll see you again, Benjamin," she breathed.

"Oh, and, Samson?" Cassandra called as the two were opening the cabin door.

He turned back toward her. "Yes?" he said shakily.

"Your wife...she misses you too."

Samson gaped in disbelief, then smiled at Malcamore as they exited the home.

CHAPTER TWENTY-TWO

THOMAS AND HIS FAMILY CREPT inside the cavern, crossing the stoned path that descended over water and led to a dry part at the back. Naomi cuddled with the two boys against a stone wall while Thomas peered past his reflection at the water glistening blue. "It's so warm," he said, sticking in his right arm, the water up to his shoulder.

"Please be careful…You don't know what's in there," Naomi whispered, clinging tighter to Jacob and Jack.

"Is it safe to drink?" Jacob asked.

Thomas scooped a handful and brought it to his nose. It drizzled out the cracks of his fingers as he whiffed, then slowly flicked out his tongue, letting a drop graze his tastebuds. The swallow sent a shocking bolt down his body like he had licked a small battery. He began choking, brushing the water from his tongue with his hands and shirt.

"No, it's not safe to drink," he whispered back.

The evening sun fell as the confusion outside, whaling alarms and uniformed shouts, had settled; the night had grown dark and cool. The beaming crystals shining underwater, reflecting off the walls, illuminated the space in the stone cave. Thomas and his family huddled, staring at the cave's entrance. The constant crackling of tree limbs and loud huffs came from outside.

"What do you think's out there?" Naomi asked.

"Animal maybe, could as well be those snake things," Thomas said.

"I'm so hungry, I haven't eaten in two days now." Jack groaned, wrapping his arms around his bone-revealing stomach, his eyes healing but still puffy and swollen.

"What can we do about food, honey? Do you have any ideas?" Naomi said.

"I could search for something. It's dark out, so maybe I can go unnoticed, kill whatever I can. They must be some kind of fruit-bearing tree or whatever it is they eat here."

"You got your gun, don't you?" Jacob said.

"Yeah, but I'm going to have to be quiet, wouldn't want them knowing where to find us, now would we? Son, you stay with your mother and Jack. I'll go out there and see what I can find and no matter what, stay in the cave and out of that water."

Thomas slowly rose to his feet. He gave Naomi a passionate kiss goodbye and hugged Jacob and Jack. He climbed back up the carved stoned path and left the cave without another glance.

The woods were a dark labyrinth of trees in the night. It seemed the ones on this side of the wall had no glowing crystals inside them. They looked like regular woods you found at a campsite down south somewhere. Texas or maybe even Mississippi, Thomas worked out the landscape in his mind for familiarity, a slow pace through crunching limbs and roots. He had only made it 100 yards before a pair of blue, glowing eyes spotted him, then scurried away into the thicket, sounds of its paw thudding against the dirt.

After another 100 yards, the pair of blue eyes returned, ruffling through the sticks. He squinted, aiming down the barrel of his Glock. The beast, whatever it was, was about to be tonight's dinner. It gave a loud howl that echoed throughout the woodland as more of the blue-eyed beasts joined in on the cry. Thomas spun, his sight jumping from oversized wolf to oversized wolf that slowly appeared from behind thick trees, snarling, slops of drool dripping from a tooth-revealing growl.

The first to leap was as big as Thomas was when standing, white with lightning streaks of gray fur. He fired three shots into its head; it whimpered and crashed against a nearby tree.

He ran.

The pack of wolves nipped at his heels as he leaped over stumps, pushed through hanging branches that would sure to leave permanent welts on his face. A wolf lunged at his back, sending him tumbling downhill, his head just missing passing trees, as the two flipped and wrestled for position. The wolf's blue eyes, menacing growl, and jaws snapped in an unforgiving cycle before Thomas's head crashed into a pile of lumber at the bottom of the hill. The pain was excruciating and shooting down his backside. He then snapped back too by the faint sight of the massive black wolf at a full sprint towards him.

It leaped at Thomas as he shielded with his arms, its blue eyes piercing down at him as it bit for his neck. Each attempt closer than the one before, globs of his drool landing on the collar of Thomas's bloodied and torn navy sweater. He screamed; another wolf lunged its sharp teeth into his side. The one at his face was angrier, and his eyes said dinner was being served. With the last heave of defense, a sudden burst of strength you get just before death takes you, forced the beast off him. He grabbed the gun from the ground and fired, not much aim taken or needed. He screamed a warrior's shout and fired until he was empty, both wolves dead on the dirt as the others temporarily scattered. Thomas, in a total rage with bulging eyes and bleeding, screamed,

"Is that all you got!" kicking the dead wolf with his boot.

A smell filled the atmosphere.

He peered up from where he had fallen after kicking the dead wolf again. Thick, gray smoke poured from a stoned chimney above him. He hadn't noticed it before, but his head had slammed into the back wall of a cabin-style home, something straight out of the first century, with an orange glow coming from inside. Thomas peeked around the corner. A vacant grass, roughly an acre, with woods that continued after. Then into the square space cut just above his head. The room was empty, almost empty, nothing but stacks of cleaned bones, animal or not he wasn't sure, nested in a pile on the floor, a fireplace tucked in the corner, and what had to be a kitchen, the edges of a massive iron pot steaming on the stove. The pains of hunger drove his feet forward as he arrived at the front of the cabin. The lot as he saw was empty but a pair of tracks that trailed the dirt and onto a created path in the woods. He peeked through the cabin's front window, to the tune of mourning wolves filling the silence. With a push on the door, it swung open.

He slowly stepped inside, the floorboards beneath him creaking as he made his way for what he hoped to be the kitchen, it was. The walls were lined with cabinets and an eating table at the center of the room. A large iron pot bubbling over a brown substance that dripped into a fire, filling the home with an unsettling stench. Burned garbage came to mind first. Opening a wooden cabinet, he found they filled one with small, silver cans; the writing was foreign, but the picture was a good reference that it was fruit or plant based, with a glowing tree and hanging fruits drawn as a label. Thomas began stuffing them into his pockets. He had reached the fifth can before the sounds of hoofing came from outside. He tiptoed for the room with the bones, hastening when the door swung open. It was wearing animal fur that draped over his body like a caveman. Like the ones he used to see on TV. It paused, turning to the kitchen, sniffing at the air.

A slammed door came from outside.

"Gosha, be ya can," a voice said.

Thomas peered out of a crack in the walls at the blue-skinned beings entering the cabin. Three more of them, each wearing a thick wool fur that stopped at the feet. His eyes followed one as it walked for the kitchen, while the others were whispering. He wiped at the sweat, turning to the window. He would have to make a run for it. When he looked through the crack again, they had disappeared. He slowly stood, backing away from the wall, the pile of bones clacking beneath his stumble.

A terrified scream came from the hallway after the door blasted open. Standing before him...

Thomas jerked up his weapon, then turned and ran, jumping through the square cut space and heading for that created path. They were giving chase behind him, shouting as he attempted to fire his gun, but only clicked its response. Through the woods, he spotted a massive lake at the end of the terrain, blanketed with a white fog.

"Please be fresh water, please be fresh water," Thomas whispered as he jumped headfirst into the cold lake. The water pushed up his nose and stung his eyes as he swam deep below the surface, kicking and forcing his way down. Beaming down on him like a spotlight, the moon showed in the sky, bursting through the clouds and onto the ripples of water. When he felt the second splash of ripples from behind, Thomas kicked and pushed as fast as his feet had ever swum in his life, or any Navy training he ever instructed. Not stopping until his footing reached the other side of the lake, he high stepped out of the water and pushed through another patch of wild growing trees. He collapsed onto his back at the edge of another cave. This one much smaller with no magical crystals inside, it was dark and cramped, perfect for hiding. He panted, soaking wet with his pockets still filled with the silver cans.

"God, I hate this island," he whispered, sliding flat, hiding between the two massive rocks.

CHAPTER TWENTY-THREE

Ashton, Jessie, Phillip, Lola, Matthew, and I all huddled together in my living room, exchanging memories about the days when we were kids.

"It was Phillip's stupid idea in the first place," Jessie said, kicking up her feet in laughter on the couch. Everyone laughed but Ashton, who was sulking from where he sat.

"Lost in the woods for almost two days! I was so scared," I said, still trying to join in on the conversation.

Phillip stretched out his feet with a loud, unbothered yawn. "It wasn't one of my brightest ideas, I admit, but at least I didn't almost burn down the school." A patch of red grew on my cheeks as I recalled that day in 7th grade science class. Mrs. Nat hadn't been clear with her instructions on the mixture of Clombozine over Pexozine. Two highly combustible crystals when melted down and combined at the wrong temperature. The smoking glass exploded, the substance landing on the class pet Whiskers, a small rodent who I think never forgave me. And also on some papers that burst into roaring flames surprisingly quickly and spread throughout the class and parts of the school. Worst day of school ever; they rushed everyone outside and had to call in the mob to put out the fire.

Matthew, from his spot on the couch, burst into hysterical laughter. "I remember that one, the pure rage on Mr. Easterling's face as he ran down the halls… Priceless."

When Mother entered the room holding an old drawing of mine, I jumped off the sofa in excitement. It was one I did of my friends when we were much younger. Far from some of my best work, but still showed I had plenty of potential.

"I keep all of your drawings," Mother said, as each of my friends admired the picture as they passed it along.

"This reminds me of something."

I ran to my room, retrieved an object out of my desk, then returned, jamming my arms into the sleeves of my jacket.

"Where are you trying to go, honey?"

"It won't take long. Guys, you coming? I want to show you something," I said, swinging open the front door. They all agreed and one after another stood, throwing arms in sleeves.

I ran back to give Mother a kiss, leaving the shouts for us to be careful behind as I closed the door.

The air was as cool as the sun was bright while we walked across the open fields of Quadrant Three. We wouldn't be taking the bus today. I led the way with quick strides through stretches of meadow grass before turning down a lone road. At the end of the trail was a barbed wire fence, and hills that sloped in the background. My pace was quick, and I took it they were losing sight of me as I slid down another hill slope.

"Hey, Rach, slow down!" Phillip called out from the back, holding onto one tree that leaned off kilter.

So far, no snakes, though I sort of worried about running into them now. Everyone was, but no one more than Phillip, who constantly found himself at the back. After a while of walking, the path had flattened once more, and we came to an enormous oak tree planted at a fork in the fields. Misplaced, like the only tree with life in its bark. I studied it, rubbing against the warmth.

"It's this way," I said, pointing to another stretch of fields. My friends were sweating and tired.

"Hey, slow down, Rach, please!" Phillip called. Matthew was standing next to him, shouting much the same. I stopped for another break as they each arrived, panting, with their hands pressed to their knees.

"Sorry I'm not trying to go so fast. I wanted to be positive we made it before dark, that's all."

"It's fine, don't let these boys slow you down," Jessie said, panting.

Lola arrived in a fight with an invisible spider she swore had fallen on her.

"Where are we headed?" Lola asked.

"My dad and I would come down here to dig for crystals. There's a cave a couple miles down."

"A couple miles, huh?" Philip said, sweat pouring down his chubby face in exhaustion. "Guess we should keep moving," he said, smiling at me as he passed. I returned the grin and continued to lead the way.

Once we grew closer to the destination, the sounds of moving waters and sniffs of fresh grass increased.

Sliding down the last grass-covered hill, we saw a stone cave tucked at the edge of the thicket.

"Whoa," Jessie said, standing next to me and looking up to the high stonewall entrance. "I did not know this was even here."

"Few do, I think. Beautiful, isn't it?" I said, looking at the cavern's first inward steps. By now the entire crew had arrived and each gazed in wonderment. Sure, they had seen a cave before, but not one that looked so magical with its crystal water and large, marbled stones.

"My dad found this place, and he would show me how to dig for crystals. The wall's not too far from here. Sometimes, we would be down here for hours. I was around ten the first time he brought me. It was like our own little haven. 'You must learn the family business, my little bug' he would say."

Rigid stones protruding from the surface acted as steps as I carefully placed my foot on a slippery rock, then leaped from stone to stone. Until I reached dry land at the other side of the cave.

"C'mon, it's a lot easier than it looks!" I shouted back at them.

Jessie took the first trembling steps.

"The trick is to not look down!"

"Thanks, Rach!"

Beneath her were the deep depths of crystal water that had no end in sight. Matthew, Lola, Phillip, and Ashton followed her actions. All of them reached the patch of dry land without getting more than their shoes wet.

"Not bad," I said, as they looked about in silence, admiring the carved stones and the water that sparkled like a bed of diamonds.

"Why is the water warm?" Matthew asked, after dipping his hand.

I didn't know why but gave an educated guess.

"It's because of the crystals that lay in the stones beneath the water. The energy they give warms it, I think."

"That's why it looks so sparkly," he said.

"So, wait, there are *real* crystals under there?" Phillip exclaimed.

"Yeah, but you won't have any way of knowing unless you go down there digging."

"Down there?" Phillip pointed to the blue expanse that got darker the further down it went. I laughed at his dramatization. "How do you even know what's down there?" he asked, staring past his rippled reflection.

I pitched my voice, low and spooky. "You don't… Who knows what creatures lurk beneath these waters?" I said, laughing. Then glanced at Ashton, who was still quiet, staring up at the high stone-work above him.

"What are you doing?" Lola shouted as I spun back to her scream.

"You just heard her! You don't even know what's in there!" Lola cried out to Matthew, who had already stripped down to his underwear and climbed up a high stoned pier, preparing to jump.

"Do it!" Phillip urged him.

"I'm prepared to go where no islander has gone before," Matthew announced, then bolted, his feet leaping from the edge of a stone.

I smiled at the sight of him launching into the air. There were no creatures in the water, as I had joked, having swum this cave many times before with my dad. But the fear that broke through my confidence was not only surprising but upsetting.

A large reptile leapt from out of the water, its mouth gaping wide, and its left eye slanted and cold.

The roar it shouted through the cavern caused the stone walls to tremble. With the opening of its enormous mouth, it swallowed poor Matthew in one bite, like he was a small fish. Then maneuvered its body in the air, nimble as a swimmer, and landed with a crushing splash. The impact caused water to shoot up to the cavern's ceiling as it swam back down to the depths below. I stood, blinking hard to dispel the vision. The sound of Matthew landing brought me back with an impact, splashing water on the others as they all laughed.

Jessie, Lola, and Phillip all followed his invitation, shouting how warm the water felt. Each stripped down to their undergarments and leaped in. *You 're being paranoid.* I joined Ashton for a seat on the rocks nearby, our knees pulled into our chests and arms around legs.

"You saw something again, didn't you?" Ashton asked. It was the first sound of his voice I'd heard all morning. Ever since our kiss, for that matter. I stared at him.

"What do you mean?"

"Visions, like from last night. I can tell by that look on your face."

"Sometimes, it's better to live in the moment, don't you think?" I asked, standing and approaching the water, then stripping down to my undergarments. "You should get in."

"I can't swim, remember?"

"I forgot you couldn't swim," I said, looking up to a fallen pebble that landed with a soft splash. After a moment's stare, I dove for the water. Ashton hung in his legs.

Once we had enough of the swim, the crew gathered around as I explained why I had brought them there.

"Guys, as you all know tomorrow is the Gathering, and since I'll be leaving, I thought I'd leave you all with something to remember me by." I headed for the back of the cave, disappearing behind a wall of stone and retrieving my hidden wooden box with a lock on it.

"When my dad and I would dig for crystals, most times we came up empty-handed. It's a lot harder than you think. But there were a few times we got lucky and after he died, I hid them here."

I opened the box, revealing a beautiful collection of crystals that sparkled in a riot of colors.

"I have five. One for each of you." I took up each crystal, handing them out and saving the last for Ashton. I passed him the whole box, and inside was a crystal along with the green stone he'd bought for me from the market. "Keep these two together for me," I whispered to him as the others were exclaiming over their gifts.

"I don't know what to say," Jessie said, holding the sparkling stone in her hand. Lola seconded her sentiments, while Phillip gawked at how rare the crystal find was, and that he bet they were worth a fortune. He changed his words once Jessie's elbow came crashing into his stomach.

"I meant they're priceless," he gasped.

"And visit here anytime," I said.

"Visit?" Matthew looked around again. "I'm considering living here. Thanks, Rachel, this was pretty awesome, this place is beautiful."

Ashton stared into the box at the pair of emeralds, wiping one of his eyes. "Hey, it's getting late. We got a long hike back," Ashton said.

"He's right, we should head back," I confirmed, suggesting the path would be impossible to navigate in the dark.

They all agreed, and we began readying ourselves for the cold walk home. The sun was setting over the Quadrant. The walk home was not as peaceful as the walk there, roads filled with soldiers and armed trucks. Ashton, who had mainly been quiet the entire day, talked the whole way home about the newfound knowledge we had discovered in the red book the night before. Jessie and the others were still not buying it.

As the hours dwindled, nightfall approached, and we were arriving back safely in the old neighborhood. The talking had become subdued as we sat around the bus stop at the end of the street.

"Damn, I'm going to miss you, Rachel," Jessie said, breaking the silence that had arisen. She wrapped her arms around me tightly and the rest joined in, drawing what minor comfort we could from the group hug.

"We can't let this happen," Ashton hissed.

"Ashton, there's nothing we can do. We've already talked about this," Jessie said.

"There's always something! We can try *something*!" he pleaded, jerking away from the hug and looking at each of us.

"Sure, you won't reconsider running away after all?" Matthew said, his tone only half-joking.

"Nah, I'll just stay brave for you guys…ya know, keep you safe."

"My hero," Jessie said, still clinging to me.

"Mrs. P is the best," Phillip said, flopping to a seat on the sidewalk. "And her cooking! I would be so fat if I lived at your place."

"*Ter*. You would be fat-*ter* if you lived with them," Jessie said, smiling at him. We all laughed at that, even Phillip. The lights from a large bus turning the corner re-silenced us. We could hear its loud motor rumbling over the quiet neighborhood.

"Guess that's us…the last bus back into the city before curfew, I bet." Jessie squeezed me in another hug, this one stronger than the one before. "You take care, Rach. We're all going to be here in the morning before the Gathering starts, okay?"

"Okay," I whispered as Jessie hurried onto the screeching bus after its doors had jolted open. Her hands wiped at her cheeks as I shooed them off through the last goodbyes, trying to smile through the pain. The doors of the bus slowly slid closed, and the rumbling motor carried my friends away for the last time.

While on my walk home, guided by the lone streetlight and the sound of Tojo howling and barking from his yard, I couldn't help but think about Ashton and that creepy book. He had a point. Something was going on behind the scenes, something that only a few knew about. But how to stop them was a different problem.

My pondering was short-lived, as an eerie feeling crept on top of my shoulders. Someone was watching me.

"Elizabeth?" I stopped and whispered, but no answer came. My house, I could see, was only a few blocks away. I quickened my steps, sight focused solely on the porch of our home. The dead grass in our yard drew nearer with every tap of my boot on the ground.

When I reached my yard, my eyes glared at the strange islander standing on my front porch. He was lanky, tall, wearing a fancy black robe and was unbothered by being spotted by me.

"What do you want?" I shouted sternly, hoping my lack of fear would defuse whatever plan he was thinking.

He took daunting steps towards me. "I'm so sorry, madam. I think I have the wrong home." His voice friendly, too friendly if that's a thing.

"Mom!" I shouted out the side of my mouth. "There're soldiers patrolling all over the neighborhood at this hour! You do know that!" I yelled.

His eerie smile was frozen to his face. "Oh, yes, I do. Like I said before, I'm so sorry ma'am. I have the wrong house. Wrong neighborhood, even. You see, I'm from Quadrant Four."

"You're a long way from Quadrant Four."

"Oh, dear. Ahh, I guess you're right. Again, I'm so sorry."

I glared at him, sure to keep my distance as he walked across the grass. He paused just before reaching the road.

"I had hoped we were starting early, false alarm. But tomorrow's the big day, isn't it?" he said with his back towards me. The glow from the lone streetlight flickered in the distance. "They'll be coming for you first, I'm sure. No need to worry though, the Gathering will come for us all. As they say. But I cannot lie. It tempted me. So you see, I had to come see you in person. Too irresistible," he said, laughing as he whistled his way down the street. "But the law is the law! I'll see you tomorrow, Rachel." He had made it to the lone streetlight before he plummeted to the ground, stiff as a board. I hoped he'd suffered a sudden heart attack. Creepy old fool. There was something wrong with him, and did he call me by my name? Before I could answer my thoughts, he arose, deformed, balancing like a four-legged beast.

He focused his sights on me, his skinny head slowly twisting upside down from where he stood under the orange glow. I back pedaled for the door as he quickly crawled towards me on four limbs, his bones clicking and snapping with every lunge. I turned and ran, reaching the steps. I could hear his snarl behind me, sense his fingers reaching for my back. It gave a loud cry as I slammed the door shut in its face. Its crackling bones crawled up the walls and onto our roof.

I ran for the kitchen, grabbing one of Mother's cooking knives. I wasn't going to be afraid anymore. Flicking on the lights in the house, I waited for a sign that he was still out there, daring him to enter the home.

"Where are you?" I whispered, glaring out of the front window.

Ashton was right. Something evil had taken over the island. As I calmed my breaths, the headlights from the old red truck shone through the window. I didn't even notice it was missing. Soon after, I could hear my mother walking up the porch steps, the jingling of her silver keys before opening the door. "Hey, Rach, you're home, that's good. I made a real quick trip to the market before curfew; the soldiers are everywhere tonight. There was talk at the market about trouble at the wall, near our Quadrant! Strange huh, for them to be having all this trouble so close to the Gathering," Mother said, walking to the kitchen and placing bags of groceries on the table. Then came the sounds of banging pots and pans.

"Some islanders are talking about coming together. Maybe the gods haven't cursed us after all. Anyway, I wanted to make you something special tonight," she said, returning to the living room and noticing the look on my face, the knife gripped in my hand. "Is everything ok?"

I nodded.

"Come on, let me run you a bath," she said, soft and reassuring. Once I had bathed and relaxed, I sat at the kitchen table drawing while Mother prepared an amazing dinner. There was no talk about the strange islander out front, none about the haunting little girl or monsters either. Maybe a new life didn't sound so bad anymore. Mother led us in a prayer, and we shared a quiet dinner with just the two of us, basking in our last night together.

CHAPTER TWENTY-FOUR

BENJAMIN FIXATED ON THE SOLDIERS as they chased the screaming Elizabeth out of the palace.

"What have I done?" he muttered, turning to the muffled cries coming from the closet. He opened the chest and reached inside, picking up the baby girl from the pile of nested clothing. Rocking her until she calmed, he swaddled her in a shirt from the pile and headed down the steps. Benjamin made his way through the screams of islanders, desperate about finding safety from the fighting happening in the streets of Quadrant One. With the baby in his arms, he stayed in the shadows. His steps took him past a church in the middle of a beautiful, open field on the outskirts. It seemed to have a peacefulness, although surrounded by war. Stepping closer, he saw several islanders were walking in and out of the church, loading up a small wagon parked out front. Their nun robes hung to the ground, and one wore a hat with a black cloth dangling from its rim.

"Ma'am!" he called out to her.

She turned to face him. "Yes?" She seemed fearless, though she looked hurried and weary.

"What's this? Where's everyone going?"

"We've got to find a new home; this place is no longer safe."

"Sure, it is. Or it will be one day, once everything's calmed down a bit. You don't have to leave."

She stared at him and shook her head, her expression of disbelief visible even behind the veil. "You've got a lot to learn, you're still a young islander." She turned away from him and began walking after the others.

"Wait!" he called to her. "Please, what do you mean?" he said, clutching the baby like an unexpected parent.

She turned back and sighed. "Sometimes things are the way they are for a reason," she said.

"Who are we to decide the fate of another? King Pius III wasn't perfect, but he was our king. He deserved better. It just doesn't seem right, if you ask me. Islanders coming together against our king. They've ruled this island longer than any of us been alive." The young man bowed his head, looking at the small child now sleeping peacefully in his arms. "Here," he said, offering the child to the nun.

Her face showed shock, then pity. "We can't take a child that young. We don't even have a home for ourselves."

"I'm not fit to raise a child. Especially this one," he said.

"Are you hurt?" She gestured to his reddened hands and his blood-spattered clothing.

"Here, just take her, please, and see to it she finds a home," he begged. His eyes followed another, dressed in the mob's uniform who was helping them load the wagon. The veiled nun followed his gaze, smiling as she grasped the swaddled baby. It did not wake.

"I'll do my best." She spun from him and joined the others without another word. He watched as she boarded with assistance, then spun the opposite direction, back towards the city.

"Hey!" a voice called from behind.

"Hey! Stop!" he shouted again, catching up with Benjamin. "You can't just leave them with your child. They don't have anywhere else to go. I'm taking them to Quadrant Three with me."

"Are you with the mob?" Benjamin asked, eyeing his attire, but the uniform looked unbattered and new.

"Yes, I am, but... I'm helping these people to somewhere safe. What the mob is doing is inhumane. I won't support it." The frustration and disgust were clear in his voice.

"I hear you, but you must listen to me. That child isn't safe with me. You have to take her with you."

"Who is she to you?"

Benjamin thought for a moment. "Um, she's my niece," he answered. "Her family was killed in the fighting."

"You seem hurt yourself." The soldier pointed to the blood on Benjamin's shirt.

"I'll be fine. Just get my niece to safety, please. I'll be okay."

The soldier nodded, and Benjamin continued the walk.

"Hey!" he called again. "I'm John, John Patterson. Feels strange taking a baby from you and not even giving you my name..."

"Benjamin Malcamore," he said with his hand extended. Bloody as it was, John did not flinch, but shook it firmly.

"Benjamin Malcamore, nice to have met you..." He looked back at the wagon. "Are you sure you can't come with us? We can't give you a ride somewhere? There's someone we can see about those wounds."

 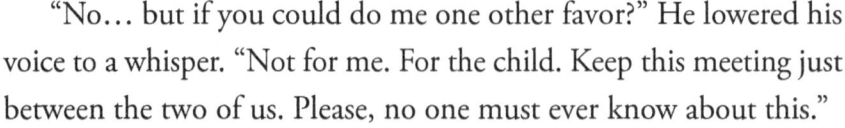

"No… but if you could do me one other favor?" He lowered his voice to a whisper. "Not for me. For the child. Keep this meeting just between the two of us. Please, no one must ever know about this."

He feared John would question, but to his surprise, John only nodded. They saluted one another with the mob's sacred salute and headed their separate ways.

CHAPTER TWENTY-FIVE

"EVERYONE, BUCKLE UP!" THOMAS SHOUTED as the minivan sped through the suburban neighborhood, then turned down Franklin street.

The earth beneath them shook.

A white Toyota slammed into a passing f-150 at an intersection. Head-on collision with the wails of metal crunching.

Thomas swerved right, then left as the van tilted with a screech before falling back down on all four tires. Naomi in the passenger seat screamed, preparing for a crash.

"Frank!" Thomas shouted. "Frank, look in my bag back there and grab my phone for me." The van swerved another hard right, then slammed to a crashing stop in the back of a parked Chrysler 300. The impact caused nylon air bags to explode from the steering wheel, smacking him in the face; his ears whistled. The yells of Frank brought him back.

"Is everyone ok?" Thomas whispered, wiping at the blood dripping from his forehead.

"We're fine, we're alive," Frank said, assisting his wife Sidney and sliding open the van door.

"Naomi?"

"I'm fine, love."

"Charlie?"

"Yeah, I'm ok, big bro." Charlie winced from the back row of the van. Each of them crawled out of the transportation and onto the street. Thomas and Frank retrieved the black duffel bags and threw them over their shoulders.

"The docks are just a few blocks away," Frank said, as they ran the crowded highway of emptied cars and trucks, piled together like a junkyard or a game of destruction derby. Dark buildings and inflorescent streetlights and nonfunctioning traffic lights. Cries from people in the backdrop drowned the quiet.

"Thomas," Naomi said. "Try your phone again, maybe you can reach Jacob, make sure he's ok."

Thomas fetched for his phone, clicking on the contact labeled "my boy."

No signal. The cell gave a non-responsive beep as he shoved it into his pocket.

They arrived at the docks.

"They're not letting anyone on, we've been here all evening!" a stranger said, crammed in-between screaming people, begging to get aboard one ship that lined the water. Military ships were no longer available, and most had already headed to undisclosed locations.

"I need everyone to form two groups! Women and children over here. Men over here!"

A marine shouted on repeat through a loudspeaker, addressing the thousands of frightened faces. The ground shook again. This time it would rival a category 7 earthquake as cement beneath Thomas's feet cracked and split open easy as a breakfast egg. Everyone gave a panicked scream. Ignoring the soldiers' orders to remain calm, they forced their way up the ramps to the cruise ships. Thomas, Naomi, Frank, Sydney, and Charlie included. A bright light tore through the night sky like a flaming rock, its beam relighting the city through hundreds of miles away from Tampa Bay, Florida. Everyone cried for cover.

Thomas awoke from a blaring alarm that rang out over the island. He had passed out, crammed between the hiding space of two large stones.

"What is with these people and their alarms?" he moaned, crawling out from the wedged spot with a bone-aching stretch. His arm and waist were still numb and the wound was still bleeding; his pockets were still filled with the cans.

"I got to find a way back to that cave," he said, peering out at the lake that seemed much wider now that the afternoon sun was shining. A wooden pier led to a forest of trees on the other side. He removed one of the five cans from his pocket.

"Let's see what all this was for." He searched for something sharp before his eyes landed on the stone hiding spot. He used its pointed end to cut into the small tin can. He held it over his mouth as a thick, orange goo dropped on his tongue. He reserved the idea to swallow, but let the taste take form inside his mouth. It was sweet, sweeter than the fresh peaches grown in China he tasted on a tour back in 2021. He emptied the can in seconds. He caught the missed slurps in his beard and brought it to his mouth, peeking in the made hole for extras.

"Best damn thing I've ever tasted," he said, securing the other cans to his pocket. Behind him, there were no more signs of wolves but other various animals that almost resembled the kind he would see back on earth if not for a few glistening furs. A deer frolicking in the distance, snorts that resembled wild hogs, flying insects, and crawling bugs.

"Ok, let's get a move on."

Constant mental notes were: watch for the blue-faced people, and most of all stay clear of those hideous snake monsters. He had pressed through beautiful stretches of fields that continued like a scrolling screen saver, or something he would see on a hallmark card. He came to a tall sign, mostly made of stone in the middle of yellow grass and pink, budding flowers. The writing was illegible; it resembled hieroglyphics carved into the walls of a pyramid.

He turned one way, whirled the other. It felt like he had been walking in circles all afternoon. He attempted to navigate via the sun from where he had fallen, but everything looked the same, and he swore he had just passed this exact sign. He was starving and confused.

Miles later...

He was lying flat on the ground, the sweet smell of the flowers tickling his nose hairs, as he laid eye level with blades of green and yellow grass. Loud hoofing came from a pair of horses kicking up bundles of dirt as they sped by, dragging an old-looking wagon filled with passengers. Once they had fully passed, he followed, sure to keep his distance. The road the wagon traveled disappeared into a stretch of hills acting as bottoms for small mountains with jagged stones and rocks. Peering up at the summit of one particular hill, he saw a reachable peak that flattened out at the top. If he reached the peak, he could at least get a good look at the landscape. The hike was painful, each clunk of his boots over unstable stones draining the last of his energy, an incline thinning the already thin air. Coming into view far in the distance, he spotted a stadium-like building, an arena with an opened roof.

"They must be the ones ringing those alarms," he whispered, reaching the flattened grass-covered peak, drenched in sweat. He glared out; the island, miles upon miles of mountains, caves, waterfalls, and frolicking animals and a massive stadium in the backdrop.

"Ty yu Ty yu!" a voice shouted from behind. When he turned, he saw the blue face, clothed in woven animal fur, standing with his glowing weapon poised at him. Thomas slowly rose his hands in the air, too tired to protest.

"Gosha peya hesy ty yu… Human," the being said, smiling at him through rotten teeth.

"Yes, me human…I'm sorry I don't understand you," Thomas said, slowly stepping closer as he inched for his gun when the islander shot. A crystalized bullet struck Thomas in the chest. The agony, half from the heat it projected, the other half from its electrical current sent rushing through his body. He lost his footing and slid down the hill side. Plunging through patches of pink and yellow grass stuffing their way into his opened mouth, he screamed to a stop at the foot of a wagon wheel, the wound appearing in his chest no doubt fatal as he closed his eyes shut.

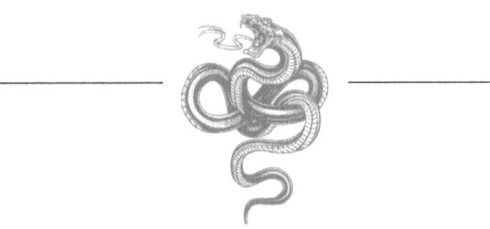

CHAPTER TWENTY-SIX

THE QUADRANT WAS DEAD QUIET with a sun like a red fireball peeking over the island.

I still hadn't slept a wink.

Today they would begin the Gathering, and I was as ready as one could be. The rules go: you may say your goodbyes, cry, grieve, what have you, but when it was time to leave, it was time. Only five islanders were allowed in a home, their way of keeping us monitored and under control. Last week's paper stated, *25 islanders scheduled to be Gathered from Quadrant Three alone.*

Twenty-five… that was a lot if you were wondering. This year's Gathering was a mixed group, it went on to say, but most of the article was about how King Theodore's Gathering idea was a seeming success until me. I folded the cloud-like comforter on my bed then took one last study of my drawings hanging on the wall, kissing the portrait of my father. I walked over to the old, wooden desk and rubbed my fingers across the rough edges, remembering when he and I built it together on my twelfth birthday, a happier time.

I grabbed my journal from out of the drawer and proceeded to the living room.

As I stood on the front porch, peering out at the lifeless roads, the sun positioned just over the neighborhood and morning dew.

"Any moment now they'll be here," I muttered, awaiting the screeching tires of the mob's bus, a burning growing deep within my belly. I should just run for it, the idea flashing in my mind. Then I imagined the mob of soldiers dragging my mother to some secret chamber in Quadrant Four. Torturing her to within an inch of her life.

Speaking of my mother, I spun towards the kitchen. I could hear her talking but couldn't make out who the other deep whispering voice belonged to.

"Morning," she said as I stepped through the kitchen's threshold. Her voice was shaky as she sipped from her mug. "We need to talk."

"What's going on? Who's he?" I asked, pointing toward the islander leaning against the back door. He looked to be in his thirties, dirty overalls and equally dirty work boots that dropped crumbs of clay to the kitchen tiles.

"I can explain, but please let me make you one last breakfast. You're going to need your strength," Mother said.

I okayed while still focused on the unknown guest. He seemed nervous and was avoiding my glare.

"Who are you?" I asked.

"I'm Noah," he said, adjusting his lean from his shoulder to his back.

An uncomfortable silence came next as the scent of breakfast filled the home. Mother slid a strip of meat and eggs onto a plate and slid it across the table.

"You got to eat."

"Thank you, Momma. Now, can you please?" I gestured to Noah.

Mother cleared her throat. "This is Noah, honey. He works with me at the Drums."

"Okay, but why is he here?"

"He's going to do a favor for me—one I can never repay him for." She looked nervous, fondling with a white rag that slammed to the sink. "There's an underground shelter-"

My fork dropped to the plate with a loud clatter. "Mom, no! We've already talked about this—"

"I am your mother! And I know what's best! I couldn't tell you before because I know how you get. I think we have everything down."

"You *think*?"

"It's going to work." Her words turned desperate. "Noah has an underground shelter in Quadrant Two. He's willing to take you there so you can hide until everything cools off. Once it does, I'll come get you and we'll escape the island together."

Noah cleared his throat and approached the table. "It's nothing fancy, let me warn you there, but it'll do. I've got enough fresh water and food to last you a few weeks."

I turned to mother. "And leave you here? Mom, they're not going to just let you hide me."

"Listen to me, Rachel! I didn't let them take you before and I will not let them take you now!"

The words nearly shocked the air out of my lungs.

"Let who take me?"

"Just listen to me, ok! Please."

I stared, puzzled. I never considered she would be the one hiding something from me. "Ok, whatever you say."

"Good." Mother left the room, feet pounding down the hallway as she hurried, then returned with a large, black bag that she slammed

215

to the table. "I've already packed some things—clothes, food, it's all in here. We've got to move fast. The Gathering starts in an hour."

I turned in my chair as muffled voices came from outside, growing louder by the minute. "You hear that?" I said, rushing to the living room window. Coming into focus was an angry group of islanders walking pass the lone streetlight.

"No surrender, no peace! No to the Gathering!" they shouted, marching in unison, signs and weapons in hand. The leader on the loudspeaker sounded familiar.

Yanking open the front door, I glared out at the growing chaos.

"No surrender, no peace! No to the Gathering!" It was Ashton, stationing the angry crowd in our yard. When he finally noticed I was watching, he ran over, out of breath but excited.

"What are you doing?"

"It's a protest, it's what I've been planning," Ashton said. "They've shut down all public transportation, Rach. The whole Quadrant is on lockdown. It's even worse in the city; I couldn't find the rest of the crew. My guess is the soldiers probably didn't let them out of the Drums. We had to walk all the way here, Rach. We won't let them take you. If they try, we're prepared to fight. All of us!" he finished in a shout, balling his fist into the air. The crowd behind him roared in response.

"That's suicide, Ashton! You will get those islanders killed!"

"Just stay behind us."

He didn't seem like he was listening to me at all as he spun and ran back for the crowd, shouting the chant into the loudspeaker. "No surrender, no peace! No to the Gathering."

I turned to Mother, afraid, when a blaring alarm rang out over the island. The Gatherings alarm was a much louder alarm than curfew call. It blasted from each section of the wall for all Quadrants to hear.

"They're starting early!" Mother gasped. "Rachel, get your things and leave with Noah, now!" I turned from the door and ran to join them in the kitchen.

After I grabbed the bag from the floor, Mother and I shared one last hug. She had to shout to make herself heard. "Listen! When they come here for you, I will keep them busy as long as I can! There will be soldiers all over this island, so you and Noah must be careful, understand me?"

Distracted by the growing ruckus outside, I glanced at the living room window.

"Did you hear me?" Mother yelled.

"You must be—"

The Gathering alarm quieted as a large bus approached the neighborhood, then came to a screeching stop in front of our home. The crowd outside chanted as Mother all but shoved me towards the back door. I pulled from her grasp and ran to the window. In fear for those innocent islanders still marching in the streets, in fear for Ashton. The lead officer stepped off the bus and spoke.

"We're only here for citizens meant to be Gathered from this section of Quadrant Three. But this protest is illegal, and I order you to disburse! If not, we will consider it a threat, and they have instructed us to react with force. You have one minute!"

The crowd grew silent.

I ran into the street, snatching the loudspeaker from Ashton, and addressed them all.

"My name is Rachel Patterson; I am the girl with the 18. I am being Gathered here today and I am asking you all to leave! Please! My family and I just want to say our goodbyes in peace. I thank you for what you are all trying to do, I really do. Thank you!" I said, looking at Ashton and then at Mother, who had crept her way to the front porch. "But please do not risk your lives or the lives of others for me. Think of your own families, your own loved ones who need and depend on you."

The tension grew to an almost physical presence.

Awareness of what was unfolding seemed to spread fast, as more and more islanders flocked to join the ever-enlarging crowd. I knew it was only a matter of time before the mob would end this spectacle.

"Have it your way!" the lead officer shouted as he aimed his weapon. Right on cue, more soldiers arrived, jumping from their vehicles, and standing at attention with weapons poised.

I looked toward Mother, whose face showed her terror. She beckoned for me to run back into the house, back to perceived safety.

Suddenly, a bomb exploded as the soldiers surged forward with a cry of pure rage.

In sheer panic, with smoke filling my eyes and screams invading my ears, I turned and bolted for the nearby fields outside of the neighborhood.

I could hear Ashton calling my name a few strides behind.

We continued scampering through the neighborhood side by side, sprinting past Mrs. Walters's house where Tojo would sleep on the lawn, usually safe and sound behind his fence, but no sight of him today. Passing the bus stop where I had said my last goodbyes to the rest of the crew, and in the near distance was the first patch of woods acting like a finish line in my mind. If we could reach the trees, it would be too hard to find us. My thoughts were racing as fast as my feet. How would I survive? What about my mother? What would happen to her now?

Just as we arrived at the fields, the first blade of grass poking at my chest, a humming bang from behind stopped me in my tracks. I turned.

"No!" I screamed as Ashton's body collapsed to the dirt.

I abandoned the escape and ran to his side, lifting his head and searching his body for the bullet penetration, then found wetness soaking his lower back and my hands came away red-stained.

The soldier was running towards us as Ashton trembled in my arms.

"They're e-e-evil… Don't let them take you. You can fight them. This is all about you, Rach, you're special," he whispered, his words barely understandable as the blood emerged from his mouth.

A pair of rough hands grabbed me from behind, and I kicked and screamed. He tossed me over his shoulder like a heavy gun and carried me back to the bus.

Screaming in uncontrollable rage, my eyes wheeled at the turmoil taking place just outside of my home. "Put her down!" a voice shouted, stern and forceful. I craned my head to stare at Mr. Malcamore from my perch. "I'm in charge here, and I said put her down *now*!" The lead soldier frowned up into his face, hesitated for the space of a second, then dropped me back to my feet.

I screamed at him in an outrage, punching at his chest with my fist. If it wasn't for Malcamore running over and grabbing my flailing hands, I would have kept going. "They killed him, they killed him!" I cried.

"Killed who?".

"Ashton! My best friend! They just shot him… They just shot him. He's dead!" Hysteria made the world reel around me; I staggered as if I were the one who they shot.

219

"Rachel!" Malcamore said, over the blaring screams. A few like Ashton had already lost their lives, lying on the ground.

"I'll take care of it, but you must go to your Gathering."

"No! I will not get on that bus! Ashton... Oh, God..."

"You must, and you will! Or the mob will kill everyone you know and burn this Quadrant to the ground. Trust me!"

I was ready to refuse again when Malcamore took something from his pocket. "Take this with you." He handed me a small bottle with a red substance inside that oozed from one end to the other.

"What the hell is this? I'm not taking that."

"You will," he said, folding my fingers over the bottle. "Drink it at your last breath, no matter what the circumstances. Your very last. Do you understand? It's your only hope."

I looked at him, confused, examined the small bottle once more, and stuffed it in the pocket of my brown trousers.

"I'll find your friend... help him if I can... but first, I must get you on that bus. We will not survive another war."

The residual smoke from the bomb still filled the air. The mob of soldiers was forcing islanders in their homes. I grappled with the thought, Ashton, abandoning my mother, and trusting this Malcamore without knowing what he had planned. I looked toward the bus that stood only a few feet away, its large motor rumbling, and the crystals illuminating the ground beneath it.

"Get on the bus, Ms. Patterson, please," Malcamore whispered. With a deep sigh, I approached the bus with slow steps. I glanced to my home to see Mother one last time, but the soldiers had it surrounded.

Forced ahead inside, some people seated, crying and staring out the windows in shock, bruised and battered. I took a spot near the back at random, the tears rolling down my cheeks.

"Samson! Samson!" I could hear Malcamore calling, yelling above the continuing din.

"Yes, young sir?"

"Search those fields and find that boy they shot! I need to speak with Rachel's mother."

Bit by bit, they cleared away the crowd. Soldiers escorted every individual named on the list from this section of Quadrant Three, if they were still alive.

Once the dust had settled, everyone accounted for. The lead officer stepped onto the bus and spoke once again.

"You are all being Gathered for your rebirth! Your life here is ending and a new one awaits you! Let's go," he said, slapping the driver on the back. The doors squeaked shut and the bus headed down the gravel road.

CHAPTER TWENTY-SEVEN

"THIS IS A MESS, ISN'T it?" Samson said, returning from the fields and approaching Malcamore, who was gazing out from the Pattersons' porch. The soldiers were still busy cleaning up the streets from the riot. The islanders they had arrested were being jammed inside waiting army trucks, while others lay awaiting medical attention.

"It is… Did you find the boy, Samson?" he asked, stepping down from the log steps.

"No, young sir. However, I discovered a large puddle of blood."

"Hmm."

"If he is alive, he's certainly lost a lot," Samson said, turning his focus to a soldier that was exiting the Pattersons' home. "What about you? Did you have time to talk to the girl's mother?"

"Yes, I spoke with her." Malcamore stared out as a vehicle sped in their direction.

"Well, what did she say?" Samson prodded.

"Never mind that now. We must head to Quadrant Four. I need to see the king, we're done here."

Samson looked curious but nodded, and they left the Pattersons' yard and headed for the coach parked out front. Just as they were about to step in, however, an armed vehicle blocked the path.

"What the hell happened here?" Lord Sanders asked, leaping from the truck, red-faced and shouting. He had arrived at the scene just a few moments too late to be of any use.

"Lord Sanders," Malcamore acknowledged.

"Don't you *Lord Sanders* me! Look at my Quadrant! Where have you been?" Sanders blustered.

"I've been here. Things just got out of hand. But everyone to be Gathered is present and accounted for."

"Word's spread about this outrageous display, and we've been having trouble with the Gatherings all throughout the Quadrants!" he huffed, now standing inches from Malcamore. "I don't know why that king of ours saw fit to put you in charge of the Gatherings for my Quadrant, but this, he will hear about! And I know you heard me calling you when you left the other night."

"He will. I'll tell him myself," Malcamore said.

"What do you mean, you'll tell him?" Lord Sanders shouted after him as Malcamore and Samson boarded the coach and shut the door.

"To Quadrant Four!" he called to William, leaning out the coach's window and leaving Sanders glaring at the chaotic surroundings.

CHAPTER TWENTY-EIGHT

THOMAS AWOKE IN THE DARK, iron chains cuffed at the wrist, naked. The ground beneath him was cold stone, the space so black he couldn't see but a few inches away.

"Help!" he screamed, jerking on chains that left little to no slack in resistance. Each tug caused them to grip tighter around his bones.

"Somebody, please help me!" Thomas pleaded.

The room was silent at the moment. His flesh pressed against the brick that made up the floor and walls. The pain was excruciating, though the hole that should be in his chest healed.

"Help me please, I've got to get back to my family," he cried, spit dripping from his mouth, peering down at the perfectly cut squares of black and gray, then down to his chest.

"They shot me... didn't they shoot me?" he said to himself, his mind madly working out the memory. The hill with the flattened top, the stadium-like building. The blue man.

"I've lost them... I can't believe I lost them. You're so stupid! Tommy. Why would you leave them alone?" he whispered, tears dropping to the ground.

"Ok, Tommy boy, time to think of something. You always think of something."

He scanned the dismal room as best he could, trying to kick the other side of the wall with his feet, a failed attempt that ended with a groaning thud.

"Ok, that was pointless." He moaned when his back slapped the ground, dragging himself up against the stonewall.

A whisper.

He peered to his right as a blue face lunged from the shadows towards him.

"KOOSHAY!" he shouted, staring in awe. He too, was chained by the wrist, growling and pulling at the shackle like a mad dog.

"Help! Please someone!" Thomas screamed. The sound of feet thudding came from outside, and a loud turning of a latch. A bright light eased through the opening sphere that rolled to its place. With the room illuminated by the white light, Thomas gasped at the dozen of chained blue face people in the room he hadn't noticed before.

"Tayyu- Human," the blue man said, holding a metallic, humming crystal-charged weapon, and aiming directly at Thomas's face. The one to his right, still growling and snapping at Thomas's neck, reverted when the soldier crammed his head with the back of the gun and scurried back to its corner.

"Yes, yes me, human. Please help me. I don't know where I am," Thomas pleaded.

"Cosha kandya Anastasiaaaaaa," he said, poking at him with the tip of the weapon.

"Anastasia?" Thomas puzzled.

"Keeya Human."

"No, no, no, Human... Help."

226

The blue man eyed Thomas for a moment before storming out, and the sphere-shaped door slowly rolled shut. Bit by bit the bright light disappeared, and the darkness refilled the cell. Thomas wept. Inside with him were growls and angered screams that grew louder, chanting in the unknown language as they pulled at their chains.

"I need to save my family!" Thomas screamed.

The next 5 minutes he would always remember passing as slow as a lifetime, when thudding feet and whispering voices returned. The sounds of the latch unbolting and the sphere-shaped door opened once again, bringing back the white light. Another blue face appeared, marching into the room with prestige. He was tall and muscular, and by tall, referring a small giant. He was dressed in a thick, wool fur with shining crystals around his knuckles and a crystal-plated crown on his head.

Thomas, sat up, naked and afraid. He could tell this was their leader.

He studied Thomas for a moment, poking at his flesh with his blue finger that felt more like being poked by a brick.

"TayuTayu… Human," he whispered. Thomas thought to choose his words wisely. In fear, he wouldn't get another chance.

"Thomas," he said, pointing at himself from the cuffs. "I'm Thomas."

"Th—omaa-sss," the Blue man said, like a toddler learning to speak. Thomas nodded and smiled. He had finally contacted someone who tried to understand him.

"My family is outside," he said.

The blue man screwed up his face, stood up straight and tall, then turned to a smaller soldier behind him. "Kissameya de Human."

"No, no, no don't, kissademimi me. I'm sorry, I'm just trying to explain that I lost my family in the caves somewhere and they're dying and I have no way to find them. And I do not know where I am. What is this place, who are you people? Why is your skin bluish? It's all just very confusing right now. And it's dark and I'm in these chains."

A beautiful blue woman walked into the cell, her hair long and knotted down to the small of her back. She was clutching a handful of crystal that formed a glowing light bulb. She approached Thomas in mid-rant, shoving the beaming lights down his throat, forcing him to swallow. It burned like being set on fire inside out. The room spun as he fell within himself. That would be the best way he would describe it later. Falling into an emptiness of existence within himself. The world he once knew, passing by like flashes in a time capsule, buildings tumbling, dinosaurs walking the earth, he continued his fall. Falling passes the end, the landing of the ice rocks, the rise of the water that destroyed the planet. He continued falling, falling past the beginning, past where man and woman were first created by a fruit-covered tree. He continued to fall, then stopped to a float in a blank space of infinity, with only the stars for company that twinkled in a ray of colors. From pink to blue and white. Thomas gagged as he began spewing out blue liquid from his mouth and nose.

"Your impurities," the large blue man said, his crystal rings and beaming crown twinkling. Thomas's eyes shot up to him in shock. "You can understand me now, I take it."

Thomas nodded, still puking up the liquids that spilled all over the stone. A space of embarrassment came when some reached the giant blue man's feet.

"Good, welcome to Anastasia, human Thomas, I am King Pius."

CHAPTER TWENTY-NINE

THE BUS BOUNCED AND JOSTLED about on the uneven roads as I sat in my seat in tears, still picturing Ashton's face. Prepared to say my goodbyes, yes, but not like this. I tried to wipe away the mourning, paralyzed by the sight of blood that covered my hands—Ashton's blood. I began wiping them on the padded bus seats, desperately trying to clean my fingers and palms.

"This may help," a kind voice spoke, hovering above me and holding a damp handkerchief, while her other hand gripped the seat for balance.

"Thank you." I sniffed, then began scrubbing with enough force to peel skin.

"Are you going to be okay?" she asked, her eyes soft and compassionate.

I shook.

"That was quite a scene back there. Almost reminded me of the war." The elder took a seat, forcing me to adjust my positioning.

Her gray puffball of hair smelled of mint, and she wore a blouse with pretty flowers woven around the sleeves. "But you will be just fine. I promise." She patted my hand in a motherly fashion. Her kindness only made me cry harder as I leaned into her welcoming arms, inhaling deep breaths of peppermint.

"There, there, young one. I'll be here with you the rest of the way. Both my husband and I."

I gasped and looked up, my tears slowing a bit. "You're Gathered here with your husband?" I asked in shock. Truly, her story should have gotten way more attention than mine.

"Yes, child. I'm Susan, and that's my husband David, over there." She pointed at an older islander at the front of the bus who was pondering out of his own window. The wrinkles forming on his forehead looked like that of someone replaying his life.

"Not my first husband, but my last." She reflected too for a moment, then smiled as her eyes brightened. "Both our times are up, as they say, so we have the privilege of being Gathered together." Her voice was firm, confident, and not at all afraid or unsure.

"But that's so sad," I said, still shocked.

"No, it's not, child. It's all about perspective. I couldn't imagine living on without him, nor could I imagine him living on without me and finding another wife–and at his age! Over my dead body. And if all this mess somehow helps our island—" She chuckled and eased herself to her feet. "Now don't cry so much, you hear. And don't worry your little heart anymore about this big, old Gathering mess."

"Yes, ma'am," I whispered. The woman nodded and began heading back to her husband's side.

"Mrs.?" I called out; a thought having struck. "You wouldn't have a pen, would you?"

"You're in luck. David!" she called to her husband, who turned to face her. "Look inside my jacket there and grab my blue pen, would you, darling? I'm a bit of a writer myself." She smiled at me while David fumbled through the jacket, tossed it back over the seat, then shuffled down the aisle to his wife.

"Here you go, child. You keep this… it's my lucky pen."

I took it, murmuring my thanks.

"And remember what I said. If you need someone to talk to, don't sulk all alone. You come find me or my husband, you hear? My David, he's a wonderful listener too, isn't that right, dear?" she asked, rubbing his back.

David remained silent but smiled, and they held hands and walked back to the front of the bus, taking their seats. I watched them for a moment, in a way, they reminded me of my mom and dad. Or how it would have been if they had grown old together. I reached into my back pocket and pulled out my little, black journal, with my name stenciled on the cover. Opening to a blank page, I wrote.

Dear diary,

I regret this might be my last chance to write. I'm headed to the Gathering now, and I've never-

I could barely get the words to the paper with all the tears filling my eyes again as the sounds of screaming and gunshots still rang in my mind. The image of Ashton collapsed and bleeding on the ground.

Ashton tried to save me today. That crazy boy almost started a war. I can't believe he's gone. And my mother, I didn't have time to say my goodbyes to either of them. But I'd rather die now than spend another day on this island.

The small bottle pressed against my leg and fell out of my pocket, landing in the crevices of the seat. I had almost forgotten about it. With a sigh, I stuffed it back in my pocket and laid the pen in the sheets of my diary. Outside, the once-bright sky had turned a steely gray. Ahead of us were stunning mountains and miles of beautiful overlapping hills and frolicking animals. This was only my second time out of the Quadrant, and I'd forgotten how beautiful the island could be.

"So, what do you think happens?" a voice spoke from the seat behind me.

I turned.

"Sorry," she whispered, covering her mouth with both hands. "That was rude of me." Her words were nervous and sporadic. "I'm Betty. Betty Davenport," she said, reaching her hand out over the seat.

"It's fine. I'm Rachel."

"Rachel Patterson, the girl with the 18. Everyone knows who you are," Betty said, pulling her hand back after we'd shaken.

"Oh," I whispered. "To answer your question, I do not know what happens next."

Betty turned and stared out at the passing fields. She muttered, "I tried my hardest, you know, to find out what happens, about past Gatherings and stuff like that. But this place is an iron vault for any actual information. I'm just so scared," she said, stroking her long, brown hair in a frantic.

"Yeah, I know what you mean. I am, too," I said, now looking with more intent. Betty seemed only a few years older than me. "What's your number? You can't be that, well, old."

"41," Betty answered, showing me her wrist tattoo. "But thanks for the compliment. I guess I still feel young inside. But that king

232

and his so-called court saw fit to give me the number 41. Guess I didn't test so well." She laughed mockingly. "Hey, can I ask you one last question? Then I'll leave you alone, I promise."

"Sure."

"Do you believe what they say? That there's another life waiting for us?" Her eyes glittered with unshed tears. "Sorry, I'm not trying to sound weird, it's just…"

"No, I understand. And I guess I believe there's another life waiting for us after this hellhole." The words gave me strength, though I wasn't sure I believed them.

"Me too…me too," Betty said, sliding back into her seat.

* * *

Drops of rain splattered against the bus, trickling down one drop at a time. The drizzle soon escalated to a pour, gushing from the sky with thunder. I had almost dozed off from watching the fields as they passed, awakened by the water splashing onto my face.

"How did this get open?" I whispered, slamming the window shut by its side latches. A sudden darkness overtook the bus, prompting unified groans and mummers as we entered a tunnel that blocked out the light.

Elizabeth, in her torn white gown and bloodless skin, was sitting beside me, staring out into the dark space. I jumped back, knocking the diary and its pen to the floor.

"I know who you are," I hissed.

She gave no answer, but only continued to stare straight ahead. The other passengers hadn't taken notice of her at all.

"I know who you are!" I said again, this time much firmer. "Your name is Elizabeth! You were the king's daughter, right? Right!?"

Her eyes turned to meet mine.

"Please, just tell me... Why are you doing this? Why are you haunting me?" I asked. Elizabeth slowly opened her mouth as a snake appeared, slithering down her cheek. "To see you again," Elizabeth said.

"Who are you talking to?" Betty Davenport asked, popping up from behind the seat.

"Huh?"

"Who were you just talking to? You said I know who you are," Betty asked again, peeking just above the edge. I may have just freaked her out even more.

"It's no one, I'll be fine." I leaped from my spot, dropping to the floor and fetching the diary and the lucky pen that had fallen.

The bus still traveled in darkness, although every few feet a glowing crystal shone on the fearful faces. I walked toward the front, taking an open seat behind the elderly couple.

"Excuse me, but where are we? I fell asleep. I was wondering what Quadrant this is," I asked.

"My guess is Four. I remember hearing about a tunnel this big, the old stadium where they used to hold games and entertainment for the king many years ago," David said.

I turned my attention to the lead officer sitting a few spots ahead. "Excuse me... Excuse me, sir, but where are we going? Everyone wants to know; we're all just scared."

"Take your seat, ma'am!" the officer ordered.

"I'm just asking—"

"Ma'am, I will not tell you again! Take your seat!" the soldier shouted, each word louder and more threatening than the last.

"Listen to the man, child," Susan whispered in warning. I nodded and returned to my original seat.

Only moments later, the bus came to a screeching stop as the soldier stood. "We have arrived at the Gathering Chambers!" he announced. "The bus doors will open. You will stand and exit the bus in an orderly fashion. Once inside, we will provide you shelter, clothes, and food. Be ready for your Gathering by midnight. Good luck to you in your next life."

I grabbed my things and did what was told as he ordered us to form a single line. I was a few paces behind the elderly couple, and Betty was standing a few paces behind me.

We exited the bus. The smell was awful, and nothing much to see but more black stone walls. Seconds later bright beams shone from behind us, the other buses arriving in a line, as more terrified cries joined the group.

At the end of the walkway was a stoned entrance, unlike any door I'd ever seen.

"Move forward!" a commanding voice said. We stepped closer when someone screamed from the back, swearing something had just slithered past their foot.

"Open chamber three!" a soldier called.

With a loud rumble, the door slowly rolled out of the way, and a sudden bright light filled the opening tunnel. I covered my eyes, shielding them from the beam.

"Move forward!" the soldier commanded.

We all walked through the entrance and into the light as the enormous door rolled back shut behind us, closing with a muffled boom.

Crammed in the bright hallway, the soldier waited until the chamber was silent before he addressed us again. "Attention, everyone! All eyes on me and listen closely. I will not be repeating myself," the soldier said, readjusting the suspenders that held his gun to his chest. "You are all about to enter the Gathering Chambers. Once you are inside, they will dispense clothes and assign you to a room. We assign rooms according to Quadrants. Go there and wait for further instructions. Questions?"

Nobody dared answer, and taking our silence as assent, he turned his back on us and shouted. "Open door three!"

I began gasping for air in a sudden panic as the door churned. I wasn't truly afraid before until now.

CHAPTER THIRTY

MALCAMORE FOCUSED ON THE STREETLIGHTS that seesawed in the rain. The squeaking and a sudden jolt from the wagon snapped him out of his deep thoughts of that dreadful night when he gave her away. He had just entered Quadrant Four with Samson, this time without invitation. Night was falling, but the once-bustling capital was now soundless and vacant.

"This is odd, young sir. I have a terrible feeling about this," Samson said, squirming in his seat.

Malcamore, puffing on one of his smokes, looked over at him from his side of the carriage. "No worries, Samson, I'll keep you safe." He chuckled, checking his pistol for ammunition.

"Go over it with me one more time if you don't mind. What's your plan again?"

"Simple. I will demand that the king put a stop to this year's Gathering. Maybe after I reveal who Rachel is, he'll be willing to spare her life."

"And you think that's going to work?" Samson's disbelief was clear on his face.

"Well…no, I don't, but still, we must try. Otherwise, they will kill her."

"She's as good as dead already, young sir. They'll never stop the Gathering."

Malcamore glared. "Don't you think I know!" he snapped.

"Forgive me."

Malcamore took another strong inhale, exhaling while staring out at the empty city. "I can't help but fear you may be right," he admitted in a softer tone as the old coach continued down the deathly quiet roads. There was no sound on the paved streets, market shops on the corners; no islanders with their evil stares, and even the kids who were playing a game of tag just a day ago were gone.

Vanished.

"Where is everyone?" Malcamore muttered, peering past his stream of smoke.

"Exactly my thoughts. It's as if they've all disappeared," Samson whispered. The churning of the coach wagon wheels slowed as they arrived at the gate outside the king's home. "Well, almost everyone," Samson amended under his breath, noticing it was the same guard from before.

The soldier stepped toward the carriage with a blank look, eyeballing Malcamore and Samson through the window.

"How are you tonight, sir? It's Mr. Malcamore and my colleague Samson. I'm sure you remember us; we were just here the other day."

"…"

"I would like to speak with the king, if that would be alright with you. I know it's a little unexpected, but I was hoping just this once—"

238

"Nobody sees the king," was the only answer as he headed back to his post.

"I never liked him," Samson whispered.

"What do you mean, no? Soldier, tell the king that Malcamore is here to see him. It only takes a second I have some important news."

The soldier returned a scowl. Malcamore hadn't noticed it before, but when the light touched the soldier's face, his eyes appeared black and empty.

"Soldier! Are you alright?" Malcamore asked.

"Nobody sees the king?" the guard demanded, repeating in the same manner. Suddenly, a gunshot blasted, signaled as a warning, the shot coming from William the driver.

Malcamore continued. "Now listen, we didn't come to start trouble, if that's what you're thinking. I would just like to sit down with the king and have a friendly chat. Now why don't you just open that gate there and we'll be on our way."

The guard made no response, not even at the gunshot.

"Nobody sees the king!" he shouted all the same.

"I think he's gone mad. Remember, Harold Wellington," Samson whispered, peeking through the window. Malcamore groaned and pulled on the handle of the wagon, opening the door. "Wait right here, Samson."

"Say no more. I'll be right here."

Malcamore approached the guard, then gestured for the driver to keep his weapon aimed. "Soldier, are you alright!?" Malcamore asked again, waving his hands in front of his face.

"Just open the gate, and let's get on with it," Samson hissed from the wagon. Malcamore back pedaled to the gate, unlatched it, and swung it open with a hard push. The soldier made no move to stop

239

him. Once he arrived back in the coach, Malcamore shouted for the driver to go forward, staring back at the unmoving guard as they passed through the gates.

"Did you see his eyes?" Samson whispered.

"Yes." Malcamore said, still watching the guard who flopped to the ground as if he suddenly died.

"What do you make of it?" Samson asked.

He turned to answer Samson. "I don't know, drugs maybe…" When he looked again, the soldier rose and crawled away, disfigured, on all fours. Samson hadn't noticed.

"Forgive me for saying so, but that didn't look like the reaction to any drug I know of. His eyes, they seemed almost…dead," Samson said.

Malcamore spun back around. "Hm. I agree," he answered, loathed to admit his own fears, and not wanting to scare Samson any further.

"It doesn't sit right, none of this seems right." Samson said.

The carriage slowed in front of the king's home as Malcamore put his plan into action. "Samson, you and the driver stay here while I go inside," he instructed.

"I won't have it, young sir. I'm going in with you."

"Not this time, old friend." Malcamore rested a hand on Samson's shoulder, preventing him from disembarking.

"Don't leave me out here by myself in the rain with old crazy eyes down there," Samson begged.

"You're not alone, Samson. The driver's with you." Malcamore chuckled.

"Keep a sharp eye, both of you, just in case we end up having to make a run for it."

"Will do," Samson said, pulling himself up straight as Malcamore shut the door.

Approaching the home, he gave the large door a knock, and it quickly opened. Standing before him was a servant in a black servant's robe, his eyes also unusually black.

"This way, Mr. Malcamore. Our king is waiting for you in his office," the servant said, his voice toned as he turned for the stairs.

When he first visited the king's home, there had been a crowd filled with laughter and drinking, a band playing soft music in the corner of one room. Now the palace, empty, seemed darker and forbidding.

Finally reaching the king's office, Malcamore hesitated before pressing forward with the palm of his hand.

There stood King Theodore, gazing out of his large window, with his wife by his side.

"Ahh, you made it. Just in time for the show. We all bet that you wouldn't return," the king said, turning to face Malcamore. "Other than you and Rose here, the entire town's completely empty," Malcamore said.

The king laughed a little. "I can explain. Take a seat, Benjamin." He gestured to the cushioned chairs.

"You were testing me, sir?"

"Can't say that I was… but we had to be sure you were still one of us." The king pulled a cigar from his pocket and lit it with a struck match. "Dear? Would you be so kind as to give me and Malcamore here some privacy?"

Rose, solemn and quiet, only nodded, her face expressionless with no returned greeting to Malcamore, who attempted to wave. His eyes followed her as she left the room.

"So, Benjamin," the king said when the door closed. He took a long puff of his cigar that flamed red at the tip. "Let's get straight to business, shall we? First, let me say good job on following through. I had my doubts, But Rose really wants you to be part of our brotherhood."

"Well, thanks for bringing that up…" Malcamore cleared his throat. "It's about the girl, my king."

"The girl with the number 18," the king mumbled. Then glared. "What about her?"

"Do you know who she is?" Malcamore asked.

"Oh… well, no, who is she?" he asked in a disinterested tone, stepping closer.

"Not just some girl who scored low on her test. She was…" He paused, knowing what the consequences would be for what he was about to say.

"The granddaughter of King Pius III," Theodore injected.

"You *knew*?"

The king took another step closer as Malcamore put his hand over the gun hidden under his jacket. The king's sight flicked downward, noticing the gesture, but ignored the threat. "Obviously, we always knew who she was, we found her during her testing," he said, leaning on the front end of his desk. "The fact she was still alive all this time was interesting, I do say, but if I'm being honest with you, Benjamin, and you seem like the type who likes it straight, the far more interesting part is this." He lowered his voice. "How in Anastasia did she survive? Because *that's* grounds for treason, Benjamin." He stared at Malcamore, unblinking, then paced the room, his steps leisurely with his hands clasped behind his back.

"Do with me what you like, but I beg you, don't kill that girl. She's the last of his family—"

"What *is* it with you and this girl, Benjamin?" The king took another long drag on his cigar.

"She's my daughter," Malcamore said.

The king gasped as he spun.

"Your daughter, you say! Oh, Benjamin, you old dirty dog you. Were you fondling with the king's daughter of all people? Which one was it? No, let me guess, it was Annabelle! Wasn't it?" King Theodore said with a grin. Malcamore solemnly nodded as the king clicked his teeth.

"You should be ashamed, Benjamin. Just when I thought you had this place all figured out. You think all this is about some girl? It doesn't matter if she is your daughter." He chuckled. "The royal lineage is over, Benjamin; I made a deal for all of their bloods and that's the end of that. The truth of it is, we could have had her killed as soon as we discovered she was alive. It was for the sake of her actual parents on her testing day, her mother begged and pleaded with me to give her more time. It was the only reason I didn't sentence her to her Gathering at that very moment. Not my problem No one's ever told her, poor girl's better off with none of you if you ask me."

"A deal with who?" Malcamore asked.

"…Her time is up, Benjamin. It's her Gathering, a beautiful moment to crossover. It's that simple. We held up our end of the bargain, and now it's her turn. It's up to the other things involved now."

"What other things?" Malcamore said, narrowing his eyes.

"Well, if you want that information, join our brotherhood. But it's just something that may crave her, you can't quite understand. Human blood and all…you get the idea."

"Human blood? There are no humans in Anastasia," Malcamore said, mystified.

The king eyed him, blowing o's of smoke in the air and stroking his beard in thought, then paused in his steps. "You didn't know...You're right about one thing, Benjamin." He pointed with his cigar like an added finger. "Let's say I believe you...that she's your daughter, but why should I spare your daughter's life? And if I did, how could you ever return such a favor?" he asked.

"What do you want?"

The king's smile escaped his face.

"Your soul." His voice turning deep and gravel.

Malcamore stood from his seat as the king's skin drew tight and peeled from his body, revealing a scaled layer of skin beneath. His eyes grew darker until they were black as a starless night and soulless as death himself.

A tapping sound came from the ceiling, like sharp nails on a chalkboard. Malcamore looked upward as a Fiend emerged from the shadows, revealing its claws and sharpened fangs. He cowered back, bumping into the chair behind him and dropping the gun from underneath his suit. The king's hands reshaped into reptilian claws with knife-like fingertips.

Malcamore let out a yell of fright and bolted for the door. The creature, the Fiend, gave a loud screech, crawling across the ceiling in a blink. It hissed, stretching open its mouth.

"I cannot force you to join, I need you to say yes for yourself. " the king laughed, his bones snaping and twitching as he spoke.

The Fiend hissed out its tongue as it crawled across the floor, chasing after Benjamin, who was backing away in the other direction, searching for an escape.

Seeing the gun, Malcamore made a wild grab for it, but the tail of the Fiend whipped it to the other side of the room with a whoosh. The king gave another horrifying laugh.

"I must be dreaming. No, this is a nightmare. I'm losing my mind. What in the Anastasia is even happening?" Malcamore yelled in shocked terror.

Squirming on the floor, he shouted, "What do you want!" "There is something in her blood, Benjamin! Something dangerous to our kind. And these Fiends here are our only hope for survival. One by one the worlds are ending; the Gods have spoken."

"She's Human?"

"And All of their siblings had the blood of filthy humans flowing through their body. Puh! They were destroying our island. A secret, kept solely by the royal family they deserve to die. But if you say yes... maybe it would buy your daughter some time. Or don't and become that thing's dinner. It's up to you."

Malcamore quivered. Every nerve in his body was telling him to flee, but there was nowhere to run.

"Yes!" the king shouted, banging on the desk while the creature thrusted his long, forked tongue out at Malcamore's face.

"The Fiends get their full, and those selected for the brotherhood get to live forever. Them the rules."

Malcamore covered his ears, attempting to block out the king's words. The Fiend slithered toward him and began wrapping him in its snake body, squeezing the air from his lungs. He struggled to breathe, gasping, looking to the king's ungodly smile fading away. His heartbeat neared a stop, his life flashed before his eyes. Growing up in Quadrant One with his father, back when the island was still at peace. Getting to know King Pius III and his family and the war he caused, the awful things he had done. The treachery.

"So, what's it going to be? She doesn't have all night," King Theodore said.

Malcamore felt more pain and heard the tiny cracks of bones protesting around his ribs. The Fiend's mouth opened wide, revealing its rows of sharp fangs. With the last of the air left in his body, he let out a strangled gasp, barely audible.

"You have a deal."

"Splendid," the king said as the Fiend uncoiled and released him from his grasp.

Malcamore let out an involuntary gasp as he collapsed to the floor, coughing, chest heaving as it allowed his airways to draw in oxygen once again.

He composed himself and crawled back up to his feet. "Now what?" he asked.

"Now, we seal the deal." The king slowly stretched open his mouth, slithering out, was a pair of small snakes, circling one another and hissing with fury, weaving back and forth about his face. They made their way down his arms, then across the desk. Slithered down the legs, then across the polished floor and finally reaching Malcamore, backing away on his bottom. He yelled in agony as they tore into his palms and crawled inside of him. He gave a back-bending squeal as his body twisted and bent in unholy positions on the floor. The feeling of the snakes multiplying and restructuring the bones inside his body. He had never experienced such pain.

"Yes! Do you feel it, Benjamin? Can you feel their power?"

Benjamin Malcamore whirled around the office. He begged for them to stop spreading, to stop reproducing.

Minutes passed that felt like an eternity. Small baby snakes and black goo spewed out of Malcamore's mouth and out onto the floor of the king's office. He rolled over on his back, breathing heavily then grabbing his wrist in pain where two snakes formed a 99 under his skin. The others slid across the floor and returned to the king, sliding inside of his opened palms.

"It's finished, Benjamin!" The king bellowed another haunting laugh as he began returning to his normal form and the Fiend climbed back up in the shadows of the ceiling. Malcamore stood with his wrists, burning with torment. His old number discarded with 99, which felt like snakes lying dormant inside him.

Regaining his wits, Malcamore snatched up his gun from the floor and pointed it at the king.

"Where is she?" he demanded.

"I'm an islander of my word, Benjamin. She's in the old Gaming chambers, the one with the tunnels. You know where that is, right? It's not too far from here. Hell, I'm sure you can smell her now if you try," the king said, gleeful and mad.

"You might make it if you hurry. Fair warning, though: no one's going to be happy about the sudden change of dinner plans. You're on your own with that. What happens next is up to you!" the king shouted, his laughter chasing Malcamore as he sprinted out the door and down the halls.

"Benjamin!" Rose called to Malcamore, running out of the house.

He skidded to a stop. "Rose, are you alright?" he said, grabbing her by the arm, staring into her eyes to see what color they were.

"I'm great, Benjamin." Rose laughed.

"And I see you are too, now." She gestured to the scar on his wrist.

"What has that! That *thing!* Done to me, Rose? Why has he poisoned me?" Malcamore asked, pulling down the sleeves of his jacket.

"Poisoned? Come now, you're being dramatic, Benjamin. He's made you immortal... immortal," she whispered. "Don't you

understand the power that gives you? Can't you feel it?" Her eyes glittered, and he realized with a sickening feeling that she was just as mad as the king. For a moment, he fought the urge to vomit.

"Young sir!" Samson called from the coach.

Malcamore shot Rose one last look and fled the house, running down the steps and into the coach. "I'll see you soon, Benjamin!" she called as Malcamore slammed the carriage door shut.

CHAPTER THIRTY-ONE

"THAT'S THE ENTIRE STORY, SPARING no details," Thomas said, sitting on the side of a large, cushioned cot, made of carved wood and linen that felt like a bear's coat. Gazing around at the decorative room, he saw pink and yellow flowers blooming and glowing out of a stoned vase next to a crackling fire pit.

"I've sent my best men looking for your family. They have that message you wrote for them to help," King Pius said, standing from where he sat next to Thomas.

Thomas looked down to his arms, then his legs, lastly his private parts. His skin, sparing no inch, was now a radiant blue.

"I'm sorry, but King Pius is it.?"

"Yes, it is."

"Can you tell me exactly where we are?" Thomas asked.

King Pius turned back and slowly paced the room, the bottom of his coat fur dragging across the polished floor. "So, your world was destroyed by falling rocks of ice, Mr. Thomas?"

"Yes, sir, it was."

"We were warned about this day, prophecies that are much older than me, about the day where your kind would come to us. We are peaceful people, Thomas, do you understand? We do not allow war on our island; we are pure and I tend to keep it that way."

"What about those monsters? The ones who live by the beach?"

"Ah, yes, we call them Fiends."

"What about them? They don't seem so pure. They ate and killed a few of my closest friends, you know. Amongst others."

"The Fiends have been part of existence a lot longer than you and I combined. This is just as much as their home as it is ours. We built that wall a few centuries back to keep them out, but my guess is, the end of your world, brought all three worlds together."

Thomas crawled out of the bed, his own smaller woven coat draped over his body. He stood next to Pius, barely measuring up to his waist, and gazed out of the window.

A loud knock came from the door.

"King Pius, sir. We've found the human's family, one woman and two boys. They are alive and being cared for at the moment."

"Good!" King Pius laughed, throwing his arms around Thomas and walking him across the room.

"Listen, Human Thomas, there is plenty of time for you to learn how things work here, if you're going to be staying. We have an opportunity to rewrite history Humans and islanders of Anastasia working together, to build a better life for us both, combining our worlds. I'm sure there's a lot we can learn from one another. Come! Let's go check on your family, then I will show you around the island. And you can tell me more about… earth." He smiled, slamming the door shut behind them.

CHAPTER THIRTY-TWO

As WE POURED INTO THE dimly lit open chamber in a massive group, most faces betrayed pure fear, the fear you would expect. My adrenaline was pumping out of my skin, flinching from the loud shouts of.

"Close the gates!" one yelled from among us, bringing all gates to a screeching locked position, the sound echoing off the facility's high walls.

The cluster of islanders surrounding me murmured in faint whispers. Someone blared a cry of desperation, calling out names I assumed were family members or loved ones.

Crammed in the crowd, I focused on a soldier climbing the steps to the second floor.

"Form two groups! One on the left, one on the right!" a soldier shouted, gesturing with his hands to emphasize the instruction. The rest of the soldiers were struggling to gain control over the room with scuffles breaking out, forcing us to elbow and cram into one another.

I picked a random line and stood by, my own emotion subdued. The elderly couple was no longer by my side; I had lost them in the shuffle and loud hollers for us to move forward.

Once the room fell silent, the guard explained one last meal was also awarded an hour before the Gathering.

As we drifted forward, I snatched the folded clothes and room number placed on a torn piece of paper. Looking down at the number written, *Room 316*. A loud rumble started. It felt like the walls and floors themselves were shaking apart. I looked up at the high ceiling. The roof slowly slid back, revealing fresh air and the night sky glistening above our heads.

"I've never seen a place like this," Betty said, walking up next to me, gazing upwards in mystery, as was everyone else around me.

"I know, it's creepy," I said, studying the retracting roof that rumbled open. The building itself reminded me of the Drums where my mother worked. Rooms that circled around, each facing the open area where we were standing.

"What's your room number?" Betty asked.

"316. What's yours?"

"I've got," Betty fumbled for her number, "323."

"Want to go search for our rooms together?" I asked. Betty nodded, and we forced our way through the growing chaos.

"Things are getting out of hand down here," she said, looking at the soldiers dragging islanders to their rooms as they kicked and screamed, some attempting to climb the walls and out of the building. But that task was impossible.

We reached a hanging sign that read: *Ones and twos, first floor. Threes and fours, second floor.*

"Looks like we're both on the second floor," I said, gripping the rail of the cold iron stairs and glaring up at the second-floor, stoned rooms that wrapped around the building.

I noticed that some were occupied and caught the occupants' eyes as I passed. Nobody smiled.

"This must be me," I said, arriving at the room with the number *316* carved above it. There was an iron cot bed in the corner and a silver bucket under a shower head hanging on the opposite wall. "Fancy," I said with a sigh.

"I'm just a few rooms down," Betty said, peeking into my cell. "Guess I'll get settled in, too, and catch up with you later?" We shared a quick hug before she left and headed the rest of the way alone.

I placed my things and clothes onto the cot in the corner. I sat and took two bounces, its hard surface made relaxing or sleeping both unachievable.

"And I thought my old bed was bad."

A loud voice spoke over an intercom that blared throughout the building.

"We will serve last meals in an hour. There will be one hour of free time before we begin the Gathering." A faint whistle and a click ended the announcement as I looked to the floor.

Thoughts of my life began swimming through my head like a pool of nightmares. My family, my friends. I glanced at the rusted shower head and silver bucket. A warm shower might be just what the doctor ordered. There was a thin black curtain for privacy, and one knob to control the water's temperature.

My mind pondered on what to expect for the Gathering as the steaming water showered over me. I cried, first a little, then a lot, the fear causing the insides of my stomach to flip and tighten. The water was steaming and rushing down into the bucket when I first felt the change in its texture. A wet, warm and soothing embrace, turning cold and thick. I ran my fingers through my hair, and they came back covered in black goo that had oozed out of the shower head. I leaped out the silver bucket that was catching the water, wrapping myself in the thin, dangling curtain after yanking it off its henges. The black goo, thicker than paint, slugged out of the faucet. Fat drops that kerplopped down into the bucket. I caught a chubby drop with my finger, examining it in awe. I'd seen this sludge before. When I turned to the entrance of my room, there was a soldier standing at my doorway, watching. He smiled, crooked and perverted.

"A little privacy please!"

He made no response, just shifted from one foot to the other and thudded down the hall.

When I was sure he was gone, I quickly dressed in the dreadful uniform they provided. *Why not?* It was a hideous jumpsuit and way too big for me. The bright orange shirt dropped down to my upper thigh and the pants were a few sizes too big as the bottom sagged over my toes. But all in all, it was actually quite comfortable.

While jotting in my journal, I heard a slight knock at the entrance. Looking up, I saw Susan and her husband David.

"Hello, it's us again," she said, holding her husband's arm like a bride to be.

"Hi."

"We've walked this whole building three times now looking for you," Susan continued. "Dreadful place. Everybody out there is a nervous mess. But at least it's a beautiful night out. That was a pleasant surprise with the roof. They're about to serve the last meals now. Would you like to come with us?"

I placed the pen in my journal and folded it shut. "No... No, thank you. I was planning to skip it. I'm not hungry."

"You don't want to meet your Gathering on an empty stomach, do you?" Susan coaxed.

As if on cue, my stomach gave a rumble, and I re-considered. Not to mention her look said she wasn't taking no as an option.

"Okay." Taking up my journal, I joined them on the walk to the eating area.

The night sky was glistening above us, thanks to the roofless view. The rain wasn't threating to start up again though I wondered if it did, if they bothered closing it. The air was cool as we stood in a crowded line for last meals. I stared at the pile of mush dropped onto my tray once we reached the front. "What *is* this?" I asked. The soldier gave an unapologetic grunt. The next added two slices of bread and what only looked like meat, but I couldn't be sure.

"Some last meal," David murmured from behind.

I looked over the crowded eating area and caught sight of Betty, who had already found a seat. She returned my wave and beckoned for me to join her.

"Betty, this is Susan and David," I introduced once we all sat.

They greeted one another, and David was about to brave a taste of the so-called meal when his wife stopped him, insisting that they say a prayer first. I smiled. It reminded me of something mother would say. I stirred my spoon around the bowl of mush and picked at the slightly molded slices of bread.

"I think I will pass on the food." I slid my tray to the side, skimming over a few pages from my journal.

"What are you working on?" Susan asked.

"It's from a book my friend found back home. He's... well, he's just back home."

"You mean the boy who started that riot?" Susan guessed; the look on my face must have given away the answer. "What's his book about?"

"You wouldn't believe me if I told you."

"Try me," Susan challenged, swallowing down another spoonful of mush. "You're not eating anyway, so you might as well entertain instead."

I tried my best to explain to them about the king's evil plot to take over the island, even mentioning the nightmares I'd been having, and about Elizabeth. They remembered her, David even recalling the day they announced she had been born.

"But these creatures, Fiends they're called, are in control and the true cause for the Gatherings, I guess."

I finished, waiting for their reaction. Betty gazed at me in awe.

"Hmm," Susan said, swallowing down the last spoonful, then patting her mouth clean. "Do you suspect those things are controlling us?"

"I'm not sure. We thought he was crazy at first, but now..."

"It wouldn't surprise me one bit!" David said, finishing his own food. "This island is beautiful, but it's tough. The food's never been plentiful... and it always seems to rain. But the islanders who called it home... things were much different when I was a child. There was a sense of... well, family, is how I would put it. Everyone on the island treated each other like family. All of that's gone to shit now," he mumbled, patting his wife's hands with watery eyes.

"We're going to spend this last hour alone, if that's okay with you two ladies," Susan said, perhaps sensing her husband's sadness and standing. Betty and I both softly smiled, and the elderly couple headed back to their room.

As soon as they were out of sight, Betty began asking more about the book. "So, these creatures, those Fiends. Can we kill them?" she asked, looking with desperation.

I shrugged. "You sound like Ashton. I'm not sure if they can be. What does it matter now, anyhow?"

"I wish you had that book with you. I would have loved to read some of it."

"Trust me, you don't. It was creepy." I stood. "I don't want to talk about it, if that's okay. Even if it's true, like I said, what can we do about it now? Maybe I'd rather not know."

"Fair enough," Betty said. We hugged again before heading off for our respective rooms.

Once back in my supposed cell, I sat on the edge of the iron cot and began thinking about my mother. I knew she was worried sick at this exact moment and not sleeping or eating. My friends—how would they handle the news about Ashton? Had someone even told them?

I reached inside the trousers and retrieved the small, red vial from the pocket, flipping it upside down and watching as the liquid oozed from one side to the other. I grabbed my journal again and wrote.

If these are my last moments, I wish to write my goodbyes properly. Goodbye to my mother, Katherine, who raised me to be respectful, loving, and kind, just like herself. Goodbye to my father, John, who taught me to be proud, brave, and strong, just like him. Goodbye to my friends Jessie, Lola, Phillip, Matthew, and Ashton. I will miss you all dearly. And last —

Before I could finish, a blaring alarm sounded throughout the facility. I gave a yelp as a voice spoke over the intercom.

"It is time to begin the Gathering! Everyone is to return to the eating area immediately!"

That was all. I placed the pen inside my journal with my name stenciled on the cover and stood. Taking one last look at the red vial, I slipped it into the pocket of the baggy pants then headed downstairs with the others.

Voices filled the building, most pitched high with terror, as people followed instructions. Soldiers walked the halls alongside us, checking to assure all rooms had cleared and calling to each other in professional tones.

"Quad one! Clear!"

"Quad two! Clear!

"Quad three! Clear!

"Quad four! Clear!"

A large rumble followed their shouts as doors slid in front of our rooms, locking them shut. Once we had all reached the eating area, I watched as they exited the facility without speaking another word.

We were now alone.

Some in attendance screamed upward at the night sky. My eyes darted around the room, searching for the elderly couple who had been so nice to me. I spotted them, crouched on the floor in pain, hugging one another.

I found a lonely spot in the corner and waited for the Gathering to begin as the chaos continued around me. Bodies began dropping to the floor, clutching their stomachs in agony.

"Can I sit with you?" Betty approached, her eyes bright with tears.

"Sure," I breathed.

Just as Betty was taking her seat, all the lights shut off in the building, leaving everyone to only the moonlight for illumination.

There were cries of panic and discomfort as the intercom spoke over us for the last time, the voice loud and echoing.

"Starting countdown. Happy Gatherings! 10... 9... 8... 7..."

My heart beat out of my chest as I glanced at Betty, who was now sobbing, curled on the floor. She screamed that something was inside her stomach.

"6... 5... 4..." The sounds of my mother screaming pierced my ears. I clasped my hands over them, begging aloud for it to stop.

"3... 2... 1... The Gathering has begun," the voice said.

A sudden silence filled the room. I turned to Betty, who now laid unconscious next to me, the black goo oozing from her mouth.

The food, I thought as the cries for help slowly faded to the sounds of loud, terrifying screeches.

"This is it." Before I could think about it, before I had the chance to talk myself out of it, I whipped the vial from my pocket, swallowing the contents in one gulp, then collapsed to the floor in a matter of seconds.

Feeling Death was painless, I thought the next moment, unsure of how much time had passed.

Opening my eyes, all pain I had ever known, withdrew. I could see Elizabeth sitting next to me—only now I could see the beautiful little girl she was when she was alive, far from the monster that had been haunting me.

Elizabeth lifted my head from the floor, and to my surprise, I floated effortlessly in the air. Glancing down, I could still see my body lying dead in the room. She kissed me on the cheek, then whispered softly in my ear. I shook in disbelief. But she returned a smile and pointed toward a door in the far hallway of the chamber.

I turned as they burst through the entrance, screaming as they searched the crowded room.

CHAPTER THIRTY-THREE

M ALCAMORE AND SAMSON STOOD AT the northern entrance of the Gathering chambers, facing a pair of massive, stoned doors with two crystalized handles.

"I'm going in with you this time, young sir! And there's no way I'm letting you tell me otherwise," Samson said.

Knowing there was no time for arguing, Malcamore agreed and begun beating at the door with a fist. The two doors groaned open as a soldier appeared before them.

"Hello, we're here for the Gathering," Malcamore said. Then grabbed him by the shirt, taking advantage of the surprise, and dragged him to the ground, knocking the soldier out cold with the back of his gun.

"Excellent job!" Samson said.

"Thank you. Now, let's go."

They entered the brightly lit facility; the space was quiet as they searched for the room where the Gathering was being held. Malcamore turned knobs on random doors that lined the hall.

Locked.

"Where the hell is everybody in this godforsaken Quadrant?" he murmured as they walked.

A young-faced member of the mob appeared from behind a certain locked door, froze for an instant, and then reached for his weapon. "State your business here!" he shouted. Malcamore fumbled for words, until the soldier glanced wide-eyed at his wrist. "Oh!" he exclaimed, his demeanor relaxing. "You're here for the feast?"

Malcamore studied him, agreeing after a brief silence. "Yes, the feast," he said, trying to sound familiar with the question.

"Right this way!" The soldier turned back for the way he came. Malcamore and Samson shared a puzzled look, but followed.

"I hear they got quite a picking this year!" he continued cheerfully, closing the door behind them. "The name's Rip, short for Ripley. I didn't have time to work the chambers myself this year, but everyone like you seems to be quite excited about it."

"Like you?" Samson mouthed.

Malcamore shrugged.

"Right through here, sir." Rip gestured to a room marked 99.

Malcamore twisted the knob and nudged open the door.

Everyone in the crowded room veered their sight to him in unison. He recognized a few from the party, even the server, Tootie, who had been flirting with him. They were naked, standing transfixed, their faces expressionless.

Malcamore slammed the door back shut. "Oh...that feast," he said, throwing his arm around the soldier's shoulder. "Tell me, Rip. Is there somewhere else we can go? Somewhere more private? Maybe get closer to the actual Gathering? Where we keep the islanders."

Rip looked at him, perplexed. "No, sir! This is the only viewing room available for your kind. When the roofs open, no one is allowed in. They get first dibs; you know what I mean, that's the rules. Should be plenty enough for you after though." He grinned.

Malcamore forced the soldier to walk alongside, away from Samson with his arm still draped over his shoulder. "No, son, I mean, I'm demanding you take us closer," he said with his gun pressed against Rip's side.

Rip looked down, stunned by his action. "Nobody's allowed in before the countdown, trust me. Until you've changed."

"Countdown?" Malcamore asked.

"Oh, is this your first Gathering, sir?"

"Yes!" he said, gun still pressed. "And for my colleague here. Our first one together. And we want to be as close to the action as possible." He spoke as confidently as he was able.

Rip, taking a quick look around to see who might watch, gave another crooked grin and agreed. "Okay, okay. I'll take you to the chambers, but you can't go inside until the feasting starts. Otherwise, I'll lose my job for sure, and I'll never get my chance to join the brotherhood."

"No worries, son. And I won't tell if you don't. Lead the way."

Rip guided them through the large facility, one unmarked door after another, then down an underground staircase.

Malcamore could feel the temperature increase as they arrived at the last door at the end of a dark hallway. "Sure, is hot down here," Malcamore said.

"Yeah, we have to keep the room at a certain temperature. It's a preference or something." Rip placed his wrist on the identifier hanging on the wall, causing a blue light to shine, and the door slid open.

"We change our uniforms and observe the islanders from here. We don't stay to watch the feasting, though. That shit ain't for the weak stomach, if you know what I mean," he said, laughing and slapping him on the shoulder.

Malcamore studied the large pane of glass that took up half the wall at the far end. He approached, giving the glass a few taps with his knuckle. "Can they see us?"

"No, it's a one-way glass, made from a specialized crystal. We can see them, but they can't see us," Rip said, with a hint of accomplishment in his voice.

Malcamore laughed as his eyes searched the crowd for Rachel. "One way, huh? I've got to get me one of these for my home," he said, scanning the room, but failed to spot her.

"What are they doing now?" Samson asked, watching the soldiers from the glass as they circled the chamber.

"Looks like they're clearing rooms… The Gathering should begin any minute now."

The door next to the one-way glass slid open as the soldiers who were clearing rooms exited the chambers.

"What are you doing?" one shouted who had stopped and taken notice of the three of them.

"Uh… this islander here, whose part of the brotherhood, wanted a closer look at the Gathering chambers," Rip said, looking toward the officer who Malcamore sensed was his superior.

"You know the rules! No contact before it begins. No special treatment."

"It's his first Gathering, Sarge. Who's it going to hurt?" Rip pleaded as Malcamore's hand slid to his pistol.

"It might hurt you a lot," he muttered.

"What did you say?" Rip said.

Without hesitation, Malcamore whipped his gun out from under his jacket and fired, killing the sergeant on the spot. Then he turned to Rip.

"Wait! Don't shoot me! Please, I really want to join the brotherhood one day," he begged.

The light behind the glass vanished.

Distracted for one crucial second, Malcamore rammed to the floor as Rip wrestled for the gun. The two scuffled until Samson helped to restrain him, allowing Malcamore to pin the young soldier with ease.

"Open that door!" Malcamore ordered.

"Are you crazy? In seconds that room will fill with huge, unkillable monsters. I'm not touching that fucking door!"

"I'm a monster myself, now open that door!" Malcamore shouted.

The soldier's fear changed to a slight gloating. "Those things love eating us, don't they? Top of the food chain they are. I can't wait until it's my turn to be like them, like you."

"What is he talking about, young sir?"

"Too bad you'll never get that chance," Malcamore whispered, then shot Rip in the face, his blood splattering all over his clothing. He looked up to the glass wall and wiping away his blood.

"Samson!" he called. "Let's go get Rachel."

Malcamore snatched the key card and a pair of flashlights from the dead sergeant as he and Samson entered the Gathering chambers.

The room was dark and in total chaos, with dying islanders curling on the floor.

"I don't see her, and what about these people? Should we save them?"

"Only if there's time, old friend," Malcamore said, searching in a panic, screaming Rachel's name. Susan caught the sounds of the shouts for Rachel and rose to her feet.

"Hey, I know her; I know Rachel Patterson." She whimpered, black goo coughing from her mouth.

Malcamore and Samson ran to her aid.

"Ma'am, are you ok?"

"It's poison, the food."

"You know Rachel, have you seen her?" Malcamore asked.

Susan strained at the words. "S-s-she's sitting over there." She pointed.

Malcamore ran across the room, stepping over the dying bodies. Finally, he reached the corner where she laid the emptied vial next to her hand.

"Samson! Over here, I've found her!" he shouted. Samson ran to join and slowly arriving behind were Susan and her husband David, still coughing in pain.

"She's already taken the vial!" Malcamore shouted, opening her mouth and pouring the blue liquid down her throat.

When nothing happened, he pressed his head to her chest. "Her heart's not beating!"

"Samson, didn't you tell me you know how to revive someone!" Malcamore said.

"Yes, young sir, but that's—"

"Try it, damn it!"

Samson got to his knees and tried to breathe fresh air into Rachel's lungs, then put both hands over her chest and pumped. "Maybe we got to work it in her system." He breathed.

Susan and David fell to the floor.

"She's not waking up.."

"Keep trying!" Malcamore said, quickly aiding to them as they shook and foamed at the mouth.

Samson repeated the process.

"Again!" Malcamore demanded.

Samson was now sweating and gasping for air himself. "Young sir... I think we've lost her."

"Try again, Samson. And don't stop trying until I tell you, damn it!" His voice cracked in anguish.

Samson pushed hard onto Rachel's belly one last time and against all odds, Rachel gave a jerk, her eyes batted open and watered, while she sucked in air in loud, sobbing gasps.

"I did it," Samson said, sitting back on his heels in shock.

"Well done, old friend!" Malcamore slapped him on the back in excitement.

"Where am I?" Rachel asked as Samson helped her to a noodled stance.

"Can you walk? We have little time. I promise, I'll explain everything to you once we've escaped," Malcamore said.

Without warning, a loud alarm blared throughout the facility.

"What's happening?" Rachel asked.

"I'm not sure, just stay close." A red light illuminated the chamber as Malcamore drew his weapon. Then the pain, almost forgotten, returned to his wrist, and he let out a shout of agony, dropping to his knees.

"Young sir!"

"I'm fine, Samson!"

"No, look!" Samson pointed upwards as Malcamore gritted his teeth, fighting for a stance. Lining the rooftop and staring down on them all were dozens of horrifying Fiends standing on hind legs. Their snake-like bodies swayed in the wind and their tongues hissed at the air. The islanders unlucky enough to awake screamed, and Malcamore grabbed Rachel by the hand and ran for the door.

"NO! Betty!" Rachel shouted as he pulled her along, followed by Samson and Susan and David, crawling to keep pace. He put the soldier's card key to the door as it slid open, bursting through, followed by the elderly couple and a few others heaving in pain. The secured door slid shut, and Rachel stopped to watch through the one-way glass. Too many to count of the Fiends poured into the Gathering chamber as they dove in through the roof's opening. They devoured body after body that did not escape, shredding them apart with their claws and fighting over the remains. One massive creature crashed against the one-way mirror, sniffing at Rachel's face and licking out its tongue. Malcamore pulled her by the hand as they ran up the stairs and through the building.

"Do you remember the way, young sir?" Samson asked, his cane tatting with the pace. "Yes, it should be this door here," Malcamore said, pushing on an unmarked door then spotting the faithful wagon and William still parked out front. Behind them was a screaming mob of naked islanders from Quadrant 4, crawling on hands and feet after them, only stopping to devour the flesh of the elderly couple and the others failing to escape. Malcamore, Rachel, and Samson all leaped inside the coach wagon.

"Go! Go! Go!" William whipped on the reins; Bubba and Coin gave a loud huff, and the wagon sped down the road, leaving behind the mob of islanders and the Gathering Chambers' lights in the background.

"We...w-we..." Rachel's voice shrunk, recalling the sickening screeches and sounds of tearing flesh.

"We must stop the Gatherings," Malcamore finished, wiping at her face.

"We are with you to the end… my Queen," Samson said.

Rachel gaped, turning for one last look at the Gathering Chambers behind them.

THE END OF PART I

ABOUT THE AUTHOR

Matthew Holmes, author of his debut novel *The Gathering (The Girl With The 18)*. He's a songwriter, poet, and a fan and author of fictional thrillers.

Matthew was born in Mississippi and currently lives in Houston, TX with his two daughters. He started writing at a very young age, his first poem, published at age 12. Courtesy of his creative writing teacher who bragged on his way with words and imagination. Although he's known for his music, he's a future trailblazer for the new wave of horror and thriller novels.

Future Thriller Novels to look for in 2021-2022:

Family Ties
The Attic Family
The Gathering (The Girl with the 18) Part II

www.ingramcontent.com/pod-product-compliance
Lightning Source LLC
Chambersburg PA
CBHW061602100726
47898CB00002B/491